Norman Waller is married with four children.
He has a smallholding in the Cotswolds that takes in
rescue animals.
He has been a Samaritan for over twenty years.

To my wife Gloria Alexandra
Without whom the world would be a
darker place

Norman Waller

FLIP OF A COIN

AUSTIN MACAULEY
PUBLISHERS LTD.

A CIP catalogue record for this title is available from the British Library.

ISBN 9781786121103 (Paperback)
ISBN 9781786121110 (Hardback)
ISBN 9781786121127 (E-Book)

www.austinmacauley.com

First Published (2016)
Austin Macauley Publishers Ltd.
25 Canada Square
Canary Wharf
London
E14 5LQ

Acknowledgments

Paul and Cynthia Bunday for their encouragement.
Mandy Bowden who gave me valuable advice on
the workings of a snack bar.

Chapter 1

The dreadful screams and shouting from number 18 Cherry Tree Road echoed the whole length of the road. Had there been a passer-by, they would have ignored it because in Cherry Tree Road, like the other roads that wove their way across the Orchard Estate, sounds of violence occurred regularly. And Cherry Tree Road, like most of the roads on the Orchard Estate, was made up mostly of small terraced houses. Drab houses of dull brick and discoloured paint, they would never have looked pretty when firstly built. Tucked into the curbs outside the dwellings was an assortment of cars that ranged from expensive new to rusting old. Occasional front gates into front gardens hung off their hinges, and many of the front gardens were littered with rubbish including old bed mattresses, rusting bike frames, piles of timber, lumps of concrete and bricks, old TV sets and obsolete electrical appliances. Here and there an occasional garden stood out because it had been looked after with loving care. Some of the houses were desperately in need of new panes of glass whilst others looked bleak because they were boarded up. Cherry Tree Road looked a sad, tired and demoralised road where violence, drugs and the planning of crimes were the order of the day.

A splash of light suddenly pierced through the darkness and torrential rain as the front door of number 18 Cherry Tree Road opened and the figure of a young woman lurched forward and stumbled into a heap on the front path.

She was just a skinny girl, probably in her late teens. Her clothing was light and ripped and was saturated within seconds from the driving rain. Her long dark hair fell across her face and eyes, one of which was almost closed from swelling and dark bruising. Nursing a painful arm she pushed herself up with a hand that was bleeding from a graze when she fell and staggered through the gate that was swinging in the wind. The figure of a powerful man in his late twenties was framed in the light of the doorway. He roared a tirade of oaths, but his words were lost in the wind. He stood there staring at the figure of the young woman as she stumbled away into the darkness.

Tom poked the dying embers of the fire. He looked at the clock and saw it said 10 o'clock. He would be leaving in a few minutes, and it would be completely safe to leave. He wasn't feeling 100%, but that was to be expected. He was still capable of doing what was needed of him. Tom was in his late fifties, but his hair was already snow white. His brown eyes were soft and kindly, and he always projected an air of calmness. He lived alone, having lost his wife Janice in a motor accident three years ago, after twenty years of blissful marriage. They had known each other from school days, and in the truest sense they were soul mates. Since her death he had endeavoured to carry on as normal a life as possible, which he knew she would have wanted. He had a good job in HR and many good friends.

Janice's tragic death was not the only tragedy in their life together. Tom had always wanted children, and when Janice gave birth to Jessica, he was the happiest man on earth. But fate struck a heavy blow when she suddenly died, from what was perceived at the time as a cot death, some months after she was born. They were both devastated. At every birthday he would walk with Janice to a particular copse where she had been buried. It was a pretty plot and was close to an area of wild flowers. The two of them would sit and share an imaginary scene of how they would have spent the day with her and what plans they were hoping for as she grew older. Janice had never conceived again, and although they had talked about adopting, time went by and it never came to anything.

He walked out into the hall and lifted his coat off a hook on the wall. He opened the front door and felt the force of the wind. He gave a grunt and left the house.

***

The young woman paused at the end of Cherry Tree Road and leant into the side of a rusting car that had been parked there for months. She tried the handle of the door, but it was jammed shut, and she sank to her knees in despair. Shivering and frozen from the driving rain, she helplessly looked around her, struggling to think of what she must do. Perhaps it was best if she did nothing but just lie down and die where she was. Her life was misery, and there was no hope of it changing. She had the means to kill herself in her pocket: pills she'd stolen from her mother when she had been living at home in that previous hell. Her bathroom cabinets had been stuffed full of bottles of pills and boxes of capsules that were enough to bring an army to its knees. She wondered what freezing to death would be like and whether it would be agonising. Would she gradually become numb and lose all feeling then simply pass away? But even as she had these thoughts, her legs had pushed her up and were moving her down the road in the direction of the town. Just getting away from Frank – that's all that mattered now.

And yet at the same time she knew it wasn't. She knew that back at number 18, a frozen dog shivering from the pouring rain remained tethered in the corner of the back yard. Murphy's long grey coat would be filthy from standing in inches of mud and his own excrement. His head would be drooping, and he would occasionally whimper. Now and then he would turn around, perhaps in a pathetic attempt to try and get some warmth, perhaps mechanically without knowing what he was doing. His sad eyes would be staring at the mud in front of him. Cindy screwed up her eyes as she pictured his protruding rib cage that couldn't be masked even by his long-haired coat. If Frank came out he would probably wag his tail expectantly but then cower into the mud as Frank swore at him. Poor Murphy. His only crime was to be born, and like her, his only hope was to die and be spared any further misery.

Perhaps she could find a night centre or a warm doorway where she could get out of the wind and rain and maybe fall asleep. Maybe she could do that. Yes, maybe pigs could fly.

***

Tom took a left and pulled into the kerb opposite a building displaying a dimly lit sign that said SAMARITANS. He switched off the engine, got out of the car and ran through the rain to the staff front door. He released the lock on the door with the device on his key ring and went in. Ben and Irene, the two volunteers he was relieving from the previous shift, already had their coats on waiting to leave. Carole, the volunteer doing the night duty with Tom, was already there and in the kitchen area making coffee. Ben and Irene shared a couple of jokes with Tom and an update on their shift then left.

Tom moved inside the ops room, where there were two small telephone booths and a computer on a desk for dealing with e-mail callers, and took off his coat. He felt the radiators and nodded his approval that they were working well. The room was sparsely furnished with a table in the middle and a second small desk with a book for logging calls and half a dozen office type chairs with varying degrees of comfort. On a wall bracket was mounted a monitor that showed through CCTV the outside of the building as well as the inside of a lobby in which callers waited before being invited into the building when they came for a face-to-face call. It gave volunteers the opportunity to quickly see whether the caller was a man or woman and any feature that might give them concern about safety. Although it was rare, volunteers had suffered assaults from drunks or nutters in the past.

Tom was briefly scanning the log when Carole came in with two mugs of coffee. 'How's that for service, Tom?' she said and put the mugs on the table.

'It's a pleasure to do a shift with you, Carole,' Tom replied with a grin. 'What a night; fit for neither man nor beast.'

Tom had not done a shift with Carole before. The duty roster, which could be filled-in up to eight weeks ahead, allowed for volunteers to do shifts at different times. This meant that their shifts could fit in with their personal lives and also allowed them to choose a shift with different volunteers – perhaps someone with whom they hadn't done a shift before. Carole was in her mid-twenties. She was comparatively new and had been a volunteer for only a year. She was employed by the local Council in the Municipal Offices. She had short dark hair and wore thick framed glasses which gave the impression that she was studious, but in fact she was athletic and regularly played hockey for a local club. She was slightly in awe of Tom who had been a volunteer for more than twenty years and had spoken to callers with almost every kind of misery and problem that one could imagine – and many that one couldn't.

It was always impossible to predict if the phone would ring as soon as one arrived on duty or whether there would be time for volunteers to have a chat. Sometimes, if the shift was quiet, volunteers could talk and get to know each other or catch up on news. One or the other of them would then start answering emails from those callers who preferred that kind of communication to the telephone. But Tom had no sooner taken a sip of his coffee when the doorbell rang, and both he and Carole looked up expectantly at the CCTV screen.

'That's unusual,' said Carole. 'It's so late for people to call here for face-to-face.'

The image on the screen was dull, and it was difficult for them to identify if it was a male or female huddled against the front door. 'We're shut for the night anyway so we can't do anything,' she went on.

'It looks like a female. I'd better go and see.'

Tom walked out of the ops room and made his way down the short corridor to the front door. He slipped the lock and let himself into the lobby into which callers would wait until being let into the building proper. The outer door was always locked at ten for the night, which meant that callers could only make contact by telephone or e-mail. The bell rang again as Tom slipped back the bolt and opened the outer door. There was an immediate blast of wind and rain that made Tom have to hold the door from pushing him backwards. In front of him was a young woman; he couldn't tell her age because her long dark hair spread across her face. She was soaked to the skin and violently shivering with the cold.

'My God,' said Tom under his breath.

'Please can you help me? I've nowhere to go,' croaked the young woman through chattering teeth.

Tom took a breath in shock at the state of the poor woman, at the same time realising his dilemma. Carole was quite right, of course; it was a strict rule that when the Centre was closed for the night callers were not allowed in.

The rule was mandatory, but to Tom this was different. The young woman in front of him was in a desperate state. If he had a shred of compassion in him, could he turn her away? On the other hand, if she came in, what the hell could he offer her anyway?

'Please,' implored the creature in front of him, and Tom could suddenly see that she was a very young woman; not a woman but a young girl in her teens.

'I'm afraid we're closed for the night. The building is locked at half past ten. I'm afraid I can't offer...' Tom stammered, but his words were cut short.

'I've heard about you... you help people.'

'We've no accommodation here. I wish I could help you, but...' Again his words were interrupted.

'I'll be no trouble.' The girl stared up at him with imploring eyes, and for a few moments Tom could only stare back in silence. Another huge gust of icy wind surged up to them and pushed water over the side of an over-flooded gutter above them so that it splashed down on to the young girl.

'You'd better come in for a few minutes,' said Tom, at the same time desperately wondering what he was going to do with the girl. 'You can't stay. It's not allowed, and I've nowhere to put you.'

'I understand,' said the girl as she stepped inside the lobby and stood there shivering as Tom closed the door behind her.

The door of number 18 Cherry Tree Road opened and spread the light from inside down the front path. Frank stood back with a shiver as the wind swirled round him then leaned forward and looked left and right, up and down the road. 'Cindy! Cindy! What are you doing?! Get back here!' he bellowed, but there was no response except the roar of the wind. Frank pushed back his hair, which reached down over his collar, and swore under his breath. What the hell was the stupid bitch playing at? If she wanted to stay out all night, then the best of luck. He wasn't going to lose any sleep over it. If she tried coming back in the middle of the night, he wasn't going to come down. She'd have to stay out all bloody night.

Tom opened the inner door to the Centre. 'You'd better come inside,' he said and led the girl into a small interview room. 'This is all we've got, but it's warm. Still very cold for April.' He reached over and put his hand on the radiator.

'Thank you.' Her voice was barely audible.

'You'd better get your jacket off and stick it on the radiator. It's soaking.'

He watched her as she eased herself out of her jacket and hung it on the radiator. Her skinny arms were bare, and he immediately saw that they were covered in bruises. The girl saw him looking and stared back at him as she pulled her hair back across her face so that he could now see that one of her eyes was completely closed with dark swelling. 'My God, you poor thing,' he exclaimed. 'You should have that eye looked at by a doctor.'

'I'm fine,' she whispered, but her teeth were chattering so violently she could barely get the words out.

'You're frozen. You're shivering…'

'It doesn't matter.'

'You'll go down with pneumonia. Wait here,' said Tom and left the room. He moved down the short corridor until he came to another small room, not much bigger than a broom cupboard. Inside were some shelves displaying assorted blankets. He lifted out two and went back to the interview room. 'You're soaked to the skin. You'd better get your clothes off and stick 'em on the radiator.'

She stared back at him with an alarmed look in her eyes.

'It's all right. You're perfectly safe here. Wrap yourself in these. I'll be back in a minute,' he said and turned to go but stopped in the half open doorway with an afterthought. 'We've no food here. How about biscuits and tea?' She nodded in reply, and he went out, closing the door behind him. As he made his way back through the ops room to the kitchen where he turned the kettle on, Carole followed him expectantly.

'What's happening, Tom?'

'Poor girl. Obviously beaten up. Soaked to the skin and frozen.'

'We can't let her stay,' said Carole with alarm.

'Don't worry about it, Carole,' said Tom calmly.

'But it's not allowed.'

'Leave it to me.'

'It's against the rules, Tom. We must ring Judy and tell her what's happening.'

'I know what the rules are, and I know what Judy will say, so let's just keep quiet and say nothing. I'm just going to give her a cup of tea.' He picked up the mug of tea and a packet of biscuits and made his way back to the interview room.

The girl had wrapped herself in the blankets and was curled up on the floor by the radiator. Tom put the tea and biscuits on the low table next to her. 'Here, get something hot inside you.'

'You're very kind,' said the girl and sipped some of the tea.

'You ought to get to the hospital and have that eye looked at.'

'It'll be all right. I'm not going there.'

Tom leant back against the wall, and there was silence for a few minutes.

'My name's Tom. Do you want to tell me your name?' he asked.

'Cindy.'

'How old are you, Cindy?'

'Eighteen.'

Tom stared back at her with a knowing look.

'Nearly,' said Cindy with a shrug.

'Who knocked you about?'

She stared back blankly. 'It doesn't matter…'

'Frank.'

Tom shook his head and looked down at the floor in despair. 'Why does he do it?'

Cindy gave another shrug but made no reply. She pulled the blankets round her and huddled into herself. She looked a mess now, but Tom realised she was probably a good-looking girl. Seeing her in her present state filled him with both anger and distress for her.

'Has he always been like it? Knocking you about, I mean?'

'No. When I first met him he was okay. He helped me – well, I thought he was helping me.'

'And?'

She shrugged. 'He got me to do things. It seemed innocent.'

'What sort of things?'

She looked back at him but didn't answer. 'I wanted to get away.'

'Why didn't you?'

'You'd think it would be easy, wouldn't you. It's impossible. He'd find me and probably kill me. He's had me in hospital twice.'

'That's terrible.'

'Don't worry. I'm never going back this time.'

'Where will you go?'

'Dunno.'

'What about family?' asked Tom helplessly.

'Jesus, I had to escape from them in the first place.'

There was a sudden tap on the door.

'That'll be my colleague. I won't be a minute,' said Tom and slipped outside into the corridor where Carole was waiting.

'Is everything all right, Tom?' she asked with an over the top urgency.

'Everything's fine,' said Tom, holding up his hands as if to pacify. 'You go back and man the phone. I won't be long.'

'If you're sure,' said Carole and walked away.

Tom opened the door back into the interview room.

Immediately he saw Cindy fumble a tiny packet in her hand which she quickly hid beneath her blankets. He didn't know what was in it, but from her guilty expression he didn't need to make many guesses.

'It's not what you think,' she said.

'We make no judgements here, but I'm concerned for you.'

'It's not drugs. I hate that stuff. Makes me ill,' she spat out the words as if determined he should not think of her as a druggy.

For a little while there was silence.

'Do I have to go now?'

'Finish your tea. Have you any friends?'

'Frank's got some but I was never allowed.'

'Where will you go for tonight? Have you tried the Salvation Army?'

'They couldn't take me. There's nowhere open.'

There was another long silence, and Tom felt his mind racing to try and come up with a solution. Carole was right; she couldn't stay. If she did and Sarah, the branch director, found out, he'd have to resign – that is, of course, unless Sarah didn't sack him.

'You may not want to do this, but what about the police station? They may be able to help.'

'You having me on? No way.'

There was a long silence again. Tom leant back against the wall, despairing at the options open to him for relieving the suffering of the young girl huddled in front of him. As a volunteer in the Samaritans, he was perfectly aware that he couldn't change circumstances in her life. Offering solutions and fixing difficulties in callers' lives was not something they did or even tried to do. And he couldn't take her in; it was simply a matter of policy.

'Do you want me to go now,' said Cindy without emotion in her voice.

Tom suddenly couldn't speak. Any words that formed in his mind simply stuck in his throat. He stared at the girl and then at the floor as if some inspiration would leap up from there.

'It's okay,' Cindy said quietly and began to reach for her clothes on the radiator.

'I'm sorry. I know it sounds pathetic, but I can't do anything more. I don't make the rules,' said Tom, but Cindy didn't recognize the agony in his voice.

'It's okay. Nothing's going to matter after tonight.'

'How's that, Cindy?'

'I'm done for. I don't care anymore; it's all too much. I'll find a hole. I've got the pills. It'll all be lovely. I can do it.'

'Is that what I saw in your hand? A bunch of pills?'

She stared back at him but made no reply. Tom felt an icy hand grip his heart. It was always the same when callers were resolved to kill themselves – the awful acceptance that the only escape from their misery was to snuff out their life by their own hand. But taking pills was fraught with problems. So often they weren't fatal, and then the person ended up with even bigger problems.

'I can't stop you taking your own life, but if you take those tablets you've got, it might all go horribly wrong, and you could end up being seriously ill.'

'It's all shit anyway.'

'You're so young. Not everyone in the world is bad. You could perhaps…' She stopped him mid-sentence with a dismissive wave of the hand and a wry smile.

'No way. You're a nice man, Tom, but that's bollocks.' She stared at him, and there was silence. The die was cast. She would be gone shortly, and there would be no way of knowing what would happen to her. If she took whatever pills she had, they may kill her or they may not. She may end up in hospital or back at Frank's, back in the hell from which she had tried to escape. The silence continued until she suddenly gave him an odd look, and he realised she meant him to turn round while she put her clothes on. A minute later she said 'okay', and handed him the blankets when he turned back to face her. He pushed them back at her and said, 'Keep them. We won't miss them.'

'No. There'll be no hot or cold when I'm done.'

'Even so,' said Tom and pushed them back into her arms. Cindy nodded in acceptance and tucked one under her arm.

'One's enough. Will you get into trouble?'

'Trouble?'

'For letting me in.'

'Of course not. I just can't let you stay the night.'

'I'll get off then,' she said and moved to the door. Tom opened it in silence and led her into the corridor. His stomach was churning, and his mind racing. This wasn't real. It couldn't be. He was actually leading this young girl out into the dead of night, a night that he had earlier said was not fit for man nor beast. Was this a dream? A nightmare? Surely it couldn't be happening. His hand was on the door to the lobby now, and he opened it. A gust of wind suddenly buffeted at the outer door. No, this wasn't a nightmare from which he would wake, it was real, and he was a principle player. For a moment he hesitated on the outer door lock, then opened it and was immediately met by a blast of icy wind and rain. Cindy stared at him with a twisted smile because of her battered face and then slipped out before he had a chance to speak. He watched her hunched body gradually become blurred and smaller as she moved farther away. Instinctively he knew something was wrong. Rules were rules, yes. But individual circumstances, individual people, a justification for breaking ranks and following the dictates of the heart: that mattered. Before he realised what he was doing, he had stepped from the doorway and was running down the road after Cindy and calling her name, 'Cindy! Cindy, wait!' He quickly caught up with her but was already nearly soaked to the skin. 'If I break the rule, would you hang on and try?' he panted and had to shout to compete against the noise of the wind. 'I've no right to ask, but if you came back and, well, hang on to the tablets. Just delay things tonight; maybe tomorrow will... I dunno, you can still do what you like... but wait one night.'

'Tomorrow won't be any different.'

'You don't know that. And what difference does one day make?'

'Why should you care?'

'Because I do.'

They both stared at each other as the rain splashed down on their faces. Cindy looked into the eyes of this man before her and felt something touch her heart – something she had never seen in any man, but something she had wished, she had desperately wanted, to see in the eyes of her father who had only looked at her with a hard and resentful stare.

'You're an odd one, Tom.'

'So I've been told.'

'You'll be in the shit. You said that.'

'Oh well, rules are there to be broken. Come on, I don't want to get soaked, even if you do,' shouted Tom and, grabbing her arm, led her back to the Centre.

***

Frank turned off the television. He finished his can of beer and stood up. His mood was foul, and he hadn't concentrated on the film he'd been watching. That little bitch still hadn't come back. Where the hell had she gone? He'd booted her out before but she'd never stayed away more than an hour. She'd be in a right bloody state in this weather, and she was useless without him. He'd fucking rescued her, hadn't he. Saved her arse, and in return she thought she could do a runner. How was that for thanks? He sat hunched over the kitchen table and thought back to the time he first came across her. It must have been a year ago by now, maybe longer. It was in the corner shop on the far side of town, the mini-supermarket run by Pakistanis. He had been in there when she came in. He knew at once she was probably homeless. She had that huddled and withdrawn look, and he had noticed straight away that she was going to try and nick something, probably food, by her furtive and nervous expressions. True enough she had suddenly grabbed a pasty and made a dash for it, but the owner had spotted her and tried to cut her off at the end of the aisle. If he hadn't stuck his foot out and sent the guy sprawling before making a dash for it himself, she would have had no chance. He'd followed her down the road for a good half-mile before catching up with her. They had stopped side by side gasping for breath but confident they were safe.

'Thanks,' she had said and grinned at him.

'Christ, you can run. You should be more careful.'

'I manage.' He knew that was the last thing she could do. It was obvious she was young and vulnerable and was still learning the ins and outs of what to do to survive. He remembered thinking she had a good body. Okay, her tits were small and she was skinny, but her hair was lovely and thick. She'd make a lovely screw and could be very useful.

'Where're you going?' he had asked.

'Why?' She had tried to act tough to give the impression she had everything under control. When he hadn't answered her it had slightly spooked her, and she'd followed up with, 'Nowhere.'

'That pie's much better hot.' She didn't reply but tried to make a dismissive swish of the hand, but when he'd begun to move off and said 'suit yourself', she had caved in and asked him to wait.

'Maybe you're right,' she'd said with a smile, and they had walked off together.

Since then it had been good. She had been a good fuck, and he had been reliable in picking up deliveries, though half the time he thought she hadn't a clue what she was doing, she was so naïve. It was only recently she had become difficult, defiant. He wasn't going to stand for that. He hadn't wanted to knock her about, but so what. She owed him and had to learn. She had nowhere to go, and he knew enough people around the place who would give him the tip off. He was going to bloody well find her, bring her back and make her pay for putting him to so much trouble. If she didn't come back by morning, she could bloody well freeze to death as far as he was concerned. He suddenly heard the dog, who was wet and shivering in the cold, wailing out in the back yard. He went out to the kitchen, opened the back door and screamed, 'Shut that bloody row. I'm going to bed and want to sleep.' He slammed the door and went up to bed.

***

As Tom poured out the coffee, he checked the clock on the wall. It said 6:40. The night shift ended at 7:30, and the next two volunteers would arrive any time after seven.

He carried the three cups of coffee into the ops room and handed one to Carole.

'Thanks, Tom. What are you going to do about the girl now?'

'Give her a hot drink and say goodbye.' He noticed her pull a face as he made his way back to the interview room. He tapped on the door and went in. Cindy was lying on the floor, huddled beneath her blankets.

'It's a quarter to seven. You'll have to go soon – before the next shift arrives. I shall be in the hot seat if they find you here.' She lifted her head as she came out of her sleep, and he could immediately see the awful state of her face. Bruises had come out on her cheeks overnight, and her eye was still very swollen.

'I'll go now if you like,' said Cindy, trying to push herself up.

'No, no. You're all right for a few minutes. Drink this, and there's a washroom and loo across the way. How does your face feel?'

Cindy gently put fingers to her face. 'Better not go in for any beauty pageants'

'You should really have your eye looked at.'

Cindy simply shrugged, as if to say she would do nothing of the sort and that the subject was closed.

'I'll come back in a few moments,' said Tom and left her to go back to the ops room.

'Has she gone?' asked Carole.

'Not yet.' Then he noticed Linda. 'Hi, Linda. You're early.'

'Hi, Tom. Carole's told me about the girl. How is she?' she said and immediately came over to give Tom a hug.

'Doing her best.' Tom was relieved it was Linda. They were good friends. Linda was about forty and had been a volunteer for about twelve years. Linda was an attractive woman with an easy going and warm heart. She and Tom had become close, often doing shifts together, and easily shared problems or difficulties in their personal lives. She had also been a good friend of Janice, Tom's wife, before she had died, and sometimes unloaded on her some of her difficulties she was having with her own marriage.

'He shouldn't have let her stay,' said Carole huffily.

'She'll be gone in a minute and that'll be the end of it.'

'Nobody else need know,' said Linda, knowing that Tom wouldn't have taken the girl in unless he believed it to be right.

'Too late for that. I've already told Judy just now when I rang in to off-load,' said Carole.

'Why did you do that, Carole? She'll tell Sarah, and Tom will be in trouble.'

'It's not what we do. I've done nothing wrong.'

'No. God forbid...' said Linda with undisguised sarcasm.

'It's okay, Linda. Carole's right. I shouldn't have done it. The Organisation would collapse if we made up our own rules as went along.'

'Well, whatever you decided, that's good enough for me, Tom,' said Linda.

'Thanks.'

'Would you like me to go and talk to her?'

'No. She's just going. No need for you to get involved, Linda. I'll deal with it,' said Tom, and he turned away and walked from the ops room back to the interview room. Cindy was waiting for him and ready to go. She pushed the blankets into his arms.

'Thanks for these.'

Tom shook his head. 'You keep them. I doubt whether they'll be used here.'

Cindy nodded and said, 'Okay, just the red one. I'll get going then,' and moved to the door. Tom followed her out to the lobby and then they both stood in the now open doorway to the building. 'It's not raining anyway,' said Cindy with a smile.

'Where will you go?'

'I'm never going back to Frank anyway.'

'Are you feeling all right?'

'I've been worse.'

'Look, if you feel you want to do anything to yourself, come and see us. Can't offer you a home or solve your problems but... well, just a shoulder to cry on. It's all we've got.'

'You gave me what nobody else has ever done. And I'm still here,' said Cindy, and Tom felt the deep emotion in her voice.

'Take care of yourself.' He smiled at her, and she was about to go when he held her arm. 'Wait,' he said and put his hand in his pocket and took out a £10 note. 'I've broken one rule so I may as well go the whole hog and break another. It's for food – do you understand? Nothing else, especially drugs.'

'I already told you. I don't touch that stuff. I carried it for Frank. He used me. I could have nicked it but I never did.' She glared at him with her one good eye.

Tom made no reply and there was silence. 'Take it.' He pushed the money at her and after a moment she took it.

'Thanks' She paused and then, softly, 'Thank you.'

Tom nodded. They stared at each other for a few moments and then she turned and began to walk away. A moment later Tom was aware that Linda was at his side.

'Do you think she'll be all right?'

'Who knows? I did what I thought was best.'

Linda touched his arm. 'You did the right thing.'

'Maybe I've done this for too long. For all I know, she'll go back to the thug who beats her up.'

'Whatever she does it'll be her choice.'

Tom smiled with a shrug. For a little while they watched Cindy until she turned the corner at the end of the road and was gone. Tom sighed. 'I'm tired. It's been a long night.'

***

Micky opened up his Micky's Snack Bar in a hurry. He had overslept and was running late. The guys would be turning up soon, and he wouldn't be ready. Micky was lucky to have the site and had got permission to have the bar parked there a couple of years ago. It was situated on the edge of a large car park serving Clarkes and the builder's merchants and next to a number of other companies on the Cannon Industrial Trading Estate. Clarkes had connected him up with electricity, and in return he gave their staff a discount. It was a bonus for Micky because it provided him with power from electricity as well as Calor gas. The site had provided him with a good flow of customers since he'd set up there, but they had increased in numbers six months ago when extensive road works had commenced close by with the construction of a massive roundabout connecting up five roads. Work was not expected to be completed for at least another year. Although there was some competition on the trading estate itself from a burger bar at the other end, Micky had got regular customers, many of whom had become his friends. Micky was a likeable and friendly guy in his late twenties. He had short, dark curly hair and a wide forehead. The line of his nose was crooked, a legacy from when it had been broken in a fight which he had been reluctantly drawn into in a pub several years ago. He had been sitting on his own drinking beer when fans of two local football clubs, neither of which he supported, attacked each other following a controversial match, and he had been mistaken for a fan of both clubs. He also had a scar along the left line of his jaw which had resulted from a bicycle accident when he was a boy. His only other distinctive feature was his slightly oversized ears which had often been the butt of jokes because they also stuck out. One of them was slightly bunched at the edge as a result of playing as a forward in rugby scrums when he was in his teens. He had always joked that his face had novelties rather than disfigurements, and though he would never have claimed to be handsome, his face seemed to have a distinctive and built-in expression of strength. He had never known his father, but he had been close to his alcoholic mother who died when she was young and he was in his early teens. He had an older brother who had gone into the army and served in Afghanistan. But when he came out of the army, he had got married and gone abroad. He hadn't seen him since and had no idea where he was or what he was doing now. Micky considered himself lucky. Apart from his snack bar, he did odd jobbing to increase his income and much of this work was physical and kept him fit. Four years ago he had managed to acquire a tiny, one-bedroom house which he boasted was not much bigger than a loaf of bread. It was in a cul-de-sac and looked over fields. By nature he was fairly shy, rarely going to clubs, and enjoyed a good book or walking across the fields. He'd recently been thinking about getting a dog.

It wasn't long before he'd unloaded the bread rolls, baps and baguettes and had the eggs, sausages, burgers, onions and bacon sizzling on the griddle. The urn was boiling and polystyrene cups were ready for the tea and coffee when the first customers turned up for their breakfast. He'd got to know what many of them liked and pre-wrapped their food in tin foil as they liked to collect it and take it away. They also collected for some of their workmates.

After the initial early customers, there was usually a slight lull, and it gave Micky a chance to get food ready for the bigger number of customers that arrived throughout the day.

At 10 o'clock Douglas and his crew arrived.

'Morning, Doug,' said Micky to the big man as he took off his helmet and wiped the sweat off his face. 'Usual?'

'Thanks, Micky. What a night.'

'Too true. You guys the same?' said Micky as he handed the bacon baguette to Andy, sausage and onions to Bob and bacon and egg to Joe and Douglas. They all took coffee and paid their money. 'How's it going?'

'Getting out some trenches but the bloody things are full of water,' said Douglas as he munched his baguette. 'One delay after another.'

As the men concentrated on their food and mumbled to themselves, Micky kept looking to the far end of the car park at an old lean-to. He had some idea that it had originally been built as a bike shed but had never been used for that purpose and was now filled with discarded cardboard boxes and lumps of timber. He had noticed when he first arrived that there was something bright amongst the junk. It stood out because of the strong red colour and he thought it looked like a blanket. As he stared across now, he saw that a girl had climbed out of the blanket and was making her way over to them. As soon as she got within a few feet, Micky and the others all stared at her and were shocked at the state of her face.

Micky found his voice. 'What do you want, luv?'

'Cuppa tea' the workmen shifted on their feet and pretended not to take too much notice. Micky poured the tea and handed it to Cindy.

'And some bacon and egg in one of those rolls.'

'You got any money?'

Cindy pushed her £10 note at him. Micky couldn't resist raising his eyebrows and exchanging glances with the others who had become embarrassingly quiet. He counted out her change and handed it to her.

'You all right, luv?' asked Douglas because he couldn't hold out any longer.

'What's it to you?' snapped Cindy. Douglas didn't answer but turned away with a shrug and began to make what was an obviously false conversation with the others.

Micky said, 'You been over there all night?'

'No. What if I had?'

Micky shrugged. 'Nothing. Just trying to be friendly, that's all.'

Cindy regretted being so hostile, but she didn't say anything.

'You got no home?' Cindy stopped munching for a moment as if thinking about an answer, but then she concentrated on her bacon and egg roll again, eating in silence. Micky felt uncomfortable, as did the men round him, which was obvious by their quiet and unnatural conversation which would normally have been full of humorous banter. This wasn't good to see – not right up close. Of course they knew that homelessness was common enough, but having this young girl, bedraggled with all her face beaten up, right in the midst of them made them feel outraged. What kind of a world was this? What kind of a country? It was definitely not good, and they all felt a deep sense of unease even though they weren't responsible. But somebody was; somebody had beaten her up. And each of them knew they were all thinking the same thing: they'd like to get their hands on that piece of shit.

Cindy suddenly threw her empty cup in the litter bin.

'Thanks,' she said and began to walk off.

'Good luck,' called out Micky without concealing emotion in his voice, and his friends felt the same.

Chapter 2

It was 9:30 before Frank was woken by a banging on the front door. He cursed and swung his legs out of the bed even though he knew whom it would be. He shivered as he grabbed his trousers and a sweater and went downstairs. He opened the door and saw Lenny standing there.

He tolerated Lenny, even liked him a bit, as much as he was capable of liking anybody. Lenny was useful. And loyal. He needed people like Lenny around him to act as a heavy and enhance his image as a man who shouldn't be messed with. Frank secretly admitted to himself that, at the moment, he was small-fry. But that was going to be temporary. He wasn't going to be a pathetic and useless piece of shit like his father who had spent all his life in and out of prison for petty crime. He had died there, and that's what he had deserved. The day was coming when he was going to hit the big time; he was going to be respected and feared all over the county. He already had a bunch of followers who were doing things for him. And already he had a wad of money under the floorboards in the box room. He was going to increase that ten times in the next few months, and he could move out of this dump and get himself a mansion. The big man who was his supplier would have to watch out because he planned to wipe him off the face of the earth when the time was right. He was going to be number one, and nobody was going to stand in his way.

'Did I get you up?' said Lenny.

'Come in,' said Frank with a wave of the hand and walked through into the kitchen. Lenny was big. He worked out regularly at the gym with the weights. He was proud of his body. His hair was cropped to within half an inch of his scalp and he had two big rings pierced through his left ear. When he was in his teens, fighting had been a pleasure for him and he hadn't minded getting some of his own medicine, which didn't happen often, but nevertheless resulted in him being left with scars on his face – one across his cheek and the other across his eyebrow. In fact he'd got both of them after he had left school when he took on a couple of nineteen year olds. He hadn't minded the scars because he left those arrogant toerags with far worse.

'Did she come back?' asked Lenny as he reached for the kettle and filled it.

'I'll find her today, don't you worry.'

'Can't believe she's got the nerve. And after all you've done for her.'

'Make the tea, Lenny. I gotta have a shit and shower. Two minutes.' Frank walked out and went upstairs to the bathroom. He stripped off and looked in the mirror. He had big shoulders and strong arms. And he was proud of his hairy chest. Everything about Frank was powerful. He pushed the fingers of both hands through his hair so that it fell back down the back of his head. Frank was not ugly, but he had a permanently intimidating expression caused partly by his dark eyes and the creases across his wide forehead. He scowled and moved into the shower, but a couple of minutes later he was out of it, dried, dressed and back with Lenny in the kitchen.

'Pretty rough out,' said Lenny. 'She'll be wanting to come back.'

'She's got to be taught a lesson.'

'I've done you two slices,' said Lenny and pushed two slices of toast across the table to Frank who spread them with butter and then jam.

'There's nowhere for her to go, Lenny. Put the word round. Someone will spot her and let us know. We'll try the usual places ourselves.'

'She's not going to go blabbing about us to anyone, is she?'

'Like who?'

'I dunno. The Old Bill?'

'Are you kidding? She hasn't got the balls.'

'Maybe she'll turn up herself. She will if she knows what's good for her.'

'She'll never survive on her own, I'll tell you that. Anyway, I'm getting low on the stuff. I need her to pick up a delivery.'

They suddenly heard the sounds of Murphy howling outside.

'I'll kill that bloody dog if he doesn't shut up. It's 'cos he knows she's gone. The fucking trouble that bitch is causing me.'

'As soon as you're finished, we'll get off then.'

Frank stuffed the lump of toast in his mouth and stood up. 'Let's go.'

They both went out.

***

Leaning forward, her head tucked into her shoulders against the wind, Cindy walked towards town. Every now and then she would stop and look back across her shoulder, wary of anyone following her. Once she had got to the centre of town with all the shops, she would have a better chance of not being found. But the feeling of being on the run scared her. With nowhere permanently safe to go, he'd eventually find her. Maybe today, maybe in a week. She wouldn't be able to go on hiding forever. For one thing, Frank had so many cronies he'd call in, it would only be a matter of time before one of them spotted her and would fall over themselves to let him know. Even those she knew who were living rough or met at some of the centres would probably snitch on her if they saw her. He'd be sure to do the rounds and question them and tell them to report to him if she had been with them. She was glad she'd found the old lean-to on the edge of the car park earlier on. She'd managed to suss it out in daylight and reckoned it would be a safe place to bed down at night without being discovered by Frank; that is, if he hadn't found her before then. She'd made up her mind about one thing. She wasn't going back to him. She'd rather be dead.

It took her twenty minutes to reach the shops and she began to move around the early shoppers. Outside one of the mini-supermarkets, she spotted Martin busking with his harmonica. Martin had occupied that pitch for years. She was amazed that he managed to survive for so long. She moved over to him.

'Hi, Mart. You okay?'

'Hi, Cindy. Your face don't look good.'

'Thanks, Mart. Done any good?'

'A few coppers. It's early.'

'You haven't seen Frank, have you?'

'No, and I don't want to.'

'Don't say you've seen me, Mart, if he comes by.'

'You in trouble?'

'I've done a runner.'

'Bloody 'ell. Take care, Cind.'

'You too,' said Cindy and walked on.

She gradually made her way round town and stopped off briefly to chat to one or two other homeless people who she knew. When she came across Robby, who was selling the Big Issue, he told her that Frank had passed by earlier and asked if he'd seen her.

'I told him I hadn't, of course.'

'The bastard's after me.'

'You'd better keep your head down. He was pretty wound up.'

'Thanks, Robby. See yer,' said Cindy and moved off again.

For the rest of the morning she moved round town, going into shops and looking out of their windows, up and down the street. It gave her a small chance of catching sight of Frank if he was nearby. She suddenly found herself outside an Oxfam shop and decided to have a look around in there. The old woman behind the counter stared at her in a funny way, and Cindy suddenly realised that it must have been because the state of her face. Her eye was still very swollen and half closed, and her cheek was going all colours of the rainbow. A number of people had stared at her as she walked along the street, and it now dawned on her why. Cindy turned away and made her way to the back of the shop where there were shelves full of books. She pretended to be looking over them to justify her being there for so long. She suddenly looked back down the shop and out of the window and saw Frank and Lenny standing there talking. Her heart began to pound as she wondered whether or not he would come inside. His conversation seemed to be intense, and he kept looking up and down the street. Cindy felt sure he must be discussing her and talking about where they should try looking for her next. She saw Lenny suddenly look up and peer into the shop, and she tried shrinking behind two other customers who were also looking at the books. Because she was so small she was able to conceal herself fairly well, but then she noticed that Lenny had put his hand on the door handle and half opened the door as if to enter. But then she heard Frank shout at him, 'Not now, Lenny. Let's get on,' and she saw Frank already moving off. Lenny closed the door again and followed. Cindy looked around self-consciously to see if anyone had noticed her state of panic, but nobody seemed to pay her any more attention. She carried on looking at the books until her heart rate had calmed down. She began to realise that Frank would not personally want to spend too much of his own time traipsing about the town looking for her. All his cronies would be on the lookout for her by now and would report to him if they saw her. As well as that, he would put the word round to the other haunts where she was known and knew other homeless. He would have probably gone home now and left it to others to find her.

She looked out of the window again and saw that it was suddenly dark even though it was only 5 o'clock. She decided she must get back to the place where she would stay the night in order to be safe. She moved out of the shop and began to walk back through town when she noticed Pam's Pantry, a cake shop that was obviously clearing up what was left over before closing up. Cindy suddenly remembered she hadn't eaten anything for God knows how long and felt hunger gnawing at her stomach. She entered the shop and spotted there was one meat pasty and a couple of artificial cream cakes on the counter. She stared at them.

'You can have 'em half price. We'd only bin them,' said the woman behind the counter, looking across her shoulder at her companion who had disappeared into a back room to see that she hadn't heard.

'Thank you,' said Cindy and gave the woman a one pound coin. The woman took the money then gave her the cakes and pasty in a bag and the one pound coin back. Cindy looked puzzled.

'Don't worry about it,' she said with a wink. 'I know what it is to have tough times.'

Cindy smiled and left the shop. She began eating as she set off down the street again. As she moved away from the shops, she began to relax a little and watched the endless stream of cars as they dawdled their way home from work. It was less than half an hour when she reached the car park. Clarkes had closed, although some lights were still on inside. There was only the odd car parked in the car park, and work on the roundabout had stopped for the day. Micky's Snack Bar was shut up for the night. She didn't notice anyone in the car park and felt she wasn't noticed as she made her way over to the lean-to. She pulled some rubbish and cardboard boxes to the side and climbed into the back. It wasn't dark yet, but she was tired. She pulled the red blanket round her and curled up. It could be worse. She'd be safe for the night.

***

It was closing time when Frank left his mates and came out of the pub. He'd had too much to drink, and he was in a bad mood. In spite of the fact that some of his cronies had asked around and visited every possible place they thought Cindy could have gone to, they had all come up blank. She had simply disappeared off the face of the earth. But Frank knew that wasn't possible, and it made him angry to think the bitch had made him look an idiot, that she had stuck two fingers up at him and done a runner. She had to be somewhere, and he was going to find her. And when he did she was going to have to suffer for it.

***

When Micky had arrived first thing to open up his van, he had deliberately looked across the car park at the dilapidated lean-to. He could tell that the junk had been moved about, and behind it he saw a glimpse of the red blanket that the girl had carried the day before. He guessed she must have been there all night again.

There was no movement, and he had assumed she was asleep. He had stood staring over at her, wondering if he should do something though he hadn't the faintest idea what. It made him feel bad inside again to think that a young girl had to live like that. This was the United Kingdom, a civilised society that he wanted to feel proud of. But this girl was living like a scavenging dog. How was it possible that this sort of thing could go on side-by-side with the rest of society living a normal day-to-day life?

As he got the griddle heated and the bacon and sausages, mushroom and onions sizzling in readiness for his first customers, he couldn't shake off his feelings about the girl. What kind of a situation must she have had to leave to make her end up sleeping rough like that? And who was the piece of shit who had beaten her up so badly? Micky didn't regard himself as a softy, but beating up young girls was out of order. More than that, it was a downright bloody disgrace, and whoever did that sort of thing needed a good hiding themselves.

As his customers started arriving, he concentrated on serving them but always keeping a lookout towards the lean-to from the corner of his eye. When Douglas and his crew turned up about 10 o'clock, they also looked across to the lean-to and saw Cindy's blanket.

'She back again, Micky?' asked Douglas.

'Looks like it. She was there when I arrived first thing,' said Micky as he started handing out their usual.

The men grunted their approval and stared towards the lean-to as they saw the blanket move and Cindy come to life.

'What a bloody state to live in,' said Bob. 'Don't seem right.'

'D'you reckon she was there all night?' asked Douglas.

'Sure to.'

'I bet you drugs is the problem,' said Andy speaking with a mouth full of bacon baguette.

'I don't think so,' chipped in Micky. 'Wouldn't have the money.'

'They get it somehow. And she had a tenner yesterday.'

'That's bugger all. Anyway, watch your mouth, she's coming over.'

They all pretended not to watch as Cindy made her way over to them. When she got to the counter she defiantly turned to stare at them head-on, and they could all see her face was still swollen with the colours caused by the bruising coming out.

'All right? Now you've had a good look. Satisfied?' She stared at them for a moment longer and then turned to Micky. 'Same as yesterday please.' She put some coins on the counter.

The guys mumbled to themselves as Micky prepared Cindy's roll with bacon and egg and poured her a cup of coffee. He gave her the roll and her change then she stood quietly eating. Micky felt uncomfortable. It wasn't in his nature to be unfriendly, and the guys were only feeling sorry for her. He liked his bar to be a happy place. 'Is your roll okay?' He smiled at her and for a moment she stopped munching and looked at him in surprise. 'Just trying to be friendly, that's all,' he offered.

'It's just a roll. It's all right.'

'Micky's proud of his rolls. Reckons they're the best you can get,' said Douglas. 'O'course we know different. But we put up with it.' All the guys laughed. 'My name's Douglas. This here is Andy; this is Joe, and the little guy's Bob. The guy up there trying to poison us all is Micky.' They all mumbled some kind of greeting as Cindy stared from one to the other, looking bewildered. When they stared back and there was a silence, she realised their expressions were one of expectancy.

'Er, Cindy. My name's Cindy.' They all grinned and jostled round her saying, 'Hi Cindy,' and then for a little while nobody knew what to say so they pretended to be concentrating on their food.

'You got nowhere to go?' tried Douglas.

'What do you think?' said Cindy still maintaining her defensive stance.

'That don't seem right. How come?'

'Boyfriend. Piece o' shit threw me out.'

Douglas put a hand to his face. 'Did he do that to you?'

She didn't answer but shrugged and looked down. 'Should have left ages ago. My own fault.'

'You didn't deserve that, Cindy.'

Again she shrugged, 'Whatever.'

Micky said, 'Are you sleeping in that lean-to tonight?' She didn't answer, and they guessed she would be. 'Where d'you go in the day?'

'Lose myself. I don't want him to find me.'

'Not much of a life.'

'Tell me about it.'

'Sorry.'

'Forget it.'

'We'd better get back, lads,' said Douglas, and the guys nodded agreement. 'See yer, Micky. You take care, Cindy.' They all nodded and started to move off.

'Cheers guys,' called Micky after them, and then said to Cindy, 'They're good blokes. Dougie wouldn't hurt a fly in spite of his size.'

'Then he must be the seventh wonder of the world,' said Cindy with sarcasm, and Micky guessed she had only ever had bad experiences with men. 'I'm gonner shove off anyway.' She turned and began to walk away.

'Take care of yourself, Cindy.' He watched her for a long time until she disappeared. He wondered what might happen to her and whether he would ever see her again.

**

Tom leaned back on the park bench and glanced at the ducks on the lake. He scratched his forehead and let out a long sigh. He had not felt so low, so unsettled, since Janice had died three years ago. He desperately needed the comfort of her presence now. She would have held his hand, and in that small gesture he would have drawn such strength. But she wasn't there, so he had to pull himself up and sort out the problems on his mind.

He would have to get down to the Centre shortly for his meeting with Sarah. He just wanted a little time to think about what he was going to say; more than that, he wanted to try and sort out exactly what he was feeling. Why was it he couldn't get Cindy out of his mind? Over the many years he'd been a Samaritan, he had spoken to hundreds of callers whose lives were in a distressing or tragic state. Like all his colleagues, he had felt sadness and true distress at their plight and, so often, frustration at not being able to solve their problems. But, as was the practice of all volunteers, he would have unloaded to his shift leader in order to leave any emotional distress behind at the Centre before returning to his daily life. Occasionally he had thought about some callers for a few days afterwards, particularly those who called several times over a period of weeks, but he had always managed to keep his emotions in check. But something different had happened during his confrontation with Cindy. The sight of her standing in the doorway in the wind and rain, frozen and her face battered, a lost and pathetic soul, not much more than a child, had touched his heart with an emotion he had not experienced before. What would be her chances of finding a decent life? If she went back to Frank, it would be one of misery. But she knew that herself, so why would she do that? It wasn't so unlikely. He'd spoken to hundreds of callers in an abusive and violent relationship who kept going back to the same partner. And if she didn't go back anyway, she'd be very vulnerable in a hostile world – living rough, eking out an existence that offered little or no hope for the future. He gave a shiver and pulled his coat round him more tightly.

He had to admit in his heart of hearts why she was affecting him so much. His daughter Jessica would have been about the same age as Cindy. What a different life she would have had: decent schooling; happy friendships; parties and a social life. Above all she would have had a loving and secure home. It was a ridiculous thought, but he felt a huge urge to try to see Cindy again and know that she was going to be all right, to know that she hadn't gone back to Frank, and that in some way she had found some kind of safe environment from which to build some kind of a normal life. Of course he knew he couldn't do anything himself, and he also knew that he was never likely to see her again. Even if she called at the Centre again, he wouldn't be there. He wondered how Sarah would take his resignation, that is, if she didn't sack him for breaking an important rule. He'd have to leave anyway, although he wouldn't tell her why. Not yet. There was still time, so there was no need. Perhaps he should be thinking more about his own problem than Cindy's. In a way, although it was completely different, it was more pressing. But like Cindy's problem, he couldn't do anything about it. Maybe he was thinking about her so much as a distraction from the worry he had about himself. It was pointless him worrying anyway, because it wouldn't achieve anything.

It was time for him to get going. He stood up and took the short walk back to his car. The Centre was only a couple of miles from the park, and when he arrived he could see that Sarah's car was already there.

Tom tripped the lock on the staff door and went into the building. Immediately to his right was the ops room where the two volunteers on duty would be answering the phones. He would normally have gone in for a quick chat, but he decided to go straight into the little room used as the director's office and talk to Sarah. She was already sitting at her desk with a cup of coffee. Sarah was in her mid-forties and had done nursing for many years. She did it part-time now. She was a handsome woman rather than pretty. Her dark hair was short, and her brown eyes gave the impression of warmth and reassurance. It was no surprise that the branch had chosen her to be the director for her three-year period because she was respected and liked by everyone.

'Morning, Tom. Do you want to get a coffee?'

'No, thanks.' Tom sat down opposite her.

'Trying to get my stuff together for the weekend. I'm off on the National Meeting for Directors. Thank goodness it only comes once a year.'

'Ahh, the burdens of high office.'

Sarah laughed, 'Of course; but then I only do it for the money.' Tom laughed too, and there was a brief silence.

'I know your job as director is not always a picnic, and I'm sorry about the business of taking in the girl for the night. It must be a first.'

'I've only asked you in for a chat, Tom, to check that everything is all right with you. You're not here to get a ticking off.'

'It set a bad precedent. I ought to resign.'

'I certainly hope you won't. That's the last thing I want you to do.'

'Look, Sarah, if you sacked me as you should do, I wouldn't take it personally. As director I realise there are some decisions you have to make for the benefit of the whole branch.'

'Oh dear, Tom, such high flown rhetoric.'

'Sorry. Look, I'm going to resign anyway.'

'But there's really no need, Tom.'

'It's got nothing to do with the girl I took in. There are other things I've got to deal with. I don't want to go into them if you don't mind.'

'Oh, Tom, you're not in trouble of any kind are you?'

'No. Not really.'

'Not really. That means there is a problem.'

'I can't say at the moment. It's complicated.'

'I'm not trying to be nosy, but you know I'd be there for you.'

'I know that, Sarah. And I promise to let you know what's going on soon.'

Sarah stood up and moved round the desk to him.

Tom said, 'I'm sorry it's so sudden.'

'I've never respected anyone's judgment more than I do yours, Tom. Come and see me at home, won't you.'

'I promise.' He kissed her on both cheeks and left the building.

***

Cindy stood in the front garden of an empty house at the end of Cherry Tree Road. The windows were boarded up and the garden was full of domestic junk. A single fir tree struggled for survival, and Cindy used it to conceal herself. She needed to get back in to where she had been living. She knew she was taking a risk and she was probably crazy, but she'd made up her mind that she was going to get Murphy out of that hellhole. And while she was there, she'd grab some underwear and clothes. The clothes she was wearing had been filthy for days, and she could smell her own body. If Murphy wasn't already dead and she managed to get him out, she had no idea how she would be able to look after him, but she'd face that problem when and if she was successful. She'd never discovered how it was that Frank had taken in Murphy in the first place. One of his cronies, Lenny, had mentioned to her that he was given to him when he was a small puppy, not much more than a ball of fur, and he had been something of a novelty for him. Judging from the time that Cindy had been living with Frank and had witnessed how he treated Murphy, she guessed that, for the three years of his life, Murphy would have suffered only pain and misery. She had often given him extra food to make up the paltry scraps that Frank used to throw him and often tried to cuddle him and bring him in the house when Frank was not around. She had to be careful because, not only would Murphy get a beating, but she would have suffered a pasting herself if he came home and discovered them. Once she had suggested that, if he didn't want Murphy, he could be taken to the animal shelter and found another home. He'd called her a bloody idiot and said that the dog was fine.

The street was quiet, and it would soon be dark. She guessed that Frank would probably be going out soon if he hadn't done so already. She would have to find a way in, but she would worry about that when she actually got to the house and was sure Frank was out. She waited until what streetlights hadn't been broken, and the occasional light from some of the houses, came on, and then she began to slowly move up the road. Every now and then she slipped into a front garden where she would not be seen by anyone in the road who happened to be walking or driving by. Frank's house was one in a line of terracing, but it was detached on one side with a narrow passageway running between his and the empty house next door. His own house was enclosed by a six-foot-high close board fence. All the bottoms of the back gardens were sealed off by a huge concrete-panelled fence, on the other side of which was the remains of a derelict warehouse and large parking space. The site had been earmarked for redevelopment ten years ago, but nothing had ever been started. There was a six-foot-high gate at the far end of the passage into Frank's garden which was always secured by a bolt at the top on the inside.

Cindy could clearly see that no lights had been switched on in the house, and that as Frank's car wasn't parked outside, she could feel fairly certain that he must be out. There was no way of knowing if he had been out all day and was due back or if he had gone out shortly before she'd arrived and would probably be out for the rest of the evening. She decided she must take the risk, knowing that if he did come back and he caught her, she was going to be in serious trouble. She heard the sound of young men's voices bantering and laughing as they approached from further down the road. As they walked past she recognised that two of them were brothers and the third their friend. They lived at the end of the road, and she had often seen them and knew that they were involved in all sorts of petty crime and possibly even more serious stuff. She guessed that they would probably be moving into the clubs later that evening and picking up or pushing drugs. As soon as they'd gone by, she gave a light spring up, caught the top of the fence and hauled herself up. She swung her legs over and dropped down the other side. Everywhere was still and quiet. In the corner where the fence joined the house, she saw Murphy emerge from his ramshackle kennel and wag his tail when he realised who it was. She quickly skipped across to him and gave him a cuddle.

'This is your big day, Murphy. We're going to get you out of here. We're both going to be free of that piece of shit Frank.' She ran her hands over his matted and filthy coat, at the same time feeling sickened by his protruding ribs.

She slipped a short length of string from her jeans hip pocket and tied it to his collar. 'I'm going to get you outside first, and then you've got to wait for me. I've got to get into the house. I won't be long. And don't make a noise.'

She led him over to the gate, slipped the bolt and stepped out into the dark passage. An old nail stuck out from one of the fence posts, and she tied the end of the string to it in a loose knot. 'Be a good boy, Murph, and I'll be back in a minute. If Frank comes back or if he's in the house, we may have to leg it pretty fast, so be ready.' She patted the dog and moved back into the garden.

She knew the layout of the house perfectly and decided, since she knew the doors would be locked, her best bet would be to try and find a window that was not completely shut. She moved up to the kitchen window and peered in. All seemed quiet and still. Even though the house was in darkness, she remained motionless and listened for any sound that might come from inside. It was just possible that Frank could be asleep. Sometimes he would crash out all day after he had been drinking heavily. It would be just her luck to get inside and wake him up. But the house was completely silent and all the windows were securely shut, so she decided that the only way would be to break the glass and release a catch of a fanlight. Her frame was tiny and would have no difficulty in wriggling through. She picked up one of the many old bricks lying around and drove it into the glass. Again she stood perfectly still, thinking that, if Frank were in the house, the noise would have woken him. All was silent. She reached through the hole, released the catch and pushed open the window. She hesitated for a few seconds then hoisted herself up on to the sill and pushed her way through the window. A small but jagged piece of glass, still fixed to the frame, nicked her shoulder and cut through her clothing down her left side. She cursed but couldn't stop to worry about that now.

She slithered on to the sink drainer and jumped down. Frank would go mad when he saw the broken glass and realised that someone had broken in. The inside of the house was very different to the outside, and Frank was very particular about keeping the place tidy. He'd had a luxury kitchen fitted, and the living room and dining room were furnished with good quality furniture. The living room was fitted with a thick-pile top-of-the-range carpet, and he'd had an over-powering but impressive fireplace put in.

Cindy began to feel confident that the house was empty but decided that, to take no chances anyway, she would get upstairs as quickly as possible, grab a few clothes and be out of the house. She skipped down the hall and took the stairs two at a time. As soon as she reached the landing, she paused. Better not get too confident. He could be in the bedroom on the bed, fast asleep. He'd certainly wake up. The door was ajar but she leant forward and strained to hear if there were the sounds of breathing. The room was deadly silent. She went straight in and made for the chest of drawers. She grabbed a pair of jeans, some underwear, a couple of t-shirts and an old denim jacket. She rolled them into a ball and tied it up with another piece of string from her pocket.

It was then that she heard voices and froze. She knew they were coming from outside the front of the house, and she ran to the window and looked down. Frank was standing outside with Lenny and looked as if he was fiddling to find his front door key. She immediately realised that if she ran downstairs she would run straight into him as he opened the front door. Her mind raced as panic set in. She was trapped and he would cut loose when he found her there. Christ, he might kill her. It wouldn't only be Frank. She would be faced with Lenny as well who would want to pitch in. She knew Frank well enough and that he was a vicious bastard of the first order, but Lenny loved handing out beatings, and she guessed that Frank would have been so mad at her that he would let Lenny have a free hand.

Frantically she looked around to see if there was some place to hide, at the same time thinking that a fat lot of use that would be. She heard the front door open and the two men enter the house. She could hear them talking but not what they were saying. If they went into the front room to watch television, she might have a slim chance of slipping down the stairs then out through the back door and making her escape across the back gardens. That is, of course, if they shut the front room door which was highly unlikely.

'Jesus Christ, Lenny, somebody's smashed the kitchen window,' she heard Frank's voice say.

'It's a fucking break-in,' said Lenny.

'The bastards.'

'Anything nicked?'

'I'll kill the bastards. Look upstairs, Lenny. They might still be in the house. I'll look down here and check if anything has been nicked at the same time.'

She heard Frank's footsteps make for the box room at the side of the hall, where she knew he kept his pile of money, together with the drugs, under the floorboards. That would have been his first panic.

Cindy could feel her heart pounding in her chest as she heard Lenny's feet jumping the stairs two at a time. Suddenly they stopped, and she realised he had paused on the landing deciding whether to go left or right. As the floorboards creaked, she knew he had moved along to the bathroom. Accepting it only gave her a pathetic chance, she lay on the ground and, because she was so small, was able to slide beneath the bed which was very low to the ground. A few seconds later she saw Lenny's feet stand in the doorway. The room was very small, and she desperately hoped he would assume there was nobody in there and nowhere to hide. Surely he wouldn't think anyone could slide under the bed, it was so low to the floor. He moved across to the fitted wardrobe and opened the door.

'Nothing up here, Frank,' he called down.

'Have a look under the bed, Lenny. They could be there,' Frank's voice shouted back, and Cindy's heart gave a leap. She was doomed.

'Nothing can get under your bed, Frank. There's nothing up here, I tell you.' Cindy watched Lenny's feet tap for a few moments as if he was having a last look round, and then they moved away and out the door.

Her heart still thumped as she heard them cursing and clumping about downstairs. They hadn't discovered her, but her situation was no better. How the hell was she going to get out? She had no idea. She might have to stay there for hours, especially if the two of them decided to stay in all night and watch television. The thought that Frank would eventually come to bed and she would still be lying underneath it filled her with horror. And then she remembered Murphy tied up outside. She couldn't leave him there indefinitely. She lay quietly trying to settle her thoughts as her heart rate began to settle down. After about half an hour, the voices downstairs became quieter and she could hear the drone of the TV. They'd obviously got a couple of beers from the fridge and were settling down for the evening. Her only chance would be to creep downstairs while they were distracted and get out the back door. Once out of the house, she could escape down the garden. She realised the likelihood of her getting past their door without them hearing her was pretty slim, but she had no choice. If they were watching a film such as a war film or gangsters where there might be loud gunfire, she would stand a better chance if she picked the right moment. Her first move would be to get out from under the bed and creep along the landing to the top of the stairs. She would be able to hear more clearly the nearer she got to them.

She eased herself out and crept towards the landing, pausing after every step to listen. She sighed with relief when she heard gunfire and loud music from the TV. Would it continue or would it stop? Should she take her chance now with the possibility of it suddenly fading as she moved down the stairs, or should she wait until it erupted again? If she waited and either Frank or Lenny came out of the room, they couldn't fail to see her and she'd be doomed. She stood motionless in indecision as her heart began to pound again.

There was a sudden soundtrack of diving aeroplanes and bombs dropping, and her feet were already skipping down the stairs. As she jumped off the last step, she grabbed the balustrade and swung round to head for the kitchen. Her haste was so great that she collided with the low table on which a telephone was placed and it clattered to the ground. The noise was deafening, and she felt an electric current whiplash her body as she stumbled on trying to keep her balance. As soon as her hand grabbed the kitchen door handle, she knew the door behind her had sprung open, and Frank was charging out.

'Come 'ere, you bitch!' he screamed. In a moment she was through the door and was certain he would never catch her now, but in the next instant she lost her footing and crashed into a metal dustbin, which toppled over, spilling its contents on the ground. She vaguely heard Murphy, still tied up in the passageway, give a bark. Blind to the pain caused by her fall, she leapt to her feet as Frank reached out and grabbed her sleeve, dragging her to the ground again. She wriggled like a ferret, and with kicking legs and flaying arms, she jerked from his grip and leapt to the side so that it slipped off her. But almost immediately his other hand swung at her with an iron fist, which missed her and thumped into concrete. He roared out in pain as his skin tore back across his knuckles. 'I'll kill you, you bitch,' he screamed and made another lunge to grab her hair. Again she wriggled and twisted out of range but saw at the same time that Lenny was already coming through the doorway to reinforce Frank.

As she went to push herself up, her hand rested on the dustbin lid and, as if instinctively, her fingers curled round the rim, allowing her to swing it in desperate panic as Frank made another wild lunge at her. The rim of the metal lid thumped hard into the side of his head causing him to lurch to the side in front of Lenny, who stumbled over him, so that they both fell in a heap. She cast aside the lid and raced down the garden before shooting through the gate. She slipped the knot fixed to the nail tethering Murphy. 'Come on, Murphy. Run! Both our lives depend on it!'

In the next instant she was racing along the passageway back to the front of the house, Murphy at her side. She heard Frank and Lenny screaming oaths into the darkness but soon they grew fainter as she sprinted down the road and away from the estate. She kept going for half a mile, not daring to look back, but eventually she reckoned she was safe. They wouldn't know which way she had gone and would give up their search almost as soon as they started. She rested her back into a tree in a grass verge at the roadside and allowed her heart to slow down and catch her breath. Murphy leant into her side. He was in such a poor condition, he had struggled to keep up with her. She knelt down on one knee and put an arm round him.

'You're going to be all right, Murph, I promise. We're going to beat this bastard. But first things first, you're hungry and cold. Me too, but we'll manage. I don't think I can get anything to eat yet, but we've got to find somewhere warm for the night. Tesco is not far. They're open all night. We'll need luck, but it's worth a try. We'll hang on for a few minutes so you can get your breath back.'

She slipped her bottom on to the ground and rested her head against the tree. Frank would be raving mad by now, knowing that she had not only broken into his house, but smashed him in the face with the dustbin lid before getting away. He'd be a laughing stock if he didn't catch her and give her the biggest thrashing of her life. She was determined that wasn't going to happen, although she didn't kid herself that he wouldn't be relentless in trying to find her. He'd have plenty of cronies out there keeping a watch as well. She'd have to avoid all her normal haunts. Maybe she should bite the bullet and leave town. But where to? And why should she? She liked this place and wasn't going to have some scumbag like Frank dictate where she should live. Live? That was a laugh. This was hardly existence.

The break-in at Frank's and the following scuffle had drained all her energy more than she realised, but it was time to move. She pushed up and set off with Murphy at her side. She kept close to the buildings and her wits about her, in fear that Frank might suddenly jump out of the pavement beneath her feet. It only took her a few minutes to reach Tesco's car park. Although it was getting late, there were still a few people wandering about with their trolleys, and it would remain the same throughout the night. She knew exactly where to find the huge bins that they used for disposing of food that was out of date or, according to apparent laws of health and safety, was not allowed to be sold for consumption. She weaved her way between the cars in the car park and managed to get round the back of the building without drawing attention to herself. She reached the bins and found they were well stocked with discarded food. Most of it was unsuitable for Murphy, but she sorted a pack of sausages and some packets of biscuits, all of which were pre-packed, and some fruit. She made her way back across the car park and quickly scanned the shop for security guards There was no way she would be able to get into the shop with a dog walking at her side. She collected a trolley, sauntered across to the far boundary of the car park and stopped on the blind side of a car.

'Now, Murph, we've got to be clever, and you've got to help me.' She untied her bundle of clothing she had retrieved and wrapped it round the dog. He was about the same size as a sheep dog but, as there was so little flesh on him, she was able to lift him without too much difficulty and place him in on the bottom shelf of the trolley. She completely covered him so that he could have been taken as a half full shopping bag. No one would suspect there was a dog wrapped up inside.

'You've got to keep still, Murph, and make no noise.'

She nonchalantly made her way back to the building and went straight into the toilets, taking the trolley inside with her. Nobody gave her a second glance. She got Murphy out of the trolley, which she pushed back out of the door, and then stepped inside a cubicle and locked the door. It was a squash for the two of them, but it was warm. She opened the pack of sausages and gave them to the dog, then munched her way through a packet of Jaffa cakes, followed by an apple. She'd eaten a lot better before, but it was enough. She curled up against the wall and pulled Murphy into her side. She knew that either security or a cleaner would be round at some stage before morning, but she was too tired to care. She closed her eyes and was soon asleep.

Chapter 3

Linda pulled into the kerb outside Tom's house and switched off the engine. In the past she had often called to see both Tom and Janice, as they were very close friends. When Janice died Tom had leant on Linda through his weeks and months of grieving, and there was very little that she and Tom could not share if they had personal problems or wanted advice. Instinctively she knew that Tom must be facing some difficulty. She could still hardly believe that he had resigned from the branch and knew that he would not have done so without good reason. She simply couldn't imagine what that reason might be and knew that it would have to be something so unexpected that he wasn't able to talk to her about it first. Tom was so committed to the Sams and had given so much to them over the years. When he'd rung her and asked her to come round as he wanted to have a chat, she would not have normally have thought this was unusual. But she could tell from his voice that something was wrong and guessed that it had to be about his resignation. As far as she knew, the rest of the branch was not yet aware of his decision to leave, and she had only been told by Sarah, in confidence, because she knew that she and Tom were so close and was worried about Tom.

She got out of the car, made her way up to the front door and pushed the bell. A moment later Tom appeared and, although he was smiling, she recognized a sadness in his eyes. He kissed her and led her through to the living room.

'It's good to see you, Linda.'

'And you.'

'Coffee or wine?'

'I've got a feeling I might need wine,' said Linda with a smile.

'I promise not to send you off drunk,' replied Tom and opened a bottle of red wine without speaking. He poured out a couple of glasses and handed one to her.

'Bottoms up.'

'Cheers.' For a few moments there was silence as they savoured the wine.

'How's Clive?'

'No headway, I'm afraid,' said Linda with a shrug. 'We're still sharing the same bed at the moment, so that's something I suppose. Not that anything happens.'

'I'm sorry. He's not, er…'

'Got a bit on the side? I don't know. If he has I'd probably be the last to know. He's on a night shift so I shan't see him until tomorrow morning.'

'He's a bloody fool.'

'Oh, I dunno. It's not all his fault.'

There was another silence and then Tom said, 'I'm sorry I didn't talk to you about me resigning, Linda.'

She brushed the air dismissively with the back of her hand. 'That's fine. No need. But I don't understand.'

'I didn't want to, but it was the right decision.'

'Sarah didn't want you to leave. Taking in that girl for the night was the right thing even though it's not allowed.'

'I've no regrets about that, and it's not why I resigned.'

'I don't understand,' said Linda, struggling to think of what could have possibly made Tom make such a decision.

'I've got cancer.'

Linda felt her skin prickle as the blood rushed to her cheeks. Her mouth dropped in shock, and for a few moments she couldn't speak.

'Tom! Oh Tom,' she cried out and immediately stood and reached out for him. She held him for a little while, and then he eased her away.

'It's all right. I'm not dead yet.'

'But Tom. How? When? I mean, how long have you known? And what does it mean?'

'Two or three months ago, I knew something was wrong. It's fairly aggressive, but I'm holding together.'

'Yes, but what does it mean? Can they treat you?'

'Oh yes yes yes.' As he spoke she could tell he was holding back on the whole truth.

'Tell me the truth, Tom.'

'Well, nobody wants to commit to an actual time scale. A year, anyway, hopefully.'

'Oh Tom, I'm so sorry,' said Linda and again put her arms around him.

'I didn't tell Sarah. I will, of course, but not yet. You're the only person who knows.'

'What can I do?'

'Nothing. I could have stayed on for a bit, but I decided to resign now while I'm doing okay.'

'How is it affecting you?'

'Not a lot of difference. I get tired quickly. But I'm not giving up on living just because I've resigned from the branch. I'm just choosing what I do more selfishly.'

'You haven't got a selfish bone in your body, Tom. I'm so glad you've told me. I shall be here for you whenever you need me.'

'I know that, Linda. There is something I want you to do for me though.'

'If I can, you know I will.'

'Now that I'm not a volunteer, it's not really allowed, but if that girl, you know, Cindy, the girl I took in, calls at the Centre again, could you let me know?'

'Of course I will,' said Linda with a slightly puzzled expression.

'It's just that I'd like to know if she's all right. I know it sounds silly but I really felt for her. You know Jessica would have been about her age had she lived.'

She reached out and squeezed his hand, 'Oh, Tom.'

'Silly, I know.'

'It's not silly. And I promise. But she may never show her face again.'

'Then we'll just have to hope she's okay. Now then. Have you eaten?'

'No. Not yet.'

'Good. Join me in the kitchen I've got smoked salmon and all the trimmings.'

'How could I possibly refuse?' She picked up her wine and followed him out.

***

Cindy sat on the park bench and watched the ducks on the pond. The sky was overcast, but it wasn't raining. She reckoned the temperature must have been about 8°C or 9°C so, as far as she was concerned, that was a blessing. She'd managed to get some cakes and pre-packed chicken breasts from the bins at Tesco so both she and Murphy's immediate hunger had been dealt with. For a while she sat there allowing her mind to drift aimlessly, deliberately avoiding facing up to what she was going to do. But eventually, if she was going to survive, she needed to get herself together and decide on what was the best way forward. Inside she had a joyous feeling that she had managed to rescue Murphy but also knew that having him with her was a responsibility and added problem for her survival. But he was going to be a loving companion for her, and she was determined not to let him go. If she remained in the town, even in the county, she knew that she would be in constant danger of Frank eventually finding her. Simply avoiding him was going to be a problem. He'd have his cronies watching the soup kitchens, hostels and care centres, ready to alert him if they saw her. She'd have to avoid most of the others she knew who were sleeping rough, because he would question them and put the fear of God into them if they didn't reveal anything they might know about her whereabouts. There was a squat in a disused factory where she had spent some time in the past. It could be an ideal place for her to hang out for a day or two until she saw which way the wind was blowing. It would be a good place to take Murphy as well because it would give him proper shelter. But the likelihood was they wouldn't want her there. Those already squatting there were very possessive and would have doubtless had a visit from Frank telling them to inform him if she turned up.

She didn't kid herself for a second that, if he caught her, he was capable of killing her. But it wouldn't be just his determination to give her a pasting that would be driving him to get her. She had been very useful to him. In spite of everything she had been reliable and, as far as it went, he trusted her. Although she was only a pawn in his business, she always nursed a sense of shame that she had played her part. She never knew the name of the source or where he lived or where he came from, though she suspected he came from the Eastern Bloc. She was pretty sure that Frank didn't know much more himself. It was the way things were. He didn't care. As far as he was concerned, all that mattered was there was a good and reliable supply of the drugs he wanted. He'd simply give Cindy an envelope with a bunch of notes inside, she had no idea how much – a few hundred, maybe a thousand – and she would take it to Carl – probably not his real name – at a point in the park. She'd sit on the bench until he came and sat next to her. She'd hand him the envelope, and he'd hand her a package. They hardly ever spoke. He'd get up and walk away, and she'd come back with the package and give it to Frank. After that she had nothing to do with it and didn't want to either. Frank would take it to his box room which was always locked, or at least should have been locked, but once he'd forgotten to lock it, and she'd seen him put it under the floor boards under a mat. He'd been sloppy in not taking his usual secretive care, probably because he'd been smashed out of his mind with booze or he'd taken a heavy dose of the drugs himself. It was obvious he mixed the drugs with another white powder before putting it into the little packets he was going to sell to his customers so that it would go further. She dreaded to think what the additive was. She'd investigated the hole in the floor where he'd taken up two short floorboards. There were money and other drugs placed there. She knew that drugs were a multi-million pound industry, and Frank was only a small time pusher, but to the source he was a regular and reliable customer. If only a few hundred quid passed hands each transaction, it was still good business. Although she was part of it, she was ignorant of the details of what was going on, and that suited her fine.

But she had to forget all that. It was behind her now, and she needed to go over her options of how she would be able to give herself a proper life. But one step at a time. She decided she'd have to risk going to the squat and try her luck. She could hardly call them her friends, but they shared a common bond, and she might be able to talk her way in. The really big question, of what she was going to do long term, she put to the back of her mind. Deep down she was determined to find a way of getting her life back on to a normal keel. Since the night Frank had thrown her out and she had found her way to the Samaritan Centre, she had put all thoughts of ending her life out of the window. Okay, she had felt what seemed like an inescapable black hole with nothing more than misery and pain ahead of her, but that was now gone. The old guy Tom showed her that there was some kindness in the world, and because he'd let her stay that one night, she'd had the chance of pulling herself together. If she threw in the towel now, it would prove that Frank and his toerag friends and her parents, who hadn't given a shit for her, had won the day. She would show the fucking world she could pull through and make a life for herself. The way things were at the moment, she hadn't any idea how, but she would do it. She stood up.

'Come on, Murphy, let's see what today brings.' They walked off.

*   *   *

Frank stared into the mirror that hung on one of the walls in his kitchen. He put his hand up to his cheek and touched the wheal. It was red and swollen and stretched across his cheek to his ear. Where it ran across his cheek, the skin was broken and had formed in a blood scab. His jaw tightened. 'Bitch!'

'We'll get her, Frank,' said Lenny who was sitting at the kitchen table drinking a mug of coffee.

'Dustbin lid. Look at that. The shit that's been in there. It'll get infected.'

'That's bollocks. It'll soon heal.'

'I'll mark her for life, Lenny. I swear to it.'

'I can't believe she had the nerve to break in.'

'Took my fucking dog Murphy. Can you believe that? He belongs to me. Me, Lenny, me!'

'You won't have to look for her. She'll come begging to be taken in again.'

'A right inconvenience, I can tell you. I need someone to pick up the gear. Carl knew her. She was good. If I use someone else, it'll arouse suspicions. People always get jumpy when changes take place.'

'You'll have to go and see Carl yourself.'

'I'm not going. Fuck that. It's worked well because he thinks I'm organized. Everything under control. He'll start wondering what's going on if I show up. Start asking questions.'

'Don't worry about it. Tell him you've dumped her. He won't care as long as long as we're still rolling.'

'That's not the point. She's putting me to a lot of trouble. I got to get her, Lenny. I really got to get her and make her pay.'

'You will, you will. She's going to stick out like a sore thumb as long as she's got Murphy with her. We'll do the rounds. Where the hell can she go?'

'She's a slippery, slimy little bitch, Lenny. A diabolical liberty, that's what she took.' His mobile phone rang. He put it to his ear. 'Yeah?'

'It's Gus.'

'Yeah.'

'I seen her.'

'Where?'

'Miller Street. Lower end of the High Street.'

'I know it. Sure it was her?'

'Couldn't miss her. Got Murphy with her.'

'Bitch. I know where she's going. Capons, the factory. It's a squat. She used to use it. I thought she might. I've been there and warned them. Thanks a lot, Gus.'

'No prob.'

Frank put his phone in his pocket. He was grinning. 'We got her Lenny. Come on, let's go.'

***

Cindy made her way along Miller Street. Murphy still looked in a wretched condition, his coat matted and with patches of dried mud, but he walked without the string lead with a little more spring in his step. Cindy was tense and kept looking back across her shoulder. They'd moved away from the shops, and there were only a few pedestrians going about their business, but the road was fairly busy with cars. This part of town was regarded as the poorer end and many of the buildings, which might have been shops at one time, were empty and in many cases derelict. Cindy wondered if they might give some shelter at night but, as they had never been used by anyone else, assumed that there must be a problem. She eventually took a left turn and then after about twenty yards took a right and entered a road with what looked like a number of lock-up garages. In point of fact, most of them were bigger than garages and were used as small businesses and workshops. Some of them were still in operation, but the one at the end, the biggest of the buildings, was Capons. Even so, the title of factory was a bit flattering. There was only a ground floor with an area about the average size of quick-fitting tyres businesses. The frontage was closed by two huge doors, but there was a small pedestrian door built into them. She made her way up the road towards Capons without anyone from the small lock-ups bothering to take any notice of her. She couldn't be sure if the building would be empty but tried to relax as she approached and then, without hesitation, pushed open the door and stepped inside. In front of her was a wide-open space that would have been the main workshop, but it had been stripped of all machinery. There was a typical concrete floor with puddles all over it from rain which had come through holes in the tin roof. To her right were three or four rooms. She walked over to one of them and pushed open the door. Inside were three young men and a girl. Two of the men were sitting on armchairs that were barely holding together. The third young man was sitting on a mattress with a young girl, leaning back against the wall. The two men were chatting quietly, but the girl and other man looked unwell and were silent. Cindy recognized the two young men.

'Hi, Pete,' she said and stared at both of them.

'Christ, we don't want you here, Cindy. Where'd you get the pooch?' His eyes flashed with alarm rather than hostility.

'I need to stay a night, that's all. Just one. I'll go in one of the other rooms.'

'They're wet.'

'Doesn't matter. I'll fix up something.'

'Is that Frank's?' asked the other young man.

'He's in a bad way, Nick.'

'I can see that. You can't stay here though. Frank's been. He said you might come. If we let you stay you know what will happen.'

'I'll keep out the way. He won't know I'm here.'

'Sorry, Cind. Too much at stake,' said Pete.

'For Christ sake, you've got to help me.'

'Get her out of here!' barked the young man on the mattress.

Cindy looked across at him with desperation in her eyes. 'No harm'll come. I promise.'

'You can't promise that,' said Pete.

'Please, Pete. Just the one night.'

'Get out!' shouted the young man on the mattress.

Cindy turned to scornfully stare at him when they all suddenly heard the screech of tyres on the road outside. Their heads jerked towards the door through which they could see the pedestrian door to the outside.

'Christ, I bet it's him. We're all fucked,' said Pete as his eyes darted with panic from one to the other.

'I'll hide in the back. Say nothing,' said Cindy as she rushed out the door, racing across the workshop, and made for the last room at the back of the building. 'Come on, Murph. And keep quiet.'

She only just managed to disappear out of sight before Frank and Lenny came through the pedestrian door and strode into the workshop before coming on into the room where the others were.

Cindy stood in two inches of water in the end room and cast her eyes round to see her options. It was totally bare. No doors. No windows. Nowhere to hide. If they came in, she was completely trapped. Instantly, panic began to flood over her. Desperately she poked her head back into the workshop to see if anywhere offered her hope of escape or at least somewhere to hide. Nothing. Then she spotted a small door in the far corner of the back wall. Could she get there, and would it open?

'Quick, Murph,' she whispered and slipped across the workshop as silently as she could. She reached the door and grasped the handle. It turned, but when she pulled the door it remain fast. 'Please, please,' she hissed to herself, and all the while her heart pounded like an express train. Again she tugged with all her strength but again the door remained jammed in its frame.

In the room where the others were, Pete said, trying to sound pleased, 'Hi, Frank.'

Frank made no reply but looked from one to the other. They all shifted anxiously.

'Has she been here?' said Frank in a toneless voice.

'Who, Frank?' Again Pete tried to sound upbeat whilst at the same time not being able to conceal the nervousness in his voice.

'You little shit. You know who I mean.'

Pete stammered, 'We don't want trouble, Frank.'

Frank took a step towards Pete, with a hard and menacing look in his eye. He stopped dead in front of him, and for several tense moments there was silence. Frank put his hand in his pocket and held up a small sachet. 'Anyone got anything to say?' For a little while there was silence.

'Out the back,' whispered the girl on the mattress. When Frank turned and looked at her, she nodded her head towards the door into the workshop.

'That wasn't so difficult, was it?' He dropped the sachet on to the girl's lap and stepped towards the door.

As soon as he appeared in the doorway, Cindy turned to see him and felt as naked as a lump of coal on new fallen snow.

'Bitch! Gotcha.' He stared across the room at her, grinning and nodding as if in cruel satisfaction at having tracked down and trapped his prey. No need for any rush. There was no escape. She was there and totally at his mercy. He could enjoy watching her tremble and cower as she visibly shrunk in terror of what was to come.

As if in a saunter, he took a couple of steps towards her and laughed with a venomous chuckle while he watched her jerk her head erratically from left to right in a wild hope that some means of escape would suddenly appear. Two more steps and he could almost smell the sweat of terror oozing from the pores of her skin. He heard her whimper but knew that inside she was screaming. Soon she would be screaming out loud. A few more steps and he was nearly there.

Cindy gave a supreme wrench on the door and it suddenly sprang open. Her heart gave a leap as she sprang through the opening and found herself in a small yard littered with lumps of old rusting machinery lying about between patches of brambles and scrub growing between huge cracks in a concrete floor. Her eyes jerked from left to right. A tall wooden fence rose either side, and a fence along the bottom boundary made up of perpendicular concrete panels eight inches wide and slotted together reached seven foot high. The panels had smooth sides and were impossible to climb and jump over because the top was extended by several strands of barbed wire – again she was trapped with no means of escape. Like a terrified gazelle, she jumped and skipped her way between machinery and brambles to the bottom end of the yard and crouched against the concrete fence. Nowhere to run, nowhere to hide; trapped in a box to await her fate. Crouching low against the concrete fence, she eased her way towards a large clump of brambles. If she could make that a barrier between her and Frank, she could use her speed and agility to flash round one side as he went the other. She'd be back through the door and away before he could grab her.

She heard him roar and saw him charge through the door, but as he advanced, Lenny came up in the rear and stood across the doorway, cutting off any chance of her escaping that way. Again Frank pulled up and stared down at her as she cringed behind the clump of brambles.

'There's no way out, bitch. I'm going to break your body so you'll never be the same. But first I'm going to put something inside you. Something big and hard and it's going right up your bum.'

Again she whimpered and slid further along the fence as if it would give her some crumb of defence. It was then that she spotted in the corner that the bottom five feet of one of the concrete panels had been broken away. It would have been impossible for most adults to squeeze through, but Cindy reckoned she was just about small enough. She made a dash for it. Frank's view of what she was doing was concealed by the brambles until she reached it. He suddenly realised what she was aiming to do and hurtled himself forward just as she started to squeeze through the gap. He made a desperate lunge at her, his fingers grasping at her clothing but without enough grip to stop her from jerking her way to the other side and stumbling on to the ground.

'Come 'ere you cow!' he screamed, but she was out of reach on the other side of the fence before he could get to her. Instinctively he grabbed the side of the opening, sticking his head through, and immediately felt Cindy's foot crash into his face. He roared in pain and pulled back, blood pouring from his mouth and split lips. Again he screamed at her but from his side of the barrier. 'I'll get you! I'll get you!'

'Not today, you won't. If you weren't such a fat gutted pig, you could have got through,' she screamed back at him and was surprised at her bravado. As far as Frank was concerned, she had always been scared and anxious in case she ever said anything out of turn, which would probably result in her getting a smack round the face. She was still terrified out of her wits but her freedom and retaliation gave her a new lifting of her spirit.

Keeping out of reach in case he tried to grab her, she bent low and peered back into the yard and saw him bending over and trying to nurse his mouth with fingers that were soaked in blood from the gash her foot had inflicted. Already his lips were beginning to bulge with swelling. He rolled around, groaning and swearing, his temper raging through his body at fever pitch.

It was then that they all heard Murphy let out a bark as he furtively began to stalk his way round the perimeter of the yard. Cindy stuck her head through the gap in the fence in a surge of panic as she realised Murphy wasn't with her.

'Come on, Murphy! Good dog, come on!'

'Get him!' screamed Frank, waving his arm at Lenny to advance and try to herd the dog into a corner.

'Come on, Murphy, come on,' cried Cindy as she watched him moving towards her from across the far side of the yard.

'Steady, Lenny, steady. Watch he doesn't make a dash.' The two men with arms spread wide eased their way forward to form an outer ring to seal off any escape. The dog began to gradually back himself into the opposite corner to where Cindy watched with a new surge of alarm.

'Leave him alone, you bastards. He's just a dog. He's done you no harm!'

'Watch him, Frank, he's gonna go for it,' said Lenny from the corner of his mouth, all the while his eyes fixed with a piercing stare on Murphy.

'Gently, gently,' whispered Frank as they both slowly eased one foot in front of the other, shrinking the space in which Murphy would have to move.

'Go, Murphy! Go!' screamed out Cindy, and immediately Murphy made a dash. But Murphy was a sick dog, a broken dog, a dog that had already had his strength and spirit beaten out of him, and he would never be able to produce a dash worthy of the name. His feeble attempt was instantly crushed by Frank, who hurled his body to the side as Murphy tried to pass. His hands streaked out and one of them caught the dog by his hind leg, bringing him down.

Frank's grip was like a vice, and Murphy could do no more than wriggle with pathetic effect.

You bastards, leave him!' screamed Cindy as she stared in utter despair at not being able to do anything.

'You want to leave me, you stinking piece of fur. Then you can leave me. You can leave the whole fucking lot of us!' screamed Frank.

He calmly climbed to his feet and, holding the dog up by his hind leg in one hand then reaching for the tail in the other, he watched him wriggle helplessly upside down. 'Goodbye.'

Still holding the dog by his hind leg in one hand and the tail in the other, he began to swing the animal round in the manner used in the sport of "Throwing the Hammer". On his second spin Frank hurled the animal with all his strength and sent him flying through the air until he crashed into the concrete panel fence with a sickening and deathly thud before bouncing off it and falling to the ground with all the life driven out of him. He lay on the ground, no more than a dead piece of skin, bone and fur.

Cindy screamed in horror, tears of terrible anguish and heartache, draining her blood in a downward gush so that she had to reach out for the wall to stop herself collapsing in a faint. Tears flowed freely down her face in uncontrolled restraint. Never had the dog given Frank anything but a wish to please, and in return he had been repaid during his short life with nothing but unspeakable cruelty. That there would never be any more suffering for him was the only small crumb of comfort that Cindy could find as she turned away. She still had to make her escape and could no longer do anything for Murphy. Through her tears she quickly looked about her and saw that she was in a narrow footpath between the concrete fence on the one side and a tall wooden fence, which concealed she knew not what, on the other. Quickly getting her bearings she guessed that if she went the one way it would lead to a road she knew as Lockhart Street which would take her on a back road back towards the town. She also remembered that towards the end of the street there was a place called The Garage. It now had nothing to do with cars but had been converted into small premises which provided a meal and facilities for a shower for homeless people. As it was Thursday she remembered it was open from twelve midday until three o'clock just for women. She could get there within ten minutes and hang out there to clean up and calm herself down. It would also be safe, for she was pretty certain Frank wouldn't want to show his face there and probably wouldn't continue looking for her today anyway. He would want to go back home and clean up his face. She imagined him looking in the mirror and seeing the swollen mess she'd inflicted on him. She didn't deny the enjoyment it had given her doing it, but it in no way diminished the crushing pain she felt in her heart for the dreadful death he had meted out on Murphy. The memory of the poor animal would stay in her mind forever. She wanted to remain and scream her hatred at Frank but knew it would be a futile gesture. She knew she had to try and be sensible and realistic, so she set off down the passageway until she reached the road. She looked left and right to see if Frank was about, but the way was clear. It only took her a few minutes before she reached the Garage and went in. She could see through a glass door that three or four other women were there sitting at a table eating a meal. She didn't recognize any of them. A young woman with a friendly smile approached her and asked if she could help.

'Would it be possible to have a shower and get the clothes I'm wearing washed?' she asked, thankful that she'd hung on to her spare clothing, still bundled in her plastic carrier bag.

'Of course you can. There's nobody in the showers at the moment. Go on through and help yourself. The water's lovely and hot. There's an adjoining room with a washing machine. You've been here before though, haven't you?'

'Yes, some time ago,' said Cindy and without adding anything more, went through the door that led to the shower. Sixty seconds later she stood with eyes closed and felt the tension ease from her body as the hot water poured down over it.

***

Frank stood in front of the mirror and stared at his face. His bottom lip was split and hugely swollen. The top one didn't fare much better. A terrible anger ground away inside him – the thought of that dirty little rat, not much bigger than a child, who had not only managed to out-manoeuvre him but had managed to inflict an injury to his face that made him look hideous. The humility was insufferable. He dare not go out and show his face. No one dare do that to him, least of all a pint-sized bitch who wasn't even worth the space she stood up in, and get away with it. If anyone discovered what she had done to him, the laughter would be heard from here to lands' end and not die down until Christmas. He wiped a smear of blood off his chin and went into his living room where Lenny sat watching the TV.

'I swear to you here and now, Lenny, that bitch is going to pay. She can't hide forever, and I can be patient. I will find her – and when I do, she's dead meat.

Chapter 4

Cindy pushed her plate away and sighed. She'd had a shower, done her washing and now she had just finished a hot meal. There were some good people in the world after all. Two other women had turned up while she had been in the shower, and they were quietly chatting to the others who were already there. They had invited her to join in, but she had politely declined, not feeling in the mood to talk with anyone.

It was good to feel clean, with her long dark hair hanging down over her shoulders. She'd have to do it up before leaving, but she'd hang on until she had to go which she knew would be soon. The trauma she'd gone through earlier had partially diminished, but she still felt sickened about what Frank had done to Murphy. She felt guilty too that it was because of her he had suffered such a dreadful fate. At the same time she knew that wasn't strictly true, but it didn't help much. It had been only a few hours earlier that she was determined to make something of her life, to fight her way out of the dead end life she was stuck in. She had said it out loud to Murphy and promised him at the same time that she would look after him and that they would find a good life together. But now the old despairing sense of hopelessness had come back. Her life was like the flip of a coin. One moment things were really bad, and then the next, something happened and everything would change. Then, just as quickly, the same pattern happened again, and then again and again and again. Would something now turn up to help her on her way, something to lift her spirits and give her the will to fight on?

While she had been in the shower, she had made up her mind about one thing. She was going to go back to the squat and get Murphy's body. She couldn't bear the thought of him being left to rot away. She would try and carry him to the park and bury him somewhere. How she was going to do that, she hadn't worked out. She didn't have anything to dig with, and she didn't know if she'd be able to carry him. There was little flesh on him, but he wasn't a small dog and would probably weigh anything up to 20 kg. Whatever the difficulties, she was determined to find a way round them.

The weather outside was overcast, and as it was mid-January, it would soon be getting dark. She got her clothes and blanket together and stuffed them into a couple of plastic carrier bags. She said goodbye to the other women and stepped out to the front reception area. The young woman who had welcomed her came up to her carrying a knapsack. She said, 'I noticed that you only have two plastic bags for your belongings. One of the public dropped this knapsack in and asked us to give it to anyone who would find it useful. Would you like it? It's not new, but it's in very good condition.'

Cindy's eyes widened in surprise. 'Thank you, that would be really useful. It's a bit of a problem hanging on to these bags all the time.'

'Good. I'm glad it's found a useful home.'

'You're very kind,' said Cindy, and after transferring her plastic bags into the knapsack and slipping her arms through the straps so it rested on her back, she nodded with a smile and left the building. The woman watched her through the window, wondering where she would sleep that night.

***

As she made her way back across town, she felt fairly confident that Frank wouldn't be out looking for her at this time. There was plenty of light from the street lighting, and many of the shop windows were lit up even though many of them were on the point of closing as it was 5:30. She guessed that Frank would be screaming and cursing as he tended the swelling that would have come up on his face from the hefty kick she had given it. If he ever did catch her, he would almost certainly killer her. It was the second time she had made a mess of his face, and nobody had ever done that to him before, least of all a female tiddler like her. She smiled as she thought about the humility he would be feeling.

As she drew near Capons, she decided to enter the way she had escaped and not let the others in the building know she was there. They would have no cause to go out into the yard, and she could squeeze her way back through the concrete fence. She had no idea where she could find a place to bury him or what she would dig a grave with, but her first task was to collect him and get him away. She reached the narrow passageway and moved down it until she reached the narrow opening in the concrete fence. She poked her head through and listened for any sound. It was dark and deathly silent. She pushed through the gap and eased her way over to where she remembered Murphy had been dumped. She stared down at his stretched out body and bunched the muscles in her face to stop herself from crying.

'Oh, you poor little boy,' she whispered. 'You never did anything but show affection to that bastard. One day we'll pay him back.'

She reached down to get her hands underneath him but suddenly went rigid. She bent her head lower and listened and realised all at once that the dog had made a sound.

'Oh, Murphy! Murphy, you're still alive. You brave boy.'

She looked around in bewilderment, not knowing what to do.

How bad were his injuries? Would she make them worse by trying to lift him, let alone carry him away? Where could she take him, and could anything be done? She had a vague memory of a vet sign down a turn-off of the High Street in town. She thought it was called St Catherine Walk. She had passed it on several occasions, and although she had noticed it, she had not paid it much attention. Would they be able to help? Would anybody still be there, or would they have closed for the night? She reckoned it must be getting near 6 o'clock. It would take her at least fifteen minutes to get there. It was her only chance.

As gently as she could, she slipped her hands underneath Murphy's body, gathered him up in her arms and held him close into her chest. Although he was thin and emaciated, he was still a fair weight, and she worried she might not be able to carry him the whole distance without stopping and so delay precious time. She squeezed back through the concrete fence and set off down the alleyway as fast as she could walk. She dare not try and run, for fear that the jogging would cause further pain to Murphy. As she made her way through the shopping area, occasional passers-by gave her odd looks, but none spoke or made any comment. She spotted a public clock secured in steel brackets reaching out high up from a shop and saw that the time was five minutes past six. Five minutes later she turned down St Catherine Walk that took her to the building displaying a veterinary sign. She was now panting, and her arms felt like lead, but she was relieved to see that there was a light on inside. She pushed open the door and went into a reception room with a counter at the far side. A young woman wearing a green tunic, who was obviously a nurse, was behind the counter.

'We're just about to close, I'm afraid,' she said not unpleasantly.

'Please, can someone look at my dog? He's seriously injured.'

'Are you registered with us?'

'For Christ's sake, please help me!'

At that moment a tall thin man with greying hair and wearing spectacles came into the reception.

'Do we have another one, Jane?' he asked the nurse.

'This young woman has just brought in her dog and –' She was cut short by Cindy.

'He's seriously hurt. Please, please help me. I think he might die.'

'Has he been hit by a car?' asked the vet, moving over to Cindy and looking down at Murphy.

'No, he's been beaten by some cruel bastard, and I've managed to rescue him.'

'You should take him to the animal shelter and deal with it through them.'

'He's dying, don't you understand? He needs help from a vet now.'

'I would like to help, but he looks in a serious condition, and we don't just take in random pets.'

'Please! I can't just let him die.'

'He'll need x-rays, and he could have internal injuries. He could need surgery, and the cost might run into hundreds of pounds.'

'I don't care what it costs. Just do what has to be done.'

'That's all very well, but are you able to pay?'

'No, I can't, not now. But I will do. I'll pay for it all one day.'

'I'm sorry. We're simply not a charity.'

'Listen!' Her voice began to tremble. 'I'll do anything. I'll come and work for you; I'll scrub the floors. You can sleep with me. I don't want money for any of it.'

'I'm sorry.'

'You bastard. You don't care about animals. All you think about is money.'

'I must ask you to leave.'

'I risked my life rescuing this dog. Yes, my life. That's worth more than money, isn't it? I was prepared to do that. All I'm asking of you is your time.'

'I don't mind staying on if you want to have a look, Richard,' said the nurse. Richard turned and looked at her in surprise and for a moment was wrong-footed. He was running a business. He simply couldn't take on cases that were potentially serious which would be expensive and get nothing for them. There was no way this girl was ever going to pay for the attention the dog would need. The animal would almost certainly have to be put down. That would be the obvious solution.

'I'll take a quick look at him. But if his injuries are too extensive, then the kindest thing would be to put him to sleep. Bring him through, Jane,' said Richard, who turned away and disappeared into a back room. Jane smiled and reached to Cindy who lifted Murphy into her arms.

'He'll do his best. Wait here.'

'Thank you,' replied Cindy and felt all her remaining energy draining from her as Jane carried the dog into the back room. She went and sat on a bench seat fixed to the edge of two of the walls. She tried to settle her mind. Once again she sensed the shattering awareness that her life was a ghastly mess – no home, no possessions, no belief in a better future. Everything was a fight, a struggle, and always accompanied with pain. She was like poor Murphy: a broken and pathetic creature hanging on to life that was always going to be filled with desperation and misery. If Murphy didn't survive, she'd sling in the towel and end it all – find a hole somewhere and be done with it. She'd heard it wasn't easy to kill yourself and didn't know how she'd do it, but she'd find some way. Christ, if it was the last thing she ever did, she'd find a way. She suddenly gave an inward smile at the irony of her thought. Then she gave an actual chuckle: bloody hell, maybe she was losing her mind as well. She leant to her side, swinging her legs up on to the bench at the same time, and curled up. Five minutes later she was asleep.

***

It was half past seven when Cindy suddenly woke to see the nurse, Jane, and the vet, Richard, standing beside her. She sprang to her feet.

'What's happened!? Where is he?'

'It's all right. He's sleeping.'

'You're lying, aren't you? You've put him down.' Cindy's voice trembled and she looked at them in horror.

'No, no. He really is sleeping. He's had an anaesthetic,' said Jane and reached out to touch Cindy's hand.

'I'm sorry. I'm just… is he going to be all right?'

'I have to tell you that, apart from his injuries, he's in a dreadful state. Even a healthy dog would have struggled to survive. How did he get such injuries?' asked Richard.

'You don't want to know.'

'Well, the individual who did this should be reported.'

'I'm dealing with it. Is he going to be all right?'

'He's got two cracked ribs; a small chip to his left femur, though it's not broken; bruising to his skull; and a dislocated left shoulder, which has now been put back and won't cause lasting damage. He's suffering from a concussion and extensive abrasions and bruising over the whole of his body. He's also riddled with worms. He's on a course of antibiotics and will need special care for several days. He will have to stay here the night. You can collect him tomorrow.'

'I'll come in the morning. And thank you. I'm sorry I shouted my mouth off.'

'I should give you a hefty bill for his treatment: several hundred pounds.'

'I'll pay it one day. I'll get the money. You'll have to wait, but I'll pay it.'

'You must go now. We closed two hours ago.'

'Can I see him?'

'Tomorrow. He's not going anywhere.' He saw she was about to protest but turned away. 'Goodnight,' he said curtly and disappeared into the back room.

'Don't worry,' said Jane. 'He'll be fine where he is for the night. You must go.' She put her hand on Cindy's arm as if to lead her to the door.

'Okay. You're right. I can't stay here, I s'pose?'

Jane suddenly looked perplexed. 'Here?'

Cindy simply shrugged, and Jane immediately understood. 'Are you homeless?'

'It's okay, I'll manage.'

'I'm sorry, he won't agree to that. There's stuff in the building that… well, it's out of the question.'

'It's okay. I'll be fine. I'll get going.'

'Have you somewhere to go?'

'Yeah, I'm fine. Thanks for doing what you did for Murphy.'

'Will you come tomorrow?'

'Of course.' She hesitated, then put her hand in her pocket and took out a £2 coin, two 50p coins and some coppers and handed them to Jane. 'I know it's not much, but it's all I've got. I'll pay the bill one day. See you in the morning.' She turned and walked out.

As soon as she got outside, a blast of cold air hit her. Of course she had somewhere to go. Yeah, yeah, like hell she had. There was only one thing for it: she'd have to make it back to the car park with the snack bar. It was only about a mile and she could make it easily in twenty minutes. With a bit of luck, her blanket would still be there, stuffed in the cardboard box in the corner. If it rained she'd be dry there, and the blanket and cardboard would give her enough warmth for the night. Good. All in all, it had been an up-and-down day. Poor Murphy had had a terrible beating, but she had at least managed to get him away, and he was in a safe place for the night. She'd think about tomorrow when it came. She pulled up her collar and set off.

Chapter 5

As soon as he had arrived to open up his van, Micky spotted the coloured blanket in the lean-to, and he knew that Cindy must have spent the night there. He wondered where else she might have spent her nights and whether she had managed to keep clear of the gorilla who beat her up. As he worked away preparing food in readiness for his customers, he kept glancing across in her direction to see if she was moving and whether she would come over. At one point he became so distracted by watching her that he nearly burnt a batch of sausages. At 10 o'clock, Douglas and his crew arrived, and they too found their gaze drawn towards the tin lean-to.

'I see little Miss Red Riding Hood has returned,' said Douglas.

'Do you reckon she's been there all night?' asked Bob.

'Must 'ave. She was there when I opened up,' said Micky as he started handing out their usual drinks and food.

'What a bloody way to live, eh. England: twenty-first century. Jesus,' said Joe as he took a huge mouthful of bacon roll.

'Probably end up on the game.'

'Fancy your chances then, Bob?' said Douglas, and they all laughed.

'She'd have to be bloody desperate to take on Bob,' added Joe, and they all laughed again.

For a little while they chatted amongst themselves exchanging usual banter, unique to workmen, whilst all the time glancing across to the lean-to in the secret hope that Cindy would suddenly rouse herself. Eventually they spotted the blanket thrown back, and Cindy pulled herself up. She stretched and looked around for a few moments. After brushing herself down, she concealed her blanket and wandered over to them.

'Hi Cindy,' said Douglas with unconcealed pleasure at seeing her. All the guys mumbled friendly noises of greeting, and for a moment Cindy was taken aback.

'Oh, hi guys.' She smiled, and they all immediately noticed the swelling that had previously closed her eye had almost disappeared. They realised that although she was unkempt and a skinny little "brat", she was a good-looking girl.

'As before, bacon roll?' asked Micky.

Cindy's hesitation was not lost on any of them. 'Er, just a cuppa tea please.'

Micky poured her tea and pushed it to her as she ferreted for some coppers, and it was then that they realised she had run out of money. Douglas grunted, caught Micky's eye and nodded his head with a wink. Micky immediately caught on and started to make up another roll. As Douglas reached across to pay him, Micky dismissed it with a sweep of the hand. He handed the roll out to Cindy. 'Here, have this one on the house.'

Cindy instantly looked alarmed and jerked her head from one to the other. 'What kind of trick is this?'

Douglas immediately held up his massive arms in a conciliatory fashion. 'Hey, there's nothing funny going on.' She stared back at him, and he could see that she still didn't understand Micky's gesture and that all her instincts were filling her with suspicion.

'Look, I over-stocked and cooked too many. Shame to bin it,' said Micky and held the roll towards her. She stared at the roll, still unsure whether or not to take it. She wasn't stupid and knew that Micky's explanation was rubbish. 'I know what it's like to have hard times. There's no shame in that.'

She stared up at him behind his counter in the bar and immediately saw the kindness in his eyes. She forced a weak smile and nodded as she took the roll. 'Thanks.' There was an embarrassed pause, then everyone made extravagant motions of eating and they all relaxed.

'Anyway, Micky's rolling in it.'

'I'd do a lot better if I had some decent customers.' They all laughed and were pleased that Cindy gave a giggle as well. Micky felt happy as he looked down on them. He loved what he did and felt the gods had been kind to him. He enjoyed the banter and serving the customers who would be coming until early every afternoon, when he would shut up shop and set off to do an odd job of work for some individual customer. He could turn his hand to most things, and although he didn't have a big range of technical skills, he was resourceful and managed to get enough work to give him an adequate income. He had a small half-truck instead of a car for travelling around, but it was a tidy vehicle and more suitable for his jobbing work.

'Anywhere you can stay in town, Cindy? With a roof, I mean?' asked Douglas.

'There's a couple of places for the odd night, but Frank'll be checking up on them so I give 'em a miss.'

'Is he the one?'

'Yeah. He'll never give up.'

'Maybe he won't bother after a while.'

'No way.'

'Why do you say that?'

'I had to rescue a dog. It's his really, but he was such a cruel bastard to him. I broke in but he caught me, and I only just escaped by smashing a metal dustbin in his face. Trouble is, he caught up with me yesterday and damn near killed poor Murphy – that's the dog. I only got away by kicking him in the face. Made a bit of a mess of him so he'll never forgive me for that.'

'Bloody hell,' interrupted Micky. 'You took a risk going back for the dog.'

'I couldn't leave him. He's had a terrible life.'

'Where is Murphy now?'

'He's safe. A vet's got him.'

The guys looked at each other in bewilderment as well as with a touch of awe at this half-pint of a girl, not much more than a child, for her gutsy spirit. None of them would claim to be saints, but all of them felt outrage at what she had suffered and frustration for having to be no more than bystanders. Three of them had children of their own, and Douglas reckoned his own daughter was about the same age as Cindy. He couldn't help feeling a genuine concern for her. Overhead the dark sky was beginning to grow even darker with the likelihood of rain. He wondered how she would survive in prolonged bad weather if she had to sleep rough continually.

'What are you going to do today?' asked Douglas.

'Watch out for that bastard. I'll be all right.'

Douglas said under his breath, 'Yeah, like hell you will.'

The guys started chucking their disposable polystyrene beakers in the bin.

'Come on, guys, some of us have got to work,' said Douglas, and they all started to move off. 'Look out for yourself, Cindy.'

Cindy nodded. 'I'll survive.'

Micky came out of his van and stood next to Cindy, and they both watched the men walk back across the car park towards the road works. 'Good bunch,' said Micky, but Cindy made no reply. 'What are you going to do now?'

'I've got to get going. I've got things to do.'

'Are you coming back to doss down over there tonight?'

'Maybe. I got things to sort out first.'

Micky noticed the uncertainly in her voice. He could see her mind was working on overtime, obviously trying to solve a problem that she hadn't revealed. It was in that moment he realised she was not only a feisty and gutsy fighter, but also a lost and vulnerable girl with the odds of successfully hacking her way through life stacked against her.

She turned away as another group of men began approaching the van.

'Wait!' She turned round and looked at him, startled by the abruptness in his voice. 'Look,' he began, but immediately hesitated and started to stumble over his words. 'If you like... I mean, if it would help... is, if you wanted to... you could sleep in here.'

'What are you talking about?'

'In the bar. It would give you some decent shelter, and you could lock yourself in so you would be safe. It doesn't matter to me. I pack up about three or four and come back in the morning.'

She stared at him with a mixture of disbelief and surprise. 'In there? Sleep? Are you serious?'

'Well, it's a damn sight better than sleeping rough over there.'

'Why would you let me do that? You don't know anything about me.'

'I dunno. Do I have to have a reason?'

'When do we get some bloody service, Micky?" called out one of Micky's new customers, and he and Cindy were jerked out of their conversation and aware of the group of men watching them.

'Sorry, mate. I'll be right there.' He turned again to Cindy. 'All you got to do is keep your head down. I've got a licence for this and they probably wouldn't allow it,' said Micky and moved away to get back into his van. Cindy stood aside as the men began crowding round the counter to be served. Micky appeared again inside the bar. He lifted a key off the wall behind him and tossed it over the heads of the workmen to Cindy who put up her hand and caught it.

'See you tomorrow, Cindy. Sweet dreams. Okay, John, what's yours? Sausage or bacon?'

Cindy stood back from the bunch of workmen, holding the key in her hand and feeling unsure of what to do. The idea of being able to sleep in Micky's bar had completely put her off balance. Surely there had to be some catch involved which she hadn't spotted. Why would he let her stay there? She was nothing to him, and he knew absolutely nothing about her. He had nothing to gain, and as far as he knew, she could steal anything of value to him in there. Apart from that she had never come across anybody in her life who did anything for nothing. There was always a price, so what did he want off her? If he wanted sex then he could take a running jump off a cliff. If it was sex he wanted off her, he'd have to ask her for it outright, and she'd tell him to his face to get lost.

She looked down at the key again and then over the heads of the workmen at Micky who was happily serving them as if he hadn't a care in the world. He suddenly looked up and saw her staring at him. He waved with a smile and then carried on serving. Maybe he was genuine. Maybe he was one in a million who was offering her something without a price tag. What the hell; why look a gift horse in the mouth? She stuffed the key into her pocket and set off towards the shopping area in town. Thoughts tumbled about in her mind. She would still have to keep her wits about her and be wary of Frank and his cronies, all of whom would be only too ready to warn him if they saw her. She'd keep well away from the most obvious places he would expect her to go, but it reduced the number of locations where she could keep her head down for any length of time. The park would be a good place as he rarely went there, and it would give her a good field of vision if he came on the scene, but her most pressing worry was about Murphy. What would be his condition now, assuming he had made it through the night? He would be an added responsibility, but there was no way she was going to give him up. One way or another she would look after him and protect him. If the vet tried any trickery or clever stunts to get him off her and send him to the animal shelter, where they'd probably have him put down, then she'd raise merry hell. How the devil she was ever going to pay him, she hadn't the faintest idea. She knew that if she had been a proper, respectable customer of his, she would have been expected to pay a whacking great bill. She wasn't stupid and knew that it would have been a few hundred pounds, even though she believed it would be a rip off. He was in business and didn't offer his services for nothing. And why the hell should he? Anyone who wasn't prepared to pay could piss off. There were plenty who would. It was a bloody miracle she had got him to do what he'd done. Of course it wouldn't make him bankrupt or kill him, but he could have dug his heels in and slammed the door in her face. Okay, it was a ridiculous thought, but she wanted to pay him and was determined that one day she'd find the money and give it him. She chuckled to herself: at least the thought was there.

She had now reached the shops and looked up at the public clock which told her the time was 10:45. She wondered at what time she should turn up for Murphy. The vet was probably dealing with a morning surgery for pets needing some sort of treatment. He'd obviously be busy, and she'd rather arrive when the surgery was coming to an end anyway. She decided to wait until about 11:30 and try her luck. She was standing next to a side street named St Michael's Parade where the local library was located. She decided to go in there where she'd be safe. Good, one step at a time.

Chapter 6

Tom walked along the path through the woods. The remains of the early morning frost had disappeared. There was no movement from the bare trees, and the silence was only broken by the occasional call from a distant cawing of a crow. The leaves underfoot had softened into the surface mud, and his steps were almost silent. His steps were slow, and occasionally he stopped and looked about him as if he was soaking up the woodland's sense of peace. He noticed his breath on the cold air, and in an odd way it reminded him that his heart was still beating and his lungs pumping – that his life was precious and he must savour it because its end was drawing near.

He finally came to a small clearing where there was placed two small heaps of stones marking the spots where his wife, Janice, and baby daughter, Jessica, had been buried. He inwardly smiled when he visualised a third heap of stones which would be placed on the ground above his own body. They would all be together again. Before Janice had died, they had often come to this spot and held hands as they fantasised about an imaginary life their daughter might have had if she had lived. Now alone, he reminded himself of the happy times he and Janice had had together. He often mumbled to her about what he was getting up to in his life. Sometimes he mentioned the tragic events that were happening in the lives of some of his callers whilst doing a shift at the Centre. On the odd occasion he would relate something more light hearted or bizarre that a caller was involved in. Today his mind was full of thoughts about Cindy. The more he had tried to dismiss his meeting with her at the Centre, the more he worried about what would become of her. It didn't matter to him that it was completely irrational, even foolish, for him to think about Jessica at the same time. He knew that Janice would understand – that she too would have felt a compassion for Cindy and be outraged that such a young person was faced with so much violence and degradation.

'I know I'm being a silly old fool, my love, but she seemed no more than a vulnerable child.' He looked down at the heap of stones as he softly spoke. 'I wish I could have done more for her, but of course it wasn't possible. She knew that. We don't give practical help anyway, and she knew that too. Of course I would have loved to have had a magic wand and solved all her problems, but that was impossible. I think about the possibility of meeting her again. If she saw me first, she would probably try and avoid me. I know that sounds silly, because I had helped her, but she might feel threatened that I was going to intrude on her life. She's never been able to trust anybody so there's no real reason why she should trust me either. I would like to know if she is all right though. If I could help her in any way, I would. You agree, don't you? It would be good to try and help her. We would have done everything we could for Jessica. I know Cindy's not ours, but she should be given a chance. I know these are just silly thoughts. I know nothing about her world, not really. I don't deny I've spoken to hundreds of people, many of them young like Cindy, whose lives are in turmoil, but that's not the same as living their life or being in the same place as them. Although we have only talked, I've sometimes felt very close and sensed their terror or pain and in some way shared their pain. But I don't really know their world, the real experience of their daily lives. If I met Cindy and wanted to help, which I'm free to do now because I'm no longer a Sam, I wouldn't know where to start. There would be such a temptation to make simplistic and arrogant suggestions as to what she should do that she'd probably laugh at me and tell me to mind my own business. I've talked to Linda about her, and as always she's such a help. She's promised to let me know if Cindy turns up at the Centre again. She's not supposed to tell me, of course, but no harm will be done. I just want to know that she's not gone back to that brute who beat her up. Yes, yes, my love, I mustn't go on so. By the way, I have another appointment with the specialist in ten days, and I'll let you know how I get on. Oh, and I've decided to paint the bathroom. The faintest tint of lavender, I think. You always liked that colour. I know you must be wondering why I should bother, but it's something I want to do. I know, I'll try not to get too much paint on the floor, and I promise to put on some old clothes.' He suddenly felt a shiver. 'I'd better be on my way. Not to worry. I'm all right. I'll come again soon.' He turned away and began to make his way back through the woods.

* * *

When Cindy left the library, it only took her a few minutes to reach the vet's. She stood outside for a few moments feeling nervous. What kind of reception would she get this morning, and would Murphy have pulled through all right? There was nothing for it: she would have to go in and find out. She pushed open the door and was relieved to see that no other customer was waiting with a pet to receive attention. There was no one behind the reception counter so she went and sat down on the wooden bench against the wall to wait. Five minutes passed, then a young woman in a green nurse's uniform appeared and spotted her.

'Can I help you?' she asked with a smile.

Cindy stood up. 'Is Jane about?'

'Yes, she's just finished in surgery. Who shall I say?'

'Oh, just say I've come about Murphy.'

''Ah, yes! You brought him in last night.' Her voice was not unpleasant, but Cindy noticed the sudden alteration in pitch. 'I'll tell her you're here.' She disappeared into a back room. A minute later Jane came in from a door on the opposite wall.

'Hi,' she said with a broad smile.

'How is he?' said Cindy, unable to hide the anxiety in her voice.

'He had a good night, and he's eaten some breakfast.'

'Can I see him? Can I have him?'

Jane took Cindy's arm and eased her to the other end of the room, away from the counter, where her colleague could not hear what they were saying.

'Are you really homeless? I mean living rough?' asked Jane with a hushed voice.

'What's that got to do with it?'

'He's going to need care. He needs rest and a warm environment. As well as that, he can only walk outside to relieve himself at the moment. His shoulder will be painful for a while. How can you help him if you're sleeping rough?'

'I can manage. I've been offered shelter. It will be warm and dry, and he can rest all day.'

Jane looked doubtfully at her. 'What do you mean you've been offered shelter?'

'It'll be okay. It's in a big van, a snack bar. He can stay in there all day.'

'Can you provide him with enough decent food? I don't think you'll be able to manage. He'd be better off at the animal shelter and offered up for a proper home.'

'No! I'm not going to let him go. I will look after him, I promise. Please help me.'

Jane saw the desperation in Cindy's eyes. 'Where is this snack bar?'

'It's where they're building the new roundabout by the Cannon Trading Estate.'

'That's about a mile from here. How are you going to get him there? He won't be able to walk.'

'I'll carry him.'

'That's out of the question. He's a very sick dog, and holding him like that would cause him a lot of pain.'

There was a silence as Cindy desperately struggled to come up with a solution that Jane would accept. 'I don't know what to do.' Now she sounded bewildered and pathetic.

'Look, I can get off for about 20 minutes around about half past three. If you come back then, I'll run you in my car. I'm probably being crazy, and Richard will go mad if he's knows what's going on, but I can see the dog means so much to you.'

'I promise I'll look after him,' said Cindy in relief.

'You can also promise that if you can't manage or there are problems, then you take him to the animal shelter or call me.'

'I will. I don't have a phone, but if I need you I'll come. And thank you. I can't pay you anything, I'm afraid.'

'You'll repay me if you look after him and stick to your part of the bargain.'

'I promise you I will.'

'All right. You get off. Best if you go now and see Murphy later.'

'But...' Cindy wanted to protest.

'No buts. I want to assure Richard everything will be all right. You've been very lucky to get such extensive treatment for Murphy without paying. Don't push it any further.'

Cindy nodded, 'All right. I'll come back at half past three. Thank you.' She felt she needed to say more, but Jane turned away and joined her colleague behind the reception counter. Cindy hesitated for a moment and then left.

Jane's colleague said, 'What was all that about?'

'Nothing,' replied Jane and disappeared into the back room.

Cindy stepped outside and leaned back into the wall of the building with a sigh.

Once again the coin had spun, and for once, luck was on her side and it had come up heads.

***

It was twenty to four when Jane drove into the car park and pulled up alongside Micky's Snack Bar. Cindy sat in the back of the car, and Murphy was on the seat next to her.

'Is this it?' asked Jane as she peered at the bar with a frown on her face.

'It'll be dry and warm in there,' said Cindy defensively.

Jane grunted and got out of the car. Leaving Murphy in the car, Cindy climbed out and followed her to the door at the end of the bar.

'It's open every day, but Micky, that's the guy who owns it, has shut it up until tomorrow morning.'

'Can Murphy stay in there all day? And what about you? If it pours with rain and gets even colder, that won't be any good.'

'It's all right. We can stay here. Micky said so,' said Cindy, knowing full well that Micky hadn't agreed to anything of the sort.

'Let's have a look inside.'

Cindy delved into her pocket and fished out the key. She climbed the two steps up to the door, pushed the key into the lock and the door swung open. There was very little light inside because there were no windows. Day light was provided when the side of the van was opened and the area from which the customers were served. Cindy ran her fingers up and down the wall inside the doorway and found a switch. She flicked it down and a light came on revealing a well-equipped unit with storage cupboards, a refrigerator and a washing up sink. On the opposite side was a large griddle plate and a work surface. The space between the two sides was narrow, limiting movement, but to Cindy it offered luxury compared to what she was used to. Although it was clean, a smell of old cooking hung in the air, and it was untidy.

'It's a bit small,' said Jane, doubtfully.

'We'll be fine. I'll stick Murphy up the end. It'll be warm and dry for him.'

'Can you stay here in the day? Is it open for business?'

'Er... yes. I help.' As soon as she said it, Cindy suddenly realised she had no idea what would happen in the day. She wouldn't be able to stay there, and Micky wouldn't want a dog in there while he was cooking.

Jane shrugged with a reluctant acceptance of the situation. 'I'm afraid I can't do anything more for you. It's no way to live, and I'm sorry. I can only wish that things get better for you.'

'You've already helped me a lot. I'm so grateful what's been done for Murphy.'

'Look after him.' She handed Cindy a plastic bag with two small packets and an envelope inside.

'These are his antibiotics and some painkillers. Make sure he takes them.'

Cindy took the plastic bag and the envelope with a questioning look. 'What's the envelope?'

'Richard didn't take your money. He said you must need it.'

Cindy nodded. 'Thank you,' she said quietly.

'I've got to get back,' said Jane. 'I hope all goes well. Don't forget, call me if you get worried.'

'I will. We shall be fine.'

Jane opened the door and moved down the two steps. She walked over to her car and got in. She started the engine and pushed the horn. Cindy waved as she drove away.

***

'I saw her yesterday,' said Gus. He was sitting at the table with Frank and Lenny in Frank's kitchen. The three of them were drinking coffee and smoking. 'Down the Millington Road.'

Gus thought of himself as number three in Frank's hierarchy – a good position. It gave him status. Frank took the piss out of him sometimes, but he always tried to laugh it off. He knew he was useful to Frank because he did a lot of running about for him which pretty much kept him in Frank's favour. Gus was only of average height, but he was overweight. He had a boyish, innocent face which belied some of the bad things he'd done on behalf of Frank. He had a crop of mouse coloured hair with an unusual streak of white through it that looked as if it was never combed. He had big full lips which, when parted, displayed a grin of good white teeth which was often evident even when he, Frank and Lenny were discussing something serious.

'What the hell was she doing down that end of town?' said Frank.

'Search me,' replied Gus. 'I only saw her for a moment. She looked as if she was heading back towards town. I was driving the opposite direction on the other side of the road, stuck in a stream of traffic that was getting a move on. I couldn't stop.'

'She's trying to keep out the way. And it's a maze down there on the Trading Estate,' offered Lenny.

'Yeah. Some empty buildings too where she could get her head down. You know: small factories or workshops that have gone bust. She could get in one of those.'

'That would be no good for her long term. She has to get out and about,' said Gus.

'She's a slippery little bitch,' said Lenny.

'I don't think you should bother with her, Frank. We've got better things to do,' said Gus. He shouldn't have said it. His opinion didn't count.

Frank reached out and grasped Gus's shirt under his throat. 'Not bother?! You see what she did to my face? Cut my cheek with a dustbin lid! Split my lip with her foot! Do you think I'm going to let her get away with that? I'm going to make that bitch pay. Do you understand? She's got to be found, and we're going to keep looking until we've got her.' Frank's eyes bored into Gus's for a few moments, and then he released him.

'Okay, Frank. I didn't mean anything. We'll find her.'

'Take it easy, Frank,' said Lenny. 'We'll get her. She's not going to be able to hide forever unless she leaves town, and I don't think she'll do that.'

'I'll take a trip down the Trading Estate and have a look around, Frank. I'll ask some of the workmen on the new roundabout if they've seen a young girl hanging around,' said Gus, falling over himself to make up for his blunder.

'Waste of time. They won't notice anything.'

'I don't know. She's a good-looking girl. They'd notice her. And anyway, I'll ask 'em to keep a look out. Spin 'em a yarn.'

'It's worth a try,' said Lenny.

'I don't care what you do. Just bloody well find her.'

'I'll get as many as I can on to it. She can't hide forever.'

'If you find her, bring her back here. I'm going to deal with her myself.'

'Don't mess her up too much, Frank. She was a good go-between. They know her, and she was always reliable. You can still use her.'

'She's got to be taught a lesson, Lenny. She's been giving us the run-around. She's marked me. I'm not having that from anybody – especially a little bitch like that.'

'Whatever you say, Frank.'

'Just get her.'

'We will. We will.'

Chapter 7

It was 6:30 in the morning when Cindy woke after having slept soundly all night. She stretched out on the floor and felt Murphy lying at her feet. She stood up and reached for the light and immediately saw that Murphy was standing on his three good legs. He gave a weak wag of his tail and limped over to her.

'Good boy. You're going to be okay. We'll look after you and you'll soon be good as new.' She opened the door and, half holding Murphy to ease the weight off his injured leg, she climbed down the two steps. The car park was almost empty. She moved round the back of the van where Murphy relieved himself, and she tucked herself into a bush that was growing at the side of the boundary fence and relieved herself as well. She looked around to see that no one had seen her and then climbed back into the van with Murphy. 'You go and lie down again, Murphy. I'll have to think about what's going to be done for breakfast later.'

She moved over to the little sink and washed her hands, then sluiced cold water over her face. She was surprised and pleased to see a small clean towel hanging on the wall with which she dried herself. She looked in the mirror fixed to the wall above the sink and noticed with a smile that the swelling round her eye had almost gone and the coloured bruising was fading. She ran her fingers through her thick, dark hair and then stuck her tongue out.

'Hm, better, but room for improvement. I've got to get a toothbrush today, Murphy. Food for you; toothbrush for me. I haven't got much money, but we'll manage.' She looked about her, wondering what she should do, when she heard a vehicle pull up. She moved to the top step and looked out. A half-truck pulled up in a car space close to the bar. Micky climbed out and unloaded two Calor gas bottles off the back. He spotted her and waved, then walked over with a smile.

'You got in all right then.'

Cindy nodded. 'Thanks.'

'How was it? Did you sleep okay?'

'Like a log.'

'Good.' He stared at her and suddenly thought how attractive she was. 'I see your face is looking a bit better.'

'Oh, thanks a bunch.'

'Sorry, what I mean is I'm glad the swelling round your eye has gone down.'

She moved back inside and he followed her. 'Bloody hell, what's that,' said Micky as he noticed Murphy on the ground at the end of the van.

'It's Murphy. I should have said. He's sick. I couldn't leave him out.'

Micky moved forward and peered down at the dog. 'What's the matter with him?'

'Frank nearly killed him, and he's suffered cruelty nearly all his life. I got the vet to treat him, but he needs time to recover. Among other things he's got a broken leg. If he can't stay too, I'll have to go. I understand.'

Micky rubbed his thick mop of hair in bewilderment. 'I don't want to turn you away, but having a dog in here... if some snotty-nosed official from the council comes round and finds out, I could lose my licence.'

'He's a good dog. He'll keep out the way.'

'Has he got to stay here all day?'

'Just for a few days, until he's a bit better. We'll get out of your hair then.'

She could see that he was having serious doubts about offering to let her stay in the bar at night. She was already taking a liberty, and having a dog round his feet while he was working was the last thing he wanted.

'I'll pay you. I can't give you money but I'll work?'

'Work? What do you mean?'

'Maybe I could help you here. You could show me what to do, and I could help. And I'll paint the van if you like. I'm good at painting. I'll give it a face-lift. You'll be pleased.' She suddenly began to get enthusiastic.

'Hold on, hold on. When you say paint, what do you mean?'

'I'll paint a scene. Cover the whole bar. You know: trees, a stream, flowers and stuff. It'll really brighten it up.'

'You can do that sort of thing, can you?' said Micky again, shaking his head with some doubt.

'Definitely. I promise you'll be pleased.' She'd done a bit of mural painting when she was very young and found that she had a talent for it.

'I dunno about that.'

'I'm not much good at anything, but I'm good at that.'

'I'll think about it. In the meantime you can help me set up for the day. I'll show you what to do. Come on, I've got to be ready for my customers,' said Micky as he opened the side of the bar. 'There's a couple of plastic crates in the back of the truck.' Before he could ask her, she was out the door and making her way to the truck. She lifted out the crates and carried them over one at a time. She lined up the rolls and baguettes and sliced them, ready to receive a

107

spread, then turned to the onions and began slicing them up. Micky quickly fell in with what she was doing and carried on the next part of the operation by placing the sausages, bacon, mushrooms and eggs on the griddle. The pair of them worked side-by-side and got a natural rhythm going, and Cindy felt that Micky was pleased with what she was doing. She'd managed to anticipate what he wanted without him having to keep giving her instructions.

His first customers turned up soon after 7:30 and couldn't resist making comments about Cindy's presence there. Most of the comments were friendly and wondered if she was going to be a permanent member of staff. Cindy felt self-conscious and worried that being there was not going to be a good move for Micky's business. She said very little but returned their comments with a friendly smile, and they in turn seemed to be pleased she was there.

When Douglas and his crew arrived around 10 o'clock, they all looked at each other in surprise when they saw Cindy behind the counter next to Micky.

'At last: you're trying making some improvement to the place,' said Douglas.

'Yeah, well I'm hoping I'll get a better class of customers,' said Micky, and the men responded with whoops of laughter and light-hearted jibes.

'You be on your guard, Cindy. He's a bit of a Casanova,' said Andy.

Micky flushed in embarrassment, looked down and pushed a burger into a roll.

'He let me sleep in here for the night so I'm just helping. I'll be gone by the end of the week,' said Cindy slightly defensively.

'He's a good hearted sod, isn't he,' said Douglas.

'Why don't you just eat your food and shut up,' said Micky, feeling even more embarrassed. They all laughed and chatted amongst each other with the usual banter, inwardly feeling pleased that Cindy hadn't had to sleep rough during the previous night. They also thought she seemed to be quick on the up-take at putting the food together and handing it out, and they liked the way she was more relaxed and smiling at them. Micky had always had a good and friendly relationship with his customers, but everyone secretly noticed there was an especially warm atmosphere with having Cindy there. They only hung around for about twenty minutes and then moved off back to their work, all of them calling out friendly goodbyes and wise-cracking at Micky. He suddenly looked at Cindy. 'Hey, you haven't eaten anything yet, have you?'

'No. But I need something for Murphy. He's got to have his antibiotics. I guess I'll have a bacon roll and a cuppa too, if that's okay?' said Cindy as she put her hand in her pocket and pulled out what money she had.

'That's okay. What are you doing?'

'I've got a bit of money left. The vet gave it back to me.' She reached out to him with some money in her hand.

'I don't want that. This won't break the bank, and you're helping,' he said and fixed up her bacon roll and put together a couple of sausages for Murphy.

'I gotta pay you. It's only right.'

'Put it away.'

'Come on, Micky, we haven't got all day.' They looked up and saw another bunch of customers waiting to be served.

'I'm on it, guys. What's it to be?' As he quickly took their orders, Cindy shoved some of her bacon roll in her mouth, gave Murphy his sausages with the medicine and was then back on the counter putting rolls and baguettes together. Before she knew what was happening, she found herself passing remarks and making friendly chat with different customers throughout the day as if she'd been doing it all her life. Some came alone, some in pairs and some in groups. They were nearly all men, and most of them were pleased to see a female presence alongside Micky, nearly all of them making predictable slightly sexist but good-natured flirtatious remarks. Cindy took it all in good heart and found herself laughing and responding with her own cheeky comments which created an even friendlier and enjoyable atmosphere round the van. Every time Cindy laughed, Micky glimpsed at her from the corner of his eye and couldn't help thinking how damn pretty she was. On one occasion he stared at her so intently he lost concentration and poured tomato ketchup on to the hot plate instead of into a roll, a mistake which was met with roars of good natured derision. As the day wore on, Micky not only noticed how well they worked together but that Cindy was smiling happily and projecting an infectious friendliness towards the customers who seemed thrilled to have her there. Gone was her hard-bitten and uncommunicative image that she displayed on the first morning she turned up at the van. He realised that she must have been fighting in some hellish life from which she was trying to escape. He had run the bar for over two years, and his routine had become almost automatic. He loved what he did but was always trying to think of ways to improve it, convincing himself in the end that he had covered all the angles. Cindy had only been there a few hours, and he realised that the whole enterprise had been lifted in a way he didn't know was possible, and it was all due to her. When the last customer of the day had gone and they'd cleared up, he suggested they finish up the small amount of cooked surplus food. They both sat on a couple of crates idly thinking about the day as they munched their food.

'You did a great job for a kid,' said Micky.

'What do you mean kid? I'm eighteen in a week,' said Cindy indignantly.

'Only pulling your leg.'

'You're not so old anyway.'

'Twenty eight.'

'Okay, you're an old man,' she said with a twinkle in her eye.

He smiled at her. 'This job keeps you young.'

'I really enjoyed myself.'

'They certainly loved you.'

She made no reply and flushed in embarrassment. For some time neither of them spoke. Micky suddenly looked at his watch. 'I gotta go. I've got to finish off a job for a customer. He gets very funny if I get there late.'

'What are you doing?'

'Fitting some cupboards. Not a big job.'

'You're clever then.'

'I don't think so. Will you be all right here?'

'Of course. And it's so good for Murphy.'

'I'm glad. I'll pick up some proper dog food on my way. He can't eat this stuff all the time.'

'Really? Thanks, Micky. I owe you plenty.'

'Forget it. It's great to have him here. I'll see you in the morning then.' He stood up. 'Don't answer the door to anyone,' he said with a smile.

'No chance of that. Thanks.'

He waved his hand and went out. For a few moments she remained sitting on her crate and then turned towards the dog. 'So far so good, Murphy."

***

The traffic was bumper to bumper and Tom waited patiently as it slowly moved forward. The development of the huge roundabout had been going on for months and wouldn't be completed for another year, but even then many wondered whether it would improve the flow of traffic. The lights turned green and Tom at last eased forward, taking the first left, and pulled into the Clarkes car park. In spite of his illness, he was determined to carry on with decorating the bathroom as he had originally intended. It was his way of showing a determination to carry on his life as normally as possible and as long as he could until the end. Apart from anything else he quite liked painting and was keen to give the room a face-lift. Clarkes wouldn't be shutting for at least another hour, and occasional vehicles were still coming into the car park. He got out of his car, made his way into the building and headed for the paint aisle. He knew the colour he wanted, but the only choice available was too dark. He thought about it for a few moments, then decided that if he mixed some white with it, he would be able to tone it to the colour he wanted. He lifted a tin of white and a tin of lavender off the shelf and turned round to make for the till when he accidentally bumped into another customer.

'Look where you're fucking going, mate,' said the man as he glared at Tom.

'I'm really sorry. My clumsiness, I'm afraid,' said Tom and couldn't help noticing the man's hair, which had a streak of white through it.

'Stupid old man. Should be locked up.'

Tom instinctively felt nervous at the man's extreme tone of aggression. 'I've said I'm sorry. It was my fault.' He moved to the side as if to move on. The man barred his way.

'I don't like your attitude. You trying to take the piss?'

Tom was about to remonstrate when a member of staff walked up to them.

'Everything all right here?'

112

'Fine,' said Tom, 'I'm just off to the till.' He quickly moved away, leaving the man with the assistant. He paid by cash and left the merchants.

As soon as he got outside, he stopped for a moment and noted that his heart was beating fast. Had he had a close shave? The guy was acting like a psycho. He gave a shudder and began walking towards his car when he stopped and stared across the car park towards the snack bar. He saw a young woman standing next to it and his heart was now suddenly beating twice as fast. Was that the girl he took in at the Centre? Was it Cindy? He slowly moved towards his car from where he could have a better view. He put the cans of paint down and opened the car boot, furtively glancing across at the girl. It was definitely Cindy. He was about to move over to her when he stopped. More often than not, if a volunteer met a face-to-face caller in the street, they usually didn't want to be recognised. Sometimes it worked the other way, but the initiative was always left to the individual. He pretended to fiddle about in his boot for a little while, at the same time sneaking views at the girl. She suddenly turned and looked in his direction and realised that she had caught him watching her. He could see that she was staring hard at him but not made recognition. There was nothing for it. He would throw caution to the window and go over to her. He didn't want to alarm her if she couldn't remember who the devil he was, so he smiled and walked slowly. As soon as he got to within a few feet, he stopped. 'Hallo, Cindy. Do you remember me?'

'It's Tom, isn't it?'

'Yes. How are you?'

'I'm fine.'

'Do you mind me speaking to you?'

'Of course I don't. Did you get into trouble for taking me in that night?'

He gave a chuckle and waved his hand dismissively. 'No, no. Everything was fine. But I've been worried about you.'

'I didn't go back. He's looking for me, but I'll never go back.'

'How are you managing?'

'I'm sleeping.' She was about to tell him that she was sleeping in the van but decided it best not to. 'I'm okay. I'm managing.'

There was an awkward silence for a few moments. He could see that she was looking better than when she arrived at the Centre the night he had taken her in but doubted that her managing, as she put it, would be giving her much of a life.

'So you're all right then?' That was a damn fool question and he knew it.

'Yeah, I'm okay. I'll tell you one thing though – you letting me stay that night made all the difference. I'd have been a bloody fool if I'd killed myself. I'm going to make myself a life one day. I don't know how, but I'm not going to be a loser.'

Tom felt his heart go out to her fighting spirit. She was going to have to drag herself out of her present life, and it would be a tough road. The contrast of what would have happened with his own daughter, Jessica, and the miserable life that Cindy was experiencing flashed before him.

'I'm glad I met you again. Just to say thank you for letting me stay that night. I'll be all right now.'

'It was nothing, and I'm glad for you. I can see now your face has healed up, you're a lovely girl. You take care.'

She gave a rueful laugh and shook her head.

'Why do you laugh?'

'That's the sort of thing that some fathers say to their daughters.

'Sorry,' replied Tom with a smile.

'Not mine though. More like a swipe in the gob.' Tom made no reply.

'I'm going in now.'

'Of course. I'm really pleased to have seen you again. Take care of yourself.'

'You too.'

Tom wanted to say more, to hang around and give her some kind of help that would make a real difference, but his coming across her so unexpectedly had put him off balance; he felt his mind floundering. Before he realised it he was back at his car and getting in. He turned and gave her a quick wave, and then he was gone. Cindy stood and stared across the car park, lost in thought. She felt happy to have met Tom again. She knew he really cared and was grateful that she had come across him the night Frank threw her out. There were some good people in the world after all.

Across the way the man with the white streak of hair came out of the building and walked across the car park to his car. He was about to get in when he saw Cindy standing over by the by the snack bar. His jaw suddenly tightened, and he quickly got into his car and took out his mobile phone. He punched the number he wanted and waited for Frank to answer. 'Frank, it's Gus. I seen her. She's here. Cindy.'

Frank's voice came down the phone. 'Well done, Gus. Where is she?'

'Clarkes car park. By the road works next to the Cannon Trading Estate.'

'Great. Keep an eye on her and see where she goes.'

Gus looked up and out of the window. He suddenly frowned.

'She's gone.'

'What do you mean she's gone?'

'She's disappeared.'

'Are you pissing me about, Gus?'

'She was there, I tell you. I saw her.'

'Well, if she was there she'd still be there.'

'I dunno where she is. She's disappeared.'

'Get after her. She must be heading back to town.' The phone went dead.

Gus scanned the car park, the muscles in his face tight with frustration. How the hell had she slipped away so quickly? As Frank said, she must be heading back to town. He turned off the ignition and spun the wheels as he left the car park.

**

When Micky turned up the next morning, Cindy had got everything ready. She'd spruced herself up as best she could and taken Murphy out to relieve himself. As soon as she heard Micky's truck, she ran out to help him carry in any crates he might have brought. The moment he saw her, his heart gave a lurch, and he couldn't believe that this girl had suddenly walked into his life. Or had she? He couldn't actually say that – not properly into his life. After all she had only spent a couple of nights in his bar and helped him for one day. She would be on the move again soon, and he'd probably never see her again, so he could hardly start imagining she had walked into his life. And even if she had, it wasn't going to go anywhere. It never did. He was no good at that sort of thing – that is, having a "thing" with someone from the opposite sex. It just didn't work for him, so he might as well put her out of his mind and concentrate on work for the day. It was a good idea, but he knew damn well that he might just as well spit in the wind because she was never going to be out his mind whatever he was doing.

'Bloody hell, you've been busy,' he said as he poked his head in the bar and saw everything shipshape.

'Reporting for duty, boss,' said Cindy, feeling excited that he was so pleased.

'How's the hound doing?'

'Great. He walked a lot better when I took him outside this morning. He'll be fine soon, and we'll be out of your hair.'

Micky nodded with a grunt. Shit! She'd be moving on sooner than he'd thought. He said, 'Okay, let's hot up the griddle and get ready for those greedy mouths.' As he spoke and moved forward, he couldn't help wondering how it was possible that only after one day with her, and not really knowing anything about her, they were getting down to a daily task as if they had been working as a team for ages.

At half past seven the first customers arrived and were reaching at the bar for their breakfast. They all greeted Cindy with beaming smiles and friendly banter, and she in turn remembered their names and spoke to them all as if they were her friends. As soon as they'd gone, there was a slight lull, then at 10 o'clock Douglas and his crew arrived. They were quickly served and stood around chatting and making jokes. They privately wondered about Cindy's past and guessed it must have been bad for her to end up homeless. They were even more concerned about her future and what would become of her. It was great to see her there, up in the bar helping Micky, but they knew it could only be a stopgap before moving on. Where that could be, they couldn't begin to imagine. None of them were softies, and all had had their fair share of troubles in their lives, but they all secretly wished they could do something for her to give her a step up in life and a decent future. They said their goodbyes shortly before 10:30, saying they'd be back at midday. As they left, other customers began arriving: some who worked in Clarkes, others who were working on the roadworks and some who were customers from traders on the Cannon Trading Estate. Every now and again there would be a lull, and Cindy and Micky would grab a drink. He'd purchased a bag of dog food, and she was touched that he was so keen to see that Murphy should be well looked after. He also insisted that she help herself to whatever she wanted. He refused her offer of money, saying she was earning her keep. They had little time to have any real conversation amongst themselves, simply passing comments to each other in the general conversations that took place with their customers. The sky above was overcast with dark clouds, and there seemed to be a murkiness that suggested the snow could start to fall at any time. It was warm in the bar, but customers were grateful for their hot drinks even though they were well wrapped for winter.

Shortly before midday there was a lull, then Douglas and his crew returned for a quick lunch. Their section of work had been delayed by some heavy plant breaking down, and they took the opportunity to have a quick break while it was being repaired. Cindy took their orders and noticed that Andy's hand was dripping blood.

'What happened to your hand, Andy?' she asked.

'It's nothing. Got hit by the digger as it swung round. My fault. It'll be okay.'

'You need something on that,' said Cindy with a touch of earnestness.

'I've got a first aid kit on the shelf, Cindy,' said Micky, nodding to the back of the bar.

'Don't worry about it,' persisted Andy as he looked down at his hand and shifted his feet with some embarrassment.

Cindy opened the first aid kit, and after taking out a wad of cotton wool, she ran it under the tap. Taking the first aid tin, she climbed down from the bar and moved over to Andy. 'Let's have a look,' she said, taking hold of his hand. She wiped the blood away and cleaned the wound with the wet cotton wool, allowing her to see that a lump of skin had been torn back above the knuckles. 'Can't leave it like that. It needs to be done properly. I'll do my best.'

'Just leave it. It'll be okay,' said Andy as he looked helplessly at the others who responded by poking good natured fun at him for getting so much attention from Cindy. She covered the wound with antiseptic and wrapped a bandage round it, then bound the whole of his hand with surgical tape to make sure the dressing stayed on. She inspected her handiwork. 'Good. I think you'll live,' she said in a business like way as she closed up the first aid tin.

'Thanks,' said Andy, holding out his hand and also inspecting what she had done for him. The men gave gentle clapping and cheers as she turned to make her way back to the bar. A moment later they were all distracted by a VW with darkened windows swerving violently into the car park. They all looked up and saw a man in his late twenties get out of the passenger seat and peer across at them. He had dark eyes beneath heavy eyebrows and a mouth with thin lips. He wore a baseball cap, beneath which grew long hair tied in a ponytail. He had a hard, unsmiling expression. After a few moments he began to walk towards them but stopped when he was about twenty metres away. 'Cindy! Gotcha, you bitch,' he roared.

'It's Frank,' Cindy whispered, and she shrunk back as if trying to hide in the side of the bar.

'Is that the one?' said Douglas, and Cindy nodded.

'Get over here. You're coming with me.' Frank advanced towards them.

Douglas turned towards Cindy and asked in a quiet voice, 'Do you want to go with him, Cindy?' She simply shook her head. 'She doesn't want to come with you,' said Douglas calmly as he turned back towards Frank.

'You keep your fucking nose out of this. She owes me.'

'I already told you: she doesn't want to come with you.'

'You don't scare me, you big ape. This is none of your business.' Frank advanced to within a few feet of Douglas who had moved forward a couple of paces to meet him. He raised his eighteen stone to his full six feet six inches. The other guys watched expectantly as the tension began to climb. They knew that, as a younger man, Douglas had played in the front row of a prominent local rugby team and was difficult to pull down even with two or three men on him. He was still immensely powerful, and any man taking him on even now needed to think twice.

'You don't seem to understand. The young lady doesn't want to come with you, and therefore she is not going to. Now we don't want trouble, so I suggest you go away and no harm done.' His calm and non-confrontational manner suggested to Frank that Douglas would be a pushover who he'd quickly put on the ground and then drag Cindy away, who had no real chance of running anywhere.

'She's coming with me,' snarled Frank.

'That's not going to happen, so please go away.'

'And you reckon you're going to stop me taking her?' said Frank with a smug sneer, and then quite unexpectedly leapt forward with a swinging fist. But Douglas was well prepared, and with enormous speed his arm, carrying an iron fist, drove forward like a piston and crashed hard into the middle of Frank's face. There was a crunch of bone as his nose shattered, and the force of the blow was so great that he was almost lifted off his feet as he reeled backwards before collapsing on the ground. In a dazed fashion he tried to push himself up as the blood streamed from his nose and mouth. Douglas was well aware that Frank was the kind of man who would normally have dismissed considerable injury and pain and come back attacking when in a fight, but his single blow had been sufficient. Eventually Frank managed to stand, but he remained very unsteady. They could tell that, although he was trying, he found it too difficult to speak and gave up the effort. The driver's door of the VW opened, and Cindy saw Lenny get out and approach them. As soon as he reached Frank, he stopped and gave him a steadying hand.

'Get him away now. And if he ever comes near Cindy again, it'll be the biggest mistake in his life.'

'You've not heard the last of this,' said Lenny.

'For your own sake, I hope it is,' said Douglas.

Frank stood for a moment choking and spitting blood. The front of his clothes were soaked in blood. He was still confused and didn't know what to do, but eventually, with Lenny's help, he turned and shuffled away to his car. Lenny opened the passenger door and helped him in before getting into the driver's seat and pulling away from the car park. Nobody spoke as they saw him drive off. The whole confrontation was over within two or three minutes.

'I don't want you to laugh, Cindy, when I tell you I'm not a man of violence, but that piece of shit had it coming to him. I think you'll be okay now.' Before she had a chance to reply, Douglas turned away. 'The rest of you layabouts had better get back to work. Come on.' He turned and started to walk away, and his crew followed, shouting goodbyes and well wishes to Cindy.

She watched them until they disappeared, and for a little while she and Micky stood in silence. Cindy eventually shook her head and blew out a long breath. 'Wow.' It was the only word she could say.

'You don't meet many people like Dougie. He's some guy, isn't he?'

'I didn't know what to say.'

'Doesn't matter. He'll just be glad you're free of that scum.' She didn't say anything and he could see she was utterly bewildered by what had happened.

'Frank won't leave it, you know,' she said quietly and with a touch of fear in her voice.

'He'll think twice before he decides to do anything. He's just a bully and therefore a coward,' encouraged Micky.

'You don't know Frank like I do. He never lets go, and he's been humiliated. He can't forgive that. He'll want his revenge.'

'Doug can look after himself.'

'I can see that, but he's put himself in danger now, all of you, because of me.'

'No, Cindy. People like Frank have to be stopped.'

'You won't stop him, Micky. He fights dirty. He knows where you are now.'

'I'm not a fighting man, but if he comes when I'm here, I won't let him harm you.' She was surprised at the intensity of his feeling.

She dropped her head in resignation. 'You guys have been good to me. I dunno why. You don't owe me anything.'

'We don't have to owe you anything. We all deserve help sometimes.'

'It's something new for me. It's never been there for me in the past. It's made me, well… a bit of a hard-faced cow.'

'No!' The word shot out with a rap. 'Don't say that about yourself. We've seen what you're like, and the guys love you. They think you're great. We all do.'

'Oh shut up,' she said, turning away in embarrassment. 'These guys over here want some service.'

Micky looked up and suddenly saw that there was a group of men waiting for service.

'Coming, guys,' he called and followed Cindy back into the bar.

Chapter 8

It was a no-brainer. Frank didn't want to go, but Lenny told him he had no choice. If he didn't go straight to the hospital and get some medical attention, see the extent of the damage, find out how much of his nose was busted, investigate the possibility of splintered bone and whether or not some of it had been rammed back further into his skull and could cause even more damage, then he was a dumb head. He had to get it sorted, it was for his own good, and Lenny thought Frank would thank him one day for getting him there.

When they pulled up at the A&E and went inside to reception, the nurse took one look at him and ushered him quickly through to a cubicle. Of course they wanted to know how he had sustained his injury, but he had no intention of telling them. It was none of their business. All they had to do was patch him up and make sure they did a proper job on him, nothing shoddy. He didn't want to look in the mirror in a month's time and look worse than what he did now. As soon as a nurse had cleaned him up, a doctor arrived and sent him down for x-ray. The result showed that his nose was broken but that no fragments had splintered off. He was taken to surgery where his nose was reset. He remained in the hospital until late afternoon and was then allowed to go home.

Lenny left him but came back that evening with Gus, and they sat with him while he unloaded a tirade of cursing against the world and a stream of vitriolic invective against the man who had put him down. He groaned at the pain roaring through his head and struggled not to throw up every time he looked in the mirror and stared at the massive swelling distorting the shape of his face, which was the third injury he had received within the last few days, the first two having come from Cindy.

'I want that car park watched every minute of every day. I want to know if she's there, why she's there, and where she goes at night. I want to know her every move and everyone who's helping her.' Frank had to pause because the effort of speaking was causing him too much pain, and he couldn't stop himself from dribbling because of the massive bruising that had spread down to his lips.

'We'll be on the case all the time, Frank,' said Lenny. 'We'll pull in Nick and Sam and set up a rota. We'll make it foolproof.'

'And I want that gorilla who did this watched. Every move. What time he gets to work. What time he goes to that burger bar. What time he goes home. And I want to know where he lives, what time he goes to bed, what time he shags his wife and what time he gets up in the morning. I want to know if he goes out and where he goes. I even want to know what time he shits.'

'We'll do it, Frank. We'll do it,' said Gus with a weird and fanatic laugh that rolled out from the back of his throat.

'His days are numbered. Do you understand? I want him ground into little bits so I can feed him to the ducks in the pond in the park.'

'It'll all be done, Frank. We'll do it.'

'That's not all. I want to know about his family. I want to know if he's got daughters or sons and how old they are.

I want to know about his wife: where she shops and what she does with her day. Do you understand?'

'Of course we do, Frank. We'll find out everything.'

'And I want that skinny little bitch brought back here. I want you to get her in a place where she can't run, where she can't scream for help, where's there's no chance of escape. I want her brought back here. And when she's back here, she's going to wish she'd never been born.'

'Dead right,' said Gus. 'We'll feed her to the ducks too.'

'Shut your mouth, Gus. I'm going to deal with her!'

'Of course, Frank. Whatever you say.'

'You guys can piss off now. I've got to get to bed. I'm done for today.'

'We're gone, Frank,' said Gus and stood up.

Lenny followed suit. 'We'll see you tomorrow, Frank.'

They both walked out without saying another word.

***

For the next seven days, the exact scenario took place. Lenny and Gus arrived at Frank's place and sat down opposite him. They listened to exactly the same as what he had told them they had to do the first night of his beating. He repeated what he had said almost word for word. He went over it again and again with pathological obsession, and when he finished telling them what they had to do and should have done already, he instructed them to give their reports of what they had seen and discovered. They told him where Douglas lived and everything about how he spent his day. They told him he set off for work at 7:15 and did a diversionary trip to pick up two of his mates, arriving at his works site at 7:30. They would get to their site works about twenty minutes to eight. They started work at 8:00 and went to Micky's Snack Bar at about 10:00 and then again about 12:30. They were back at work by 1:00.

They currently finished work at 4:30 when it was nearly dark. He dropped his mates home before arriving at his own house by 5:00. They told him that Douglas's road, Vernon Street, on the northern side of town, was fairly wide and it also had wide grass verges. It was the kind of road that accommodated a variety of people who had reasonable jobs. Douglas parked his car in his garage, but there were cars parked in the road at intervals.

They told him that his wife did her shopping at Tesco and also spent a lot of time in the garden. There were two children: a girl of about sixteen and a boy about fourteen. Both went to Wingate Secondary, about half a mile away.

Frank had questioned them more about the details of the width of the road, grass verges and parked cars because they had a bearing on what he was planning, though he hadn't told Gus or Lenny anything about what that was.

He questioned them too about Cindy, pressing them to give him every detail.

'The main thing we've discovered is that she sleeps in the snack bar,' Lenny told him.

'Sleeps there? Jesus, she must be well in with that cloth-eared guy who serves behind the bar,' said Frank.

'She spends all day there helping. When they close down about 4:30, he goes off and she shuts up for the night.'

'There's one other thing. You won't believe this, Frank,' said Gus. 'She's got that dog with her.'

'Murphy? Can't be. I killed the little bugger.'

'It's him all right, and he looked pretty good to me,' agreed Lenny.

'I want her. And I want that dirty little animal too.'

'We'll get 'em Frank. You say the word and we'll get 'em.'

For seven days, the same conversation. For seven days, the same questions and the same answers. For seven days, Frank spent every moment working out how he was going to get even.

***

Cindy rolled up her bedding and put it away in the corner of the bar. Today was her eighteenth birthday. She opened up the side of the bar and saw the sun creeping up between the buildings. It was going to be a nice day – frosty but sunny. She felt happy. She knew her future looked bleak at the moment, but as far as day-to-day living was concerned, her life had completely turned around in such a short time. She had managed to get away from Frank so far and had begun to think that he might not, after all, try to track her down again. In her heart of hearts, she didn't really believe that and knew that she must be constantly on her guard. She knew him too well to ever believe he would give up making her pay. Frank was such a mad bastard, he wouldn't be put off by Douglas's threat of doing him serious harm if anything happened to her. Anyway, she wasn't going to let thoughts about Frank spoil her day. She had a quick wash in the tin bowl and looked at herself in the old mirror. All the swelling on her face had gone, but she frowned at what she saw. She'd been told by some in the past that she was good looking; some had even said she was a real beauty (probably guys who had wanted to get into her knickers), but she couldn't see it. Her hair was long, thick and naturally wavy, and she acknowledged she had good bone structure, but so what? That didn't amount to anything much. Her nose was too small and turned up. She didn't care for that very much. She stuck her tongue out and squinted closely into the mirror through half closed eyes. What she needed was a shower, so she decided that she'd try and fix it with Micky for her to get away back to the garage and use the shower facilities she'd made use of before.

She glanced at her watch and saw that it was 6:45. Micky would arrive by 7:30, so she had plenty of time to get everything ready. She now had it all under her belt and was able to handle everything as if she'd been doing it for years. More than that, she had made sure the place was spick and span and had finally persuaded him to buy some paint so that she could decorate the outside of the bar. She had been surprised by her natural artistic talent and had made a spectacular start of painting a scene of palm trees and sunshine, which drew praise from Micky's customers. All in all, at a very basic level, she was getting her life together and feeling good about herself. By the time he arrived, she'd have everything up and running; the bacon, sausages, onions and anything else he was experimenting with would be ready on the griddle. Everything would be ready for those who turned up early for breakfast before starting work. By the time Douglas and his crew and many of the other workers arrived, everything would be going with a buzz. There was always terrific banter with jokes and leg-pulling, but Micky had noticed that all the men had cut back on the worst of their swearing. Subconsciously they felt a kind of protectiveness towards Cindy. It was a way of indicating they had a care for her and not right that they should give free reign to their coarseness. If some of them had thought about it consciously, they might have realised that she'd had to live for a long time in a world where coarseness was at the milder extremity of her daily life. On the rare occasion when one of them accidentally let slip the foulest choice of a swear word, he would quickly retract with a polite nod and quick word of apology to her. She would respond with a wide smile that told them it was okay but that she was touched that he should care and want to give her such respect. Micky was thrilled that the men liked her so much and that she had become part of his world, but the reason wasn't because it was good for his business. He had felt himself being drawn towards her with a different kind of affection to theirs. Every morning he came to catch up with her and see that she was okay, his heart rate would quicken. Every night he would go to sleep thinking about her, and every morning when he saw her, he couldn't take his eyes off her. In spite of his determined efforts to concentrate on the job at hand, she would be such a distraction for him that he would lose track of what he was doing and get what was ordered mixed up. Sometimes he had noticed she too looked back at him in a way that he interpreted as having that special kind of intimate affection, but he couldn't be sure if that was just wishful thinking or whether it was real, and he would secretly torment himself with hope. He was far too shy to express his feelings openly to her, but if he thought that his friends, particularly Douglas, had not picked up the telltale signs, he was mistaken. Nobody said anything, but to most of them it was clear that Cindy and Micky were dead right for each other.

At half past seven Micky pulled up in his half truck and entered the bar.

'Everything ready, boss,' she said with a huge smile.

He stared at her, thinking that he was looking at the most beautiful girl in the world. He wanted to rush forward and take her in his arms and tell her she was the most wonderful person he had ever met. In fact he did say 'that's wonderful' in a warm and hugely enthusiastic way, but he could only allow it to sound like a response that he'd use to anyone. Nevertheless, she beamed her pleasure at his praise and beckoned him closer so that he could inspect her layout on the griddle. Before he realised what he was doing, he put a single arm around her back and gave her a squeeze, but again it could be interpreted as no more than a comradely gesture. If there was the suggestion of anything more, it was lost on her, mostly because she was so wound up with the excitement in her role as a good helper. And she had every reason to feel that life was good. After all, he had been really kind to let her sleep in the bar at night, and she was thrilled that he had obviously got complete trust in her. Sometimes he had even taken a back seat and allowed her to run the show with both the cooking and serving. He must have known that she could easily have creamed off some of the money without him knowing, but she had never felt that he doubted her. He had actually given her money. Initially she had refused it, saying that she was indebted to him and that he owed her nothing. In a boyish way he had implored her not to think he was giving her charity – it was because she had earned it. Because of her presence and the way she dealt with everyone, his business had not only got more customers, but there was always a friendly atmosphere around the bar. The icing on top of the cake was Murphy's recovery. He'd put on weight and his coat began to shine. He had such a gentle nature, and when he was outside the customers loved him.

'You're the best member of staff I've ever had. Here, happy birthday,' said Micky with a wide grin. Cindy turned round to him and saw he was holding a package wrapped in coloured paper towards her.

'For me?!'

'Of course for you.' He could see she had been taken completely by surprise. When the hell had she ever been given a present? She nervously held out her hand to take it, almost as if she was scared it would bite her.

'Jesus, thanks. How did you know it was my birthday?'

'A week ago you told me you would be eighteen in a week. I just guessed it was today.'

'I should learn to keep my mouth shut,' she said with a smile.

'Open it.' He moved in closer to her, peering down at the package with such excitement he could have been mistaken for the one receiving the present. She tore off the wrapping, revealing a small cardboard box. She lifted the lid and, with wide eyes and a gasp, took out a mobile phone.

'Micky! Bloody hell!' She began turning it over and fiddling with it with such excited fingers that she nearly dropped it. 'These things are brilliant. I know people have them, but I've never had one. Well, I had nobody to ring.' Her eyes glistened in wonder as she flipped open the lid and started running her fingers over it. 'This is the most amazing present I've ever had.'

'My number's in the menu so you can always call me. And I can call you too.'

'Thank you, Micky. I'm overwhelmed.' Like an excited child, she kept staring at it.

'There's money in it, but it's pay-as-you-go. It's the simplest deal. You shouldn't have to use it much, so what's in there should last for some time.'

He watched her, thinking how much he would love to take her in his arms and tell her he would give her the whole world if he could.

'Oh, Micky, that's so kind of you. I don't know what to say.' She stared at him in bewilderment but then suddenly flung herself forward and threw her arms round his neck. 'Thank you. Thank you.' He held her for a few moments, feeling intoxicated by the pressure of her body against his, and then she eased herself back and turned her attention once again to her present. He was thrilled at her happiness and how she had responded to him, but he knew that her hug was no different from what he might have received from a sister if he'd had one.

He suddenly looked up. 'Christ, the guys are coming. Are we ready?'

'I'm on it.' She spun round and started flipping bacon, sausages, onions and eggs on the griddle and lining up the rolls. She was so engrossed in what she was doing that she hadn't noticed Douglas and his crew come right up close to the bar and stand in a line with grins all over their faces. Why were they here so early?

'Why are we waiting? Why are we waiting?' they called out in unison.

'Hey, you guys are so early. Why are you so early?' She stared down at them as if to scold them for not warning her the day before when she realised they all had wide grins on their faces.

'Happy birthday. Happy birthday. She's a jolly good fellow. Eighteen and never been kissed.'

She rocked back on her heels wide-eyed and completely stunned. She couldn't speak and stared at them, her mouth agape. Joe reached up and handed her a posy of flowers. 'Happy birthday, Cindy.' In a daze she took the flowers off him. Immediately Andy followed with a large box of chocolates, and then Bob with a package of coloured paper. She took the gifts and opened Bob's package, revealing a long woollen scarf. 'If you ever have to sleep rough, it'll help to keep you warm.' The guys grinned and nudged each other as they saw how overwhelmed she was.

'Oh yeah, I got something too,' said Douglas and handed her a small cardboard box. Cindy turned and looked at Micky as if to say, 'Look at all this. What's going on? It had to be you who told them it was my birthday. Why are they doing this?' He smiled back and nodded at her to open her present and enjoy herself. She lifted the lid and lifted out a small circular cylinder.

'Christ, it's pepper spray.'

'Keep it under wraps. I'm not sure they're legal, but if any bastard tries it on with you, don't hesitate to use it.'

She stood back in a daze while Micky handed out their rolls. They were all chattering and giggling like a bunch of kids who'd just been given a big bag of sweets.

'I don't know what to say to you guys except I love you all. You've made this the happiest day of my life.' As she spoke they looked away because they could see she was close to tears.

'Mind what you're doing with that spray. We don't want you getting it mixed up with the tomato sauce,' blurted Andy, and they all laughed.

'You'd think old Micky would give everything on the house today,' said Joe.

'Yeah, dream on,' Micky called back.

For a little while they stood around cracking jokes and pulling Cindy's leg. Other customers arrived and picked up what was going on and joined in the general banter, but eventually they made their way back to work whilst calling out their good wishes to Cindy as they went.

She and Micky watched them go, affected by the excitement that had generated around the bar while the men were there, and as the day wore on they both continued to experience a warm glow – she because of the show of affection the guys had expressed for her and he because he was thrilled to see her so happy. Customers came and went. Some knew it was her birthday, and those that didn't were soon made aware. All wished her well and spent their brief time at the bar chatting and joking with her. She couldn't remember ever having been so happy, but knew it was all because of her new found friends. For the first time in her life, she had abandoned the need for distrust; for the first time she had experienced the giving and receiving of affection and it made her feel, also for the first time, much more like a whole person. What else could there possibly be in life to make her feel happier? Even so, with her mind reeling from one excitement after another, she found herself occasionally looking back and recollecting the misery of her past. She scarcely remembered her father (except that he used to hit her), who left her mother when she was about seven, and the man who moved in as her new partner was nothing more than a brute. Alcohol and abuse, both physical and sexual, became the order of the day, and eventually she was taken into care and gradually moved through the spectrum of foster homes. In one or two she had found some comfort but in the end had to move on due to reasons that had nothing to do with her. Whether they were or not didn't matter because she always felt that each move was another rejection. Through it all she'd had a fantasy that one day she could escape into a world where there would be laughter and she could feel safe. What she had felt today, what she was feeling now, meant that in some magical way that dream had come true. Micky and Douglas and Joe and Andy and Bob were the closest she had ever come to having a family, and whatever the future held for her, she would never forget them.

After the last customers of the day had come and gone, she cleared up with Micky, chatting excitedly to him, repeatedly telling him how much she had enjoyed herself. She was continually distracted by picking up her phone and drawing him to her side so that she could show him. When they had finally completed the cleaning up, discussed what food stock they would require for the next day and it was time for Micky to set off and leave her alone, she was not down-hearted. She had decided that she would definitely go into town and get to the garage for a shower. After that, she planned to go for a walk along the river and watch the ducks. It was something she had always wanted to do but in all her life had never managed to achieve. As a child, pictures and children's books about the countryside, especially the river, had fascinated her, but the chance of experiencing them in real life had been impossible. When she had moved in with Frank and suggested they take a walk along the river, he had derided her and said that he had better things to do than waste his time on such a pointless activity. Well, nobody was going to stop her now even though it would soon be dark.

As she cast a final look over everything, making sure it was all shipshape to a standard that Micky had come to marvel, he returned to the bar after carrying out empty gas bottles and rubbish to his truck.

'All done, Micky.' She stood in the doorway smiling at him. 'Do you need me for anything more?'

He didn't reply but remained still, looking up at her with a tense expression on his face. She immediately sensed his mood and knew something was wrong. 'What's the matter?'

'Where are you going now?'

'Just going into town. I'm gonna just... I dunno.' She didn't want to mention the shower. She shrugged her shoulders and wondered where this was going.

'Yes, but what are you going to do, and what time will you come back?'

'I don't know, Micky. Have I done something wrong?' She suddenly felt vulnerable and defensive. Had she overlooked something? He had never questioned her like this before.

'Of course you haven't; it's just that...' He began to stammer, and she knew him well enough to sense that something was worrying him, something that he was struggling to get off his chest.

'It's all right, Micky. Tell me what's on your mind.'

'I worry about you. You help me here and do a wonderful job. You go away when we're done and come back to sleep. In the morning I turn up and everything is ready.'

'I love helping. You know that. And I'm so grateful I can sleep here.'

'No; I don't want you to.'

Immediately the atmosphere froze. She stared at him and felt a glaze seeping across her eyes. Within moments her feelings of elation had suddenly plummeted to a sense of sickening doom. Was her joy to be a flash in the pan? Had it all been a fantasy that had now come to an end? Was she now back in the world of reality where betrayal, distrust and rejection were all that she had previously known?

'I thought it was okay. I won't come back if you don't want me to.'

'You don't understand. I don't want you to come back because...' but he couldn't finish his sentence.

'Because what, Micky? Tell me.'

'Because I want you to come and live with me. I've only got a tiny little place, but it's mine, and it's warm in winter, and you'd be always safe, and it would be a proper home for you, and you wouldn't have to hang about in the streets, and I've got a proper bathroom, and you could use it every day, and I could cook you meals, and I wouldn't knock you about like.' She leant forward and gently put her hand on his mouth. He stopped speaking and he stared at her.

'You're serious, aren't you?'

Micky looked down and began fiddling with his hands. He knew he was no good at this; he never had been and he never would be. Why is it some guys could simply deliver the patter without turning a hair? He felt the palms of his hands become damp and his shirt stick to his chest.

'Don't get the wrong idea now. Okay, I like you, but I'm not going to... well, I mean you know... I don't want you to think that I'm going to try and...'

'I'd love to, Micky. I'd love to come and live with you more than anything else in the world.'

He stood in total silence, his mouth agape, and his hands beginning to shake. She moved in closer, and with closed eyes, tilted her head upwards. 'If you kiss me, that will seal the deal.'

He blinked in hesitation and then, his heart pounding at the wall of his chest, he leaned forward and touched her lips with his own. He immediately felt her body melt into his own, and he instinctively wrapped his arms around her as if she had become the most precious thing in his life.

Chapter 9

Linda took her time driving to visit Tom. She couldn't make up her mind whether she felt pleased or anxious about his request for her to visit him. It was quite normal for her to drop by and see him from time to time, and she often spoke to him on the telephone, but there was something in his voice when he rang her and asked her to call by that alerted her he had something important to tell her. She wondered if it was because she knew him so well that she was able to detect that something unusual was afoot. Maybe it was something subtler than that. Maybe it was because, after years of being a Sam volunteer, she had developed that sixth sense which could tell if a caller was hiding something much more important than what they were actually calling about, something they wanted to get off their chest but couldn't bring themselves to reveal.

She pulled into Oliver Road and stopped behind a car that was already parked outside Tom's house. She ducked her head and peered towards the house, wondering if he already had a visitor or whether it was someone randomly parking. A moment later the front door opened and a woman stepped out. Linda could see her having a quick word with Tom, standing in the doorway, before moving away to her car and then driving off. Tom spotted Linda and waved, beckoning her to come on in. He waited for her as she made her way up the garden path and then greeted her with a kiss. 'Hi. Come in,' he said and led her through to the kitchen. 'Coffee?'

'Please. How are you?'

'I've two got important bits of news to tell you.' He filled the percolator and put coffee in it. He had never liked instant coffee.

'To do with your visitor?'

'She's a health visitor. They're really looking after me now.'

'You deserve it.'

'It's only recent. She's a very nice lady. Probably make a good volunteer.'

'How often is she coming?'

'Whenever. Twice a week seems plenty.'

'The NHS isn't so bad.'

'I agree. Nothing's perfect. Do you want to go in the living room or are you okay in here?'

'Here's great, Tom,' said Linda and pulled up a chair to the table. She felt there was something slightly odd about their conversation. What they were saying was perfectly normal, but it just seemed slightly stiffer than what both of them were accustomed to.

'I hope the news is good,' said Linda.

'Fifty-fifty,' said Tom with a smile so she guessed the bad news wasn't too bad.

'Okay. Don't keep me in suspense any longer, Tom.'

'I've seen her.'

'Who?'

'Cindy. You know: the girl I took in that night.'

'Crumbs! Where?'

'I saw her in the car park by Clarkes, next to the Canon Trading Estate.'

'Did you speak to her?'

'Yes. I wondered if I should but it was okay. I think she was pleased to see me.'

'That doesn't surprise me. How is she?'

'She's fine. Well, you know what I mean. Relatively speaking.'

'I'm so pleased, Tom. I know you've been worried about her and this means a lot to you.'

'I admit it. I know it's ridiculous, but I admit it.'

'Of course it's not ridiculous.'

'She's a fighter, Linda. She's still got no home, but she's not going back to the thug who beat her up.'

'What about her future, Tom? It's not going to be easy for her.'

I know. I wish I could help her.' The percolator stopped bubbling, and he turned away to pour out two mugs of coffee. 'No sugar but milk, is that right?'

'Perfect.'

He turned back and handed her a mug before pulling up a chair on the opposite side of the table.

'Is that plausible? Helping her, I mean?' said Linda with strong doubt in her mind.

'I know as volunteers we never give practical help. It's not what we do anyway, even if we could, and that's fine. What we do is great, but I'm not a Sam now so I should be able to do something.'

'Don't take this the wrong way, Tom, but she's not actually your responsibility.' Linda spoke as gently as she could though she knew he wouldn't take offence.

'I know, I know. But if Jessica had lived, she would have been about the same age. She would have had such a different life. I simply have this urge to help this Cindy, who, through no fault of her own, has had a rough deal in life.'

'You've got a lovely heart, Tom.'

He smiled and waved her compliment aside with a sweep of his hand.

'I suppose it's a fantasy really. I don't know what I could do, and there are bound to be practical difficulties that get in the way that I hadn't even thought about. There always are.'

'If she's as gutsy as you think she is, she'll make out anyway.'

'I hope that's true. I shouldn't worry, but I can't help it.'

'If she gets into trouble, maybe she'll call on us at the Centre again.'

'Yeah. I hadn't thought of that. Let me know if she does, Linda.'

'You know I can only do that if she agrees to it.'

'I know, I know. Only do it right.'

'From what you've said I don't suppose she'd mind anyway.'

'At least she's in a better place than she was before. That's something.'

'It's not for me to tell you what you already know, Tom, but we can't fix most of the wrongs that come to us.'

'Oh, I know. I've only been rambling on because I feel so frustrated about some of our callers and never being able to help. In spite of everything, I'll forget about this Cindy soon enough.' He gave a wistful smile, and for a little while they both remained silent.

'You said you had two bits of news. I assume that was the good bit of news. The fact that you've seen Cindy, I mean. What's the other bit?'

He stared down at his mug of coffee, fingering it on the table. The mood in the room suddenly changed, and Linda realised that something was wrong.

'Tom, is something wrong?' she said gently.

He tilted his head to one side and stared at her.

'What is it, Tom?'

'The lady you saw – the health worker – she's new on the scene. It seems that after all I may not have a year.'

'What do you mean? What's happened?'

'It's aggressive. More than was realised. Two months. That may be optimistic.'

Linda's body went rigid. 'Two months. Oh, Tom. Tom.' She reached across the table and took his hand. 'That's terrible.'

'Not so bad once you've got over the shock. Two months. A year. It's less time but doesn't change anything much.'

'But how are you coping? Here? On your own?'

'I'm doing fine. For the moment anyway. The nurse is keeping a close watch on me. When things get really bad, my doctor has made arrangements for me to get into the Sue Ryder Hospice. I shall be well looked after.'

'I can't believe it. You look so well.'

'Yes. That seems to be a trick it plays.'

'What can I do? Is there anything I can do?'

'Having you around is a huge help, Linda. I know you'll help me get through this.'

'I'll see you daily, and you call me day or night. I can be here in 15 minutes.'

'Thank you. I'll try not to call you in the night. Clive might not be too happy about that.'

'Don't worry about that. He probably wouldn't notice if I wasn't there anyway.'

'I'm sorry. You've got your own problems without having to cope with mine.'

'Rubbish. You're my greatest friend. And Janice was too. I loved her, and I love you. Now is there anything I can do at the moment?'

'As a matter of fact there is. I've laid out a plan of action and a number of things I want done when I'm dead. I'd like you to go through them with me. Bring your coffee into the other room. It's all written down. I'd like to know what you think, and I'll tell you what I would like you to do.' He stood up and walked out. Linda followed him.

***

Micky took a sharp left, drove to the end of the cul-de-sac and pulled up in front of the last house. It backed on to fields and was tiny. Cindy thought it was exactly as he had described, not much bigger than a loaf of bread. The building was constructed in old wire-cut bricks that were now weathered and displaying different shades of their original colour. The front door, fitted with old-fashioned hinges and painted dark red and barely six feet high, was slightly to the side instead of being in the middle of the front wall. The windows, with wooden frames also painted in dark red, were very small, and the roof consisted of small old clay tiles that were still as hard as iron. Sitting in the passenger seat, Cindy looked at the house with wide eyes.

'Is this it, Micky?'

'I know it's small but…'

'It's wonderful.' She jumped out of the cab and looked up at the house, her eyes now shining with excitement. Murphy was at her feet. 'It's so pretty.' She opened the small front wicker gate, ran up the path and peered through one of the windows. 'Come on, Micky, I want to see inside,' she beckoned him with the excitement of a child. He followed her up the path, smiling at her pleasure, and unlocked the door which opened immediately into the living room. The room was not as small as one would have suspected from an outside viewing, and this was because it stretched the whole width of the house. The floor was made of red quarry tiles and softened by two colourful mats. Into one wall was built a small but open brick fireplace, in front of which was a well-worn sofa. Behind this were a small wooden planked table and two upright chairs. An old Welsh dresser rested against the wall opposite between two windows, and a staircase came down at the side of the third wall. A doorway into the fourth wall opened into the kitchen, the only other room downstairs in the house.

'I love it. I love it,' she blurted as she moved around, poking the sofa and trying to take in everything.

Micky walked into the kitchen. 'What do you think of this then?' She came and stood beside him and jerked her head from side to side, trying to see everything at once. A modern sink and drainer were immediately in front of her, below a window that looked out on to the back garden and fields and woodland beyond. The room was big enough to house a small refrigerator and a reasonably modern gas cooker, and there were lots of pots and pans hanging on the walls. Various jars and assorted kitchen utensils laid around on random surfaces. 'I'm a bit untidy, I'm afraid, but I keep the place clean,' he said as he opened the kitchen door at the side of the house, where there was an outhouse in which he indicated a fairly old washing machine.

'It's not brilliant, but I've got more or less everything I need.'

'I think it's wonderful. I can't believe it.' She went and held his arm, 'Micky, this is the most wonderful day in my life. This couldn't be better.' She had a sudden afterthought. 'It's all right, isn't it? To have Murphy? To keep him with us?'

'Of course it is. If there's not room for the three of us, then you'll have to go.' He stared at her with a wide grin.

'I hate you too,' she said, matching his grin and hitting him in the chest.

'There's more to see upstairs, but I'm starving. Let's have something to eat, and then I'll show you the rest.' He went back into the kitchen and opened the fridge. 'How about some steak? I've got a lump in here.'

'Fantastic. Can I help?'

'In the freezer in the outhouse, there's a bag of chips. Is that okay?'

She immediately started back for the outhouse. 'Can't think of anything better.'

'Shouldn't take long; I'll get the oven going hot.' He fired up the oven and rummaged in the fridge as she went for the chips. As soon as she returned he started pointing in all directions. 'There's some plates in there, and in that drawer you'll find cutlery. What do you reckon on courgettes in garlic? I could fry them and grill the steak.'

'Never had 'em, but I bet the queen of England couldn't do better.'

'I can do a bit better than just frying up sausages and bacon,' he laughed happily as he busied himself, and she began laying the table in the living room.

'I've got a bottle of wine in the bottom of the dresser, and there's glasses up top. Dunno if the wine's any good, but I'm game if you are,' he called out to her.

'I'm on it,' she called back, and when she'd finished laying out, she began walking round trying to immerse herself in all her new surroundings with its knick-knacks and furniture, enjoying the excitement of knowing that it was all going to be part of her life. She reached up to a shelf and inspected his collection of CDs and wasn't surprised that he had a lot of Dolly Parton. She looked around the room until she found a player and put one on low volume.

Micky put his head round the door. 'Do you like her?'

'Of course I do, if you do,' she grinned back at him, and after he'd disappeared for a moment, he returned with two plates which he put down on the table.

'Come on. Let's get stuck in.'

They both sat down and she stared at her food. 'You're a bloody marvel, Micky.'

'It's your birthday. And you need building up. You're as thin as a rake.'

'I shall get as big as a house.'

'No you won't. We'll do lots of walking. That's if you want to, I mean.'

'Of course I do. And we can take Murphy.'

'Definitely. He'll love it. When the summer comes it will be better. We'll have more time.'

'I can handle the bar when you've got other work. I know what to do, and you can trust me.'

'Of course I trust you, and you're brilliant at it. With you helping me we'll be a fantastic team. If I can get round some of my other jobs, we'll make a lot more money.'

'I won't let you down, Micky. I'll do my best at the bar.'

'Don't be silly; you're better at it than me, and all our customers love you.'

'Well you taught me what to do, and I enjoy it so much. The men are great fun, and Dougie and his crew were so kind to me today.'

'They know you've had a rough deal and think you deserve better.'

'My life has changed so quickly. I still can't grasp it.' She suddenly went quiet and looked down as if lost in deep thought.

'What's the matter?'

'I often think of the night I went to that place and talked to that guy who took me in for the night. It was amazing to see him again.'

'I'm glad you did.'

'I had nowhere to go, and I was soaked and frozen stiff. Frank had damn near killed me, and I wanted to die. Didn't seem much point in going on, and I had a load of pills.'

'Thank Christ you didn't.'

'I would have done, you know – if he hadn't taken me in. He wasn't supposed to, but he told me there was no problem.'

'I'm sure he knew what he was doing.'

'In a way I'd like to see him again. He was such a nice old gentleman. Well, not really old.'

'I expect you can. You could go back to the Centre where he took you in. I'll come with you if you like. I'd like to meet him too and thank him.'

'Would you really, Micky? That would be brilliant.'

'Settled then. Come on, let's have some pud.' He picked up their plates and headed for the kitchen.

'Pud? Bloody hell, Micky, I'm stuffed.'

He came back a few moments later with a tray carrying two plates and a bowl. 'You haven't lived until you've eaten my trifle.'

She leaned forward and peered into the bowl.

'What's in it?'

'It's only simple – assorted fresh fruit on sponges, then the custard covered in whipped cream.'

'Sounds beautiful.'

'That's not all. I do what they do in posh houses. I laced it with sherry. Read it in a magazine. Tastes fantastic.' He spooned out two portions and gave one to her.

She looked down at it and her eyes lit up. 'What a feast, Micky.'

They ate in silence except for groans of delight as they demolished the trifle, finally scraping their bowls clean. As soon as they'd finished, they sat back and grinned across the table at each other.

'I'll wash up 'cos you got the meal,' she said and stood up.

'No. We'll do it together.' He cleared the rest of the table and followed her to the kitchen where they both washed and dried the dishes, she, full of fun, occasionally flicking soapy water at him, and he, retaliating by flicking the tea towel at her. He hung it up, and she dried her hands.

'Do you want to see the rest of the house now? Upstairs?'

'Oh yes, yes please.'

'There's not a lot.'

I shall love it. Lead on.' She gave him a gentle push, and he moved to the stairs and began to climb up with her close behind. At the top there was a small landing. He opened a door on his right, which revealed a bathroom shower, bath, wash basin and toilet. The floor was polished floorboards. She followed him inside and looked around.

'Oh, Micky, a bathroom. This is bliss.'

'The shower gives you hot water, but there's only hot water coming from the taps in the wash basin and bath when the boiler's on. I've got to replace it before the winter because it's always breaking down.'

'Just to get in here each day. You can't imagine what that means.'

'You'd better come and look at the bedroom.' He led her out of the bathroom to the other side of the landing and into the bedroom. It was large: as big as the room downstairs. In the middle of the wall facing them was a window which, like the kitchen below them, looked out over the back garden and beyond to the fields and woodlands. There was a chest of drawers in the corner and a stand-up cupboard next to it which he'd made himself and in which he hung up jackets and trousers. In the middle of the room was a double bed.

'Single bed was never big enough for me,' he said and suddenly began to feel a little embarrassed.

'Is this the only bedroom?'

'Um... well, yes. But you can have this bed, and I'm going to sleep downstairs on the sofa.'

'I can't let you do that, Micky; this is your bed.'

'I'll be all right. I wouldn't expect you to sleep on the sofa.'

'I'm definitely not going to agree to you sleeping down there while I'm up here in your bed.'

Micky looked dejected. He wanted everything to be perfect for her and hadn't expected this problem. 'What are we going to do then?'

She stared at him and realised he was upset and struggling to come up with the right answer, an answer that would make her happy.

'Oh, Micky, you lovely man, what planet have you come from?' she said gently and slipped her arms round him. 'I'm sure it will be big enough for both of us.'

She pressed herself into him and held him tightly. A wave of love for him poured over her. She had been physically, sexually and emotionally abused throughout her young life. Any experience of sex had meant she was nothing more than some man's object to satisfy his lust. She had been the victim because she had been the one there. Had it been another girl, it would have made no difference to the man, that girl would have been the victim instead. There had been no feeling, no love. She had had to cope with rape, physical injury and rejection. She had been scorned by betrayal, lies and cruelty. Every day had been nothing more than a challenge for survival. Yet there now stood in front of her a man who knew nothing of this; a man who was strong and whose only fear lie in his timidity that he might hurt her; a man who had shown her nothing but kindness and tenderness. She felt a passion surge through her body which she wanted to express to him as an expression of the feelings in her heart rather than for just the pleasure she knew her body would enjoy. She felt his heart pounding against the side of her face, but then she eased back and looked up until he looked down and met her eyes.

'I must have come from a planet for idiots, but I didn't dare hope that, well, I love you, you see, and I didn't think that.' He was stopped in his tracks by her pressing her lips against his, and she felt his arms wrap around her.

Chapter 10

It was almost a month before the injuries to Frank's face had healed to a degree that satisfied him enough to go out to all his normal haunts, but the new shape of his nose had changed his face forever. Every time he looked in the mirror, he was reminded of the man who had done it to him and what he was going to do to him in revenge. There were others who would have to pay as well. They would all have to learn that to cross him would be to make the biggest mistake of their lives. The big-eared goon who served at the snack bar, he would definitely have to pay because Lenny had found out that he was shagging Cindy and got her to move in with him. In the last month he had been able to find out everything about him – where he lived, what other work he did and where he spent his spare time. He had taken Cindy off him, so he would have to pay severely. And of course Cindy would have to pay. Each one of them. Each one of them, one by one, would have to bear terrible pain, terrible suffering. He would be the instrument of their suffering, and he would enjoy it. The first one would be the heap of lard that had broken his nose and disfigured him for life. He would have his body broken beyond repair unless, of course, he died in the process. It wasn't always possible to tell the final outcome when punishment was carried out. Sometimes it could be a very fine line between life and death. It was of no consequence. Either outcome would be satisfactory. More than that, either outcome would, not would, that was the wrong choice of word, but WILL fill him with joy. And that moment was now very near. After all, he had spent the whole month laying out his plans. There had been no urgency. Dragging out the planning and simply thinking about it had given him constant pleasure. Lenny had given him even more details about the target's daily life and he had even visited the road himself where he lived and watched the house and all the goings on around it. He made special note that the target left the house every evening between 10:00 and 10:15 to walk his dog down the road. He would come out of the front door, turn right and walk twenty yards before crossing the road at the point where a sycamore tree was growing out of the grass verge. The dog usually lifted its leg on the tree causing the target to pause. Then he would walk across the road and turn right and continue until he reached the T-junction about 200 yards away.

He would then cross the road and come back down the other side. The occasional car was parked in the road as the same side as his house. He and Lenny had noted that very little traffic came up or down the road at night. Perhaps the odd one or two, as occupants to some of the houses returned home. The target's routine was perfect. The location and site was perfect. The plan was perfect. And now he was ready to put it into action.

***

There was the squeal of brakes and smell of burning rubber. Micky curled his fingers round the safety belt until his knuckles went white, and he closed his eyes.

'Jesus Christ, Cindy! I thought that was going to be the end of me.'

She turned towards him and grinned. 'Sorry. I got a little bit confused.'

Micky looked skywards and blew out a long hiss of air, then he relaxed his shoulders and laughed. 'Jenson Button and Lewis Hamilton have got nothing on you.' He shook his head as if in despair.

'I've got to learn. You're not going to give up on me, are you?'

'No, but I think that's all my nerves will stand tonight.' She leaned across to him and kissed him on the cheek. 'Sorry. I meant to have moved my foot and pushed the brake. I just had a mental blockage.'

'It's okay. You're doing well. It's only your second lesson.' She leaned across at him and kissed him again.

'You're so lovely, Micky; I might get to like you,' she grinned.

'A transit truck is not the easiest vehicle to learn to drive in. You've got the hang of it pretty quick. You just need practice.'

She pulled into the kerb and stopped. 'You drive now,' she said and slipped out of the driver's seat, moved round the front of the vehicle and got into the passenger seat as he eased himself out of it. For a moment they both sat in silence, thinking about the lesson she had just had.

'Micky, can we do something,' she said with a touch of seriousness.

'Yeah, what is it?'

'You know the place I went to, the night that guy, Tom, took me in? It was the Samaritan Centre.'

'Yeah.'

'We're quite close to it. It's in Warwick Street. Can we go round there? If Tom's there I'd just like to see him. Just tell him about you and that I've got a lovely little place to live.'

'Course we can. I'd like to meet him too. Thank him. But will he be there?'

'He may not be. But we can try, and if he isn't, maybe I can leave a message.'

'Okay,' said Micky and turned on the ignition and pulled away. He drove into Warwick Street and pulled up opposite a sign that said SAMARITANS.

'I feel a bit nervous about going in now,' said Cindy, peering across at the building.

'They're the last people to bite your head off.'

As they continued to stare across the road in thought, Linda came into sight, making her way towards the Centre. They paid her no attention until she reached the Centre and turned to go in. Cindy jumped out of the truck and called out, 'Excuse me!'

Linda stopped and turned to face her. 'Hallo.' She smiled at Cindy.

'Sorry to bother you. Do you work here? I mean, are you one of the...?'

'I belong to the Samaritans, yes. Can I help you?'

'No, it's all right. Well I mean, I visited here some time ago. I spoke to someone – he told me his name was Tom – and, um, I had nowhere to go and he let me stay the night.'

'Yes, I know who you mean. I remember. Is your name Cindy?'

'Yes. I just wanted to, well, leave a message, I suppose, to thank him and, er, is he there by any chance?'

Linda paused for a moment, took a breath to speak and then paused again.

'No, Cindy. I'm afraid he left.'

'Oh, will he be here tomorrow?'

'He's not coming back. I'm sorry to say he's very ill.'

Cindy looked alarmed. 'What do you mean very ill?'

'I'm afraid he's dying. He's in a hospice.' As soon as she said it, she felt a sudden panic, wondering if she had

155

said too much. It was personal information about Tom, and he probably wouldn't have wanted her to know about his condition. In any case, volunteers never disclosed information about themselves.

Cindy felt her cheeks prickle as the blood jumped to her face. She touched Micky's arm and looked at him questioningly, as if he would have a complete understanding of what Linda was saying.

'Dying? Why is he dying? He's not an old man.'

'He has cancer. It's very sad for all of us.' Linda felt her cheeks burning as she realised in embarrassment the blunder she was making. It was unforgiveable what she had revealed.

There was another long silence and Linda could tell that Cindy was trying to get a mass of thoughts together. Micky took her hand. 'You okay?' he asked very gently.

'I wanted to tell him… I wanted him to know that I'm living with Micky. I'm happy. I'm getting on.'

I'm really happy for you, and I know he will be too. I'll tell him.'

Cindy looked at Micky again, this time questioningly, as if he would agree with what she was going to say. 'I s'pose. I mean, do you think I could see him? Go to the hospice, I mean?'

Linda couldn't escape it. She'd dug a big hole for herself. Why had she opened her mouth? Was it because Tom had showed such a real interest in the girl to the extent that it seemed natural for her to know about his illness? It was too late now anyway. She'd have to keep going.

'Do you really want to do that?' asked Linda.

'I do, yes. Except that, well, he may not be glad to see me. I mean, I'm not his family. I'm not even, oh I dunno.'

'I think he would love to see you, but I have to warn you, he's very sick. I saw him earlier today, and he actually talked about you.' Maybe she hadn't said too much after all. He would almost certainly want to see her even though he was very ill.

'Really?' She looked up at Micky and smiled. 'He was so kind to me.'

'Cindy will never forget his kindness,' said Micky.

'It's the Sue Ryder Home off Victory Street.'

'I know it,' said Micky. 'I did some work for someone along that road.'

'Say you're a good friend.'

'I will, and thank you.'

'Where are you living?'

Micky spoke, 'I've got a tiny little place at the end of Bush Lane; it's a cul-de-sac at the foot of Costers Hill. I'm the last house on the left. It's very small,' he added as if embarrassed by the size of his property.

'It's not small. It's lovely. I love it. We both love it.'

'I know where you mean,' said Linda. 'I go along Bush Lane sometimes. At the end there is an access through the hedge that leads up to the hill.'

'That's it,' said Micky.

'I've often noticed your little house. It looks lovely.' She smiled at both of them and they smiled back. 'I have to go inside now to see somebody. But I won't be long, and I shall be going back to see him again myself. Take care of yourselves. Come and see us if you ever need to.'

'I'll look after her,' said Micky.

'Goodbye,' said Cindy as Micky eased her away and back to the truck. Linda turned and made her way into the Centre.

As soon as Micky and Cindy had got into the truck, Cindy said, 'She's a nice lady.'

'Yeah. They're probably all nice.'

'Can we go and see him now, Micky?'

'Of course. We may as well while we've got the time.'

He turned on the ignition and pulled away.

***

It was 7 o'clock when Gus turned up at Frank's. Lenny was already there. He pulled up a chair at the kitchen table and took a can of beer that Frank pushed across the table at him.

'He's home. They all are. Wife and two kids. I managed to wander by. The two kids are watching telly with grub on their laps. He and his wife were eating out the back. His car's put away so he won't be going out.'

'Well done, Gus. Looks like it's tonight then,' said Frank.

'Can't see it getting any better,' added Lenny.

'It's going to piss with rain later.'

'Doesn't matter. Better for us. If anyone comes along, it'll be harder for them to see.'

'I'm really looking forward to this.'

'You're not coming with us, Gus. It's just Lenny and me tonight.'

'Oh no, Frank. I want to be there to see him get it.'

'We'll let you know all about it. You've done really well, but we don't want three of us there. If you get us a set of wheels and be here by half past nine, then you will have done more than enough.'

'You know I can do that all right, Frank. I won't let you down.'

'I know that. And you know what we want. It may not be that easy.'

158

'I'll manage, don't you worry.'

'I wish I could give you more time, but it would have been taking a big risk if you nicked it too soon before we want it. We want the whole thing finished and done with before the owner's discovered it's gone and reported it to the old bill. I know I'm being fussy, but we mustn't have any slip ups.'

'Dead right, Frank. That's perfect planning.'

'Get to the brick works by half past ten. We shall be there by then, give or take.'

Better park in Brick Street and walk the last bit. The car won't be noticed there. Don't forget the can of petrol. If all goes well we should be having a drink in the club well before eleven.'

'I'll have a close look at Tesco and West Road car parks. There'll be a big choice, and I'll make sure I get the right vehicle.'

'Good idea, Gus.'

'I'll get off then,' said Gus and walked to the door. 'This is going to be a great. Payback starts tonight.' He grinned and walked out.

***

Micky took a left and pulled into the drive that led up to the Sue Ryder Hospice. It was a long, curved drive, but even though it was dark, they could see, beyond the artificial lighting, well maintained grounds of grassland and trees on either side. It gave them both a feeling of peacefulness. The building, which was large and impressive, had obviously been a home for a wealthy family of landed gentry many years ago and had now been converted into the kind of hospital that cared for the dying or very seriously ill.

Micky pulled into a parking space at the side of the building and switched off the engine.

'Are you okay about this?' he said and placed his hand on her lap.

'Yeah, I want to see him. Do you think I'm being silly?'

'Of course not. He was very kind to you.'

'I can't tell you how bad I felt that night. Really bad. Oh, I dunno. It's just that he was so gentle with me. I'd never experienced that before. I know it sounds crazy, but in my dreams he was just like the kind of person I'd want as my father.'

'Has he got a wife or family? They may be there.'

'I don't know. I don't know anything about him.'

'Doesn't matter. Let's go in anyway.' He nodded at her, and they both got out of the truck. The entrance was a large front door, but it was off the latch so they pushed it open and went in. They found themselves in a large open hallway which still retained many of the house's original characteristics. It seemed to bear no relationship to a hospital where one expects to see nurses and doctors flitting about from treatment rooms and wards. The walls were of wooden panelling and the atmosphere was quiet and restful. Ahead of them was a counter, and behind it a woman was speaking on the phone. They approached her and waited until she had finished her call. As soon as she hung up, she put the phone down and smiled at them.

'Can I help you?'

'Is it possible to see Tom?' As Cindy asked the question she suddenly realised she had no idea what Tom's surname was.

'Is that Tom Elliott?'

'Er, yes,' said Cindy and looked at Micky for some reassurance.

Micky quickly spoke. 'To be honest, we don't know his surname. He's a good friend, but we only know him as Tom.'

'It must be Mr Elliott because we only have one Tom here. You're welcome to see him, but I think he's probably asleep.'

'We won't be long, and we won't disturb him,' said Cindy.

'If you go through that door, it's the second room on the left,' said the receptionist, pointing the way with her finger.

'Thank you,' said Micky and took Cindy's arm to give her reassurance as he detected her nervousness. When they reached the door, they spotted a dispenser on the wall requesting them to take a squirt to sterilise their hands. They both complied and moved on to the second room on the left down the passageway. Cindy pulled at Micky's arm and stopped.

'I don't know what to say.'

'If he's asleep you won't have to speak. I'm sure he'd be pleased to see you anyway.' Cindy nodded and they both went in. There was only one bed in the room and it was on the far side. They both approached quietly.

Tom was slightly raised with the support of three or four pillows. His arms were thin as sticks and lay stretched out on the covers in front of him. His eyes were closed. Cindy felt her jaw tighten at the sight of his face which had a grim pallor. She had thought he had a thick thatch of hair, but it now seemed very thin and lank. His eyes were sunken, and his cheekbones seemed to erupt from his face from what appeared paper thin skin. She looked up at Micky and swallowed, trying to overcome her shock. He simply smiled back at her and held her hand.

'Do you think we had better go?' she whispered.

'In a minute.' As Micky finished speaking Tom's eyelids fluttered and he slightly opened his eyes. He stared up at them, and they could see he was trying to identify who they were.

'Hallo, Tom. It's Cindy. Do you remember me?'

He suddenly formed a half smile and gave a kind of nod even though his head remained on the pillow.

'Cindy.' He spoke in a whisper.

'I'm sorry to see you so ill, Tom.'

This time he shook his head as if to say not to worry.

'This is Micky. He's looking after me. He's got a little house, and I'm living in there with him so I won't have to go back to Frank.'

Tom smiled again with a nod.

'She's going to be all right. We haven't got a lot, but we've got each other and that's enough for us,' said Micky.

Tom mouthed the words, 'Thank you.'

'When you're better we want you to come and visit us,' said Cindy.

Again Tom smiled with a nod but then moved his hand as if to reach Cindy's. She reached out and slipped her fingers into his palm. She felt his grip tighten a little, and then he closed his eyes. She and Micky just stood still in silence, looking down at him. There didn't seem a need to speak. She understood that he knew they were there and it was giving him comfort. For a long five minutes, neither of them moved. They simply sensed that, although Tom knew he was close to death, he displayed an aura of peace. Cindy momentarily put her free hand up to her face as she felt a tickle and realised it was a tear running down her cheek. She wiped it away but remained holding his hand in silence.

Micky gave her a gentle nudge, suggesting that it might now be time for them to go. Cindy nodded, then bent down and gently kissed Tom on the cheek. "Thank you for taking me in on that night,' she whispered. He didn't move and she eased her hand from his. They both stood for a moment longer and quietly walked out.

Cindy stopped at reception. The woman looked up. 'Thank you for coming.'

'Do you know…' Cindy faltered for a moment before going on, 'Do you know how long the gentleman will live?' As soon as she had asked the question, she felt it was something she shouldn't have.

'I'm afraid I can't tell you that. I don't know.'

Cindy nodded. They thanked the woman and made their way out to the truck. As soon as they got in and slammed the doors shut, they sank back into their seats, but neither spoke for a little while. Micky stared out into the darkness beyond the lighting and tried to collect his thoughts. He knew that Cindy had been greatly moved by Tom's simple act of kindness on the night he took her in. He understood, too, that that single act had ('like the flip of a coin,' as she would put it) set in motion the path that she had since travelled. A lot of things had happened to her, but she had fought like a tiger and managed to escape. She may have been small, but she had the heart of a lion, and it was one of the reasons he couldn't help loving her. Not bad, he thought: fights like a tiger and has the heart of a lion. He grinned inwardly at the odd combination. Anyway, he was determined to make sure that nothing bad was going to happen to her again. She had experienced very few acts of kindness in her life. Tom had represented the kind of man she wished for her own father to be, and that was probably one of the reasons she felt drawn to him. He wondered what family Tom had and whether or not he had a partner or children. He had seemed to really care about Cindy, so maybe she was the kind of daughter he never had. Of course that was ridiculous, but then stranger things happened in life, so maybe it wasn't so ridiculous.

'It seems so unfair. I mean, he isn't an old man,' Cindy said in a voice barely above a whisper.

Micky nodded. 'He's a good man too.'

There was another silence when a car came up the drive and parked beside them. Linda got out.

'It's the lady from the Centre. I'm going to speak,' said Cindy as she got out and came round the truck to meet Linda. 'He looks terribly ill,' she said.

'I'm afraid he hasn't got long, Cindy.'

'I wanted him to know it was me, that I'd come to see him. But I don't know if he recognised me.'

'I'm sure he did. He wanted to get to know you better, and I'm sure he would have done if he was going to live.'

'Is there nothing they can do for him?'

'Not anymore. They've done all they can. He's not in any pain, and he knows the end is near.'

'Does he have anybody? I mean, was he married or did he have any children?'

'He was married but his wife died about three years ago. He had a baby daughter but she died when she was only a few months old. She would have been about your age now.'

'So there's nobody.'

'He has many close friends. Those who know him love him.'

'I know he hasn't died yet, but I would like to come to his funeral.' She looked questioningly at Micky who had come to stand by her.

He nodded. 'Of course.'

'That's kind of you. I know where you live now. I can call by.'

'Thank you.'

'We'd better go. We mustn't hold you up.'

'My name's Linda. Take care of yourselves. Goodbye,' said Linda and walked off towards the front entrance.

'Let's go home,' said Micky.

'Yeah. But I'm glad we came.'

They both got into the truck and Micky drove off.

***

Gus pulled up outside Frank's just before 9:30. He was happy. He'd got what he considered the perfect motor: a ten-year-old Range Rover with bull bars on the front. Frank would be pleased. He'd picked it up from the Tesco car park without the slightest hiccup. He'd watched the owner, an old guy and his wife, get out and go into the store. He reckoned they'd be in there for at least twenty minutes, maybe more, so there was plenty of time for him to get it to Frank's and for Frank to be away on the job well before discovering it was stolen. Breaking into the car had been as easy as shelling peas for Gus.

He slammed the door shut and made his way up to the house, quietly whistling to himself. He pushed opened the letterbox flap and called out. 'It's me, Frank. Gus.' A moment later Lenny appeared and let him in. Frank had moved into the living room and was stretched out on a sofa.

'Sorted,' said Gus with a wide and smug grin.

'What you got?' asked Frank.

'Range Rover, with bull bars.'

'Perfect,' said Frank.

'It's dirty as well. Can't even read the number plates.'

'Even better. Good job, Gus,' said Frank and stood up from the sofa. 'We'll get off straight away. You make sure to meet us at the brick works by ten thirty, Gus.'

'I'll be there. I've got the petrol.'

'Good. Here, take these,' said Frank handing Gus his car keys. Gus took them and handed him keys to the Land Rover.

'I'll drive, Lenny. Let's go.' They grabbed their coats and moved out.

***

It took Frank a little more than twelve minutes to cross town. He turned south until he came to the roundabout which gave him access to Vernon Street. He moved down it slowly and stopped twenty-five yards back from number 68, where Douglas lived. He turned off the engine and switched off the lights. The area was enveloped in a murky drizzle, almost fog, for which Frank nodded in quiet satisfaction. He and Lenny sat back and prepared to wait. If Gus's snooping had been accurate, which Frank believed it would have been because he had been on the job for at least a couple of weeks, then Douglas would walk his dog out just after 10 o'clock. He decided that as soon as he saw the front door open, he'd start the engine and let it idle in readiness.

'Be sod's law if he does it differently tonight,' said Lenny.

'I don't see why he should. Relax, Lenny. It'll be a pushover,' he suddenly laughed, 'If you see what I mean.' Lenny sniggered too.

'This is only the first, Lenny. We'll take 'em down one by one.'

'It's that little bitch I want to see get her comeuppance.'

'She will. And that will give me the greatest satisfaction of all.'

He stopped speaking as they both heard voices and turned their heads to try and discover where they were coming from. Frank looked in his side mirror and saw a couple of young lads approaching on the pavement. They were larking about, playfully pushing each other and laughing at the banter between them.

'Drop your head below the sill, Lenny. Best if they don't see us and wonder what the hell we're doing here,' said Frank. They both slipped down on their seat and ducked their heads as the two lads walked by. Lenny and Frank couldn't see them as they walked by, but they didn't hear them make any comment or notice a falter in their steps, so they guessed their presence hadn't been noticed. They sat up again.

'Five to,' said Lenny. 'Shouldn't be long now.'

'Good. Once we've got him down, we can drive to the end of this street and turn into Windsor Road, get half way down it and get away through Lock Street. We'll pick up the main road and be at the brick works a few minutes later. It'll be easy. Clean. No fuss. Mission accomplished.'

The hour hand reached ten on Frank's wristwatch. He leant forward on the steering wheel and peered through the gloom in the direction of number 68. Any time now the door should open and the big guy should appear. A car suddenly approached from behind, drove on a little way and parked on the same side as number 68, two doors further on.

'Shit!' said Frank. 'Why do they have to come now?' He watched as a man got out from the driver's side, a woman from the front passenger seat, and another couple got out from the back. They stood under the streetlight laughing and chatting on the pavement. 'Get out! Get out!' screamed Frank, but it was almost a silent scream hissed from the back of his throat.

'If he comes out now, we're fucked,' hissed Lenny.

'Shut up!' snapped Frank as he thrust his head forward to try and get a better view of what was going on. 'Why don't they go inside and fucking talk?!'

The front door of number 68 opened and the big man was framed in the hallway lighting.

'He's coming, Frank.'

'Shut up! I can see.'

'We'll have to call it off.'

'Wait!'

'We don't want to do this with a bloody audience in the front row.'

'Will you shut it, Lenny, and wait.' Frank's heart began to pump hard as he realised his plan could face disaster if he tried to carry it out with people having a grandstand view. Why the hell couldn't they do their yapping inside the house?

The big man shut his front door and walked down his front garden, opened the gate and, holding his dog on the lead, began to walk away down the street towards the group of people two doors away.

'We can't do it, Frank. Let's go.' Frank began to breathe heavily but made no reply. His whole body was taut with a mixture of frustration and readiness. He turned on the ignition key but didn't fire up the engine. Then he turned it back again. His nerves were making him neurotic.

'What the fuck are you doing, Frank? We can't do it now!' hissed Lenny and grabbed Frank's arm in panic. Frank pushed him off with a maniacal snarl. 'Wait!'

The big man drew level with the group of people and began chatting. Frank lowered his window a couple of inches and caught snatches of their conversation.

'How's work, Doug?'

'Could be better if the weather improves.'

'I bet. Rather you than me.'

'How's Julie?'

'She's fine.'

'Going to rugby on Saturday?'

'Definitely. See you there.'

Frank hissed, 'Get on, get on. Get your fat arses off the street.'

'We're going inside while you men gossip,' said one of the women as she took the other one's arm and led her up a front garden path.

'We'd better go in too, Doug,' said one of the men.

'See you again. Cheers,' said the big man as he turned to continue walking down the street. Frank turned on the ignition, and the engine fired and began to quietly hum.

The two women reached their front door and fiddled with a key in the lock. A moment later the door opened and light shone out from the hallway. They stepped inside, but the door remained open.

'They haven't gone in yet, Frank.'

'They're in. We're all right, Lenny. He's not there yet.' Frank very slowly eased the nose of the vehicle out from the kerb and pulled wide of the car parked in front of him. He didn't turn his lights on, and from a distance of twenty yards, he would appear no more than a large blurb in the darkness and murky drizzle.

The big man continued down the street until he got to the big tree in the verge and paused while his dog lifted his leg against it. The two men who'd been chatting had got half way up the front path and could be clearly seen by the light spilling from the open front door.

'Any second he'll start to cross the road, Lenny.'

'No, Frank. Those guys still haven't gone in.' Lenny's voice was now raised in panic.

'Fuck them,' snapped Frank and eased into the middle of the road.

'Frank, no!'

The big man turned to step into the road, but his dog had discovered an interesting smell and pulled back. The dog suddenly lost interest and followed the big man. Frank's foot hit the floor and the vehicle surged forward. By the time the big man had reached just past half way across the road, Frank was doing about just under 40 miles an hour. The big man started to turn when he was struck with a thud by the Land Rover. His body was catapulted into the air and crashed on to the nearside kerb. He made no sound and lay still with blood leaking from his body and spreading dark patches across his clothing. The Land Rover sped away into the darkness. The two men who were about to enter the house turned and immediately sensed their blood beginning to race round their bodies.

'Oi!' screamed out one of them. It was an instinctive reaction, but he knew immediately it was a pathetic and useless response. They both rushed back down the garden path and saw the fading shadow of the vehicle, the make of which neither could identify, disappear into the gloom. Across the road the dog was barking by the body lying in the kerbside.

'Call an ambulance, John,' said one man and bent down over the body. 'It's okay, Douglas. You're going to be okay.' The words had no conviction and came out automatically. John had turned away and was jabbering into his mobile phone.

'...Vernon Street. I'll wait here. Please be quick. The vehicle didn't stop.'

'They're on their way, Phil. Those bastards never stopped. Where the hell did they come from?'

Phil ignored the question and slipped his coat off to lay it over Douglas. 'The ambulance is coming Doug. You're going to be all right.'

'I'll call the police, Phil,' said John and punched the emergency number again on his phone.

'What's happened?' called out a voice, and this time it was from one of the women coming out of the house.

'It's poor Douglas, Mary. He's been knocked down.'

'My God. Is he all right?'

'Doesn't look like it. He's alive though. Ambulance is on its way.'

'I must tell Julie. I'll break it to her gently. She'll be terrified.' Mary turned back on her heels and ran to number 68. As soon as she got there, the front door opened and Julie stepped into the framed light.

'What's happened? I could hear shouting,' asked Julie.

'Julie, Douglas has had an accident. A car has hit him.' Julie stifled a gasp.

'Is he all right? Where is he?'

'John's called an ambulance,' said Mary, and the two women ran over to where Douglas was lying on the ground. Julie bent down over her husband and placed her hands on him, not knowing how she should place them for fear of hurting him.

'Oh, Duggie. Oh my God.'

The others stood by helpless and in shock. The sound of the ambulance siren could be heard in the distance. A little dog stood by Douglas, looking from one to the other.

***

'Bloody 'ell, Frank. I think you killed him,' said Lenny as Frank weaved the Land Rover across town.

'With a bit of luck.'

'Those guys hadn't gone inside. D'you reckon we were spotted?

'Don't talk bollocks, Lenny. What the hell does it matter anyway? We'll be shot of this crate soon, so nobody will be any the wiser.'

'Worked like clockwork Frank.'

'Planning. That's the secret. Planning and patience. Cindy and Big Ears will be next.'

I can't wait.'

'Patience, Lenny. Patience.'

They moved across town, and as soon as the shops were behind them, they turned south taking several turns until they reached Brick Street. Frank drove slowly down it in second gear just to be certain they went quietly. He relied only on his parking lights. As soon as they got to the end, he saw his own car tucked into a lay-by at the entrance to the brick works, which today, after fifty years of being demolished, was no more than a piece of derelict wasteland. Gus had faced it towards them so that they could get away quickly once they'd done away with the Land Rover. They drew level and Frank lowered the window.

Gus spoke first. 'How did it go?'

'Perfect. With a bit of luck we killed the bugger.'

'You're a genius, Frank. You're bang on time too.'

'Seen anybody?'

'No. Place is like a morgue. I've stuck a couple of plastic cans over on the right,' said Gus.

'Two?'

'I thought one to chuck over it and the other one could be dumped inside. It should explode.'

'Good thinking, Gus. Leave no trace. Give us a couple of minutes. As soon as you see any flames, start the engine.' He slipped into gear and slowly drove on into the brickyard. They parked close to the cans of petrol and got out, leaving the doors open. Lenny picked up one of the cans and, after unscrewing the lid, began pouring the liquid over the interior of the Land Rover. As soon as he had emptied it, he took the other can and dumped it on the floor behind the front seats. Frank slammed the doors shut.

'All set, Lenny?'

'I'm ready.'

'Do it then.'

Lenny took a box of matches from his pocket and stood next to the vehicle. He struck a match and flicked it through the partially open window. There was an immediate flash of flames.

'Let's go,' said Frank and began to trot away back to his car. Lenny drew alongside him. By the time they reached his car, the Land Rover was engulfed in flames. They got in Frank's own car, and Gus began to move up the road. A moment later there was an explosion. The three of them grinned and set off to celebrate.

Chapter 11

Micky swung the truck off the main road and pulled into the Clarkes car park. As usual there were already one or two vehicles parked, belonging to employees of the company. He drew up in his usual place close to the snack bar. It was 6:45 in the morning. The weather was overcast, but the murky drizzle from the night before had lifted. Micky leant across from the driver's seat and gave Cindy a kiss on the cheek. 'Work time,' he said and climbed out of the truck.

'Coming, boss.' She got out and followed him, Murphy close behind. Once they'd got inside the bar, everything went like clockwork. Murphy hid himself away in a corner and watched as the two of them set about their chores in readiness for the first customers. A system had evolved between them so that they didn't get in each other's way, and even if Cindy was left to run the show herself, as often happened if Micky wanted to be on a job elsewhere, she was able to handle everything automatically. As well as that, she loved the work as much as Micky. Not only did she love the work, she revelled in at last experiencing some regularity and order in her life, something that she'd never had before meeting Micky. Her earlier life was always looking over her shoulder, trying to escape physical or sexual abuse, constantly looking out for danger, and always searching for an opportunity to escape and find a better life.

Now she had found it and was sharing it with someone who loved her.

They soon had the rolls, baps and baguettes cut and buttered and the griddle hot and sizzling with sausages, bacon, onions and mushrooms. Shortly before 7:30 they were ready for business.

'Here comes the first lot,' said Micky as a group of three men approached the bar. Food and drink were passed down and money exchanged as the usual chatter about football, work and rubbishing the politicians bounced off one to the other against a background of laughter. As always the atmosphere brought some relief to the tedium or stress of the work that most of the men were experiencing, and the hot food and drink to combat the cold and bleak winter weather gave true enjoyment during their short breaks.

Just after 10 o'clock, Joe, Andy and Bob wandered over to the bar. There was no sign of Douglas.

'Hi, guys. Dougie let you over here unsupervised?' asked Cindy with a smile.

'Dougie's not here,' said Andy.

'Oh yeah? Skiving off work today?' said Micky.

'No, poor old Dougie's had an accident,' said Bob. 'He's pretty bad.'

Cindy suddenly felt alarmed and put down her spatula. 'What do you mean? How bad? What accident?'

'He got run over last night.'

'Bloody 'ell. Where?' asked Micky.

'Taking his dog for a walk. Along where he lives.'

Micky and Cindy looked at each other in dismay as they tried to take in the news.

'What happened?' asked Cindy.

'We don't know,' said Andy. 'Julie rang me first thing, that's his wife, to tell me Dougie couldn't pick me up, that he'd had an accident last night when taking the dog out.'

'Jesus,' said Micky. 'How bad is he?'

'He's bad. They took him to the Royal.'

'He's not going to die or anything is he?' Cindy's voice had a cry of panic.

'Dunno. Julie couldn't tell me anything. She'd been there all night but had just got home. He was still unconscious.'

'We must go and see him, Micky. Tonight after work.'

'Of course we will.'

'You can't do that,' said Andy. 'Nobody can go except Julie and his kids until he's regained consciousness and the doctor says.'

'Poor Dougie.' Cindy looked in devastation at Micky.

Micky said, 'Does Julie know how it happened? What about the driver?'

'The bastard never stopped.'

'No! Are the police on to it?'

'I think they turned up,' said Bob, 'But we don't know anything more.'

'We'll go and see his wife, Julie, Micky. I'd like to meet her. Just let her know how sorry we are – that we care about Dougie.'

'Good idea,' said Micky.

'Where does he live, Andy?'

'Vernon Street. Number 68.'

'I know Vernon Street,' said Micky. 'We'll go later.'

The mood round the bar suddenly changed and everyone remained quiet. Even after Andy, Bob, and Joe had returned to work and the flow of customers came and went all day, the mood remained subdued. Ever since the day that Douglas had stood up for her against Frank, in such a dramatic way, Cindy had felt a fondness for him even though she didn't really know much about him. As far as she was concerned, he was just a lovely guy. It filled her with anguish to know that such a terrible accident should have befallen him. As the day wore on, she couldn't stop herself from arguing in her head about his chances of making a full recovery, or even whether or not he might die. She knew the arguments she put forward, and then countered, were stupid because she knew absolutely nothing of what had happened or how serious his injuries were. Was it a big vehicle? How fast was it going? Would Dougie's size and fitness make any difference? Could he have head injuries and maybe brain damage? Would he be left a cripple? Would the police catch the driver, and what bloody difference would that make to Dougie anyway? The thoughts went round and round in her mind all day, but in the end she had no answers and continued to nurse the pain of worry.

When the last customers had come and gone, they cleared up as quickly as they could. When everything was ship-shape and put away, Micky locked the door of the bar and set off for Dougie's.

'I have a bad feeling, Micky,' said Cindy.

'I know you're worried, but you're letting your imagination get the better of you. Dougie's tough.'

'I hope you're right. But being hit by a car isn't the same as by another human.'

'Sounds as if they got him into hospital quick and he's made it through the night, so that's a plus. And anyway, they're pretty shit hot today. He'll pull through.'

She was grateful for his positive note but had got into the habit during her life of expecting the worst. The remainder of the journey they were silent until Micky said, 'This is Vernon Street. Even numbers are on the right.'

He drove slowly until they reached number 68. He pulled up opposite on the opposite side of the road. Micky peered across the road at the house. 'Looks quiet. Maybe she and the kids are at the hospital,' he said.

'Let's try anyway,' said Cindy and got out of the truck. He followed her across the road and she rung the front door bell. They only had to wait a moment before the door was opened by a woman of about forty-five. She had a kind face with soft brown hair down to just above her shoulders. She wore no makeup and looked tired.

'Hi. My name's Micky and this is Cindy. We're friends of Dougie. He comes every day to my snack bar and…'

She cut him off. 'Oh yes, he's told me all about you.'

'We don't want to intrude but wanted know how Dougie was?'

'Come on in. I've been at the hospital most of the day and am going back later. My son and daughter are waiting there.' She led them through to the living room and sat down in an armchair. She indicated for them to sit opposite on the sofa.

'How is he?' asked Cindy.

'He still hasn't come round. I don't really know how bad he is. The doctors say he is stable, but he's got a lot of injuries. Broken leg. Broken arm. Broken pelvis and ribs. But I'm mostly worried about his head injuries. That could be really serious.'

'I couldn't believe it at first when Andy told us,' said Cindy.

'When did it happen?' asked Micky.

'Last night. He took the dog for a walk as he always does just after ten. This is a very quiet road. My neighbours who live a couple of doors away had just arrived home.

Suddenly this car came from nowhere. They didn't really see it until it had gone by and was disappearing through the drizzle. It seems odd, but according to them they didn't notice that it had any lights on.'

'Really?! That is odd. They couldn't tell you anything about the vehicle then?'

'No. The police have virtually got nothing to go on. It certainly wasn't anybody who lives down this road, but it's not usually used as a through road either. They think it might have been stolen. They're checking out reports.'

'Are you okay?' asked Micky. 'I mean there's nothing we can do, I s'pose.'

'No. It's kind of you to call. I'm trying to be positive. I've got good neighbours. I have the children. We're a close family. I'll get word to you when I have any news.'

'Thank you,' said Cindy. 'When he comes round we'll definitely go and see him.'

'Thank you. I'm going off to the hospital shortly.'

'We'll be on our way then,' said Micky and stood up. Cindy also stood.

'Doug has told me such a lot about you two. He's very fond of you,' said Julie and led them out to the hallway. She opened the door. 'When he comes round I'll tell him you called by. It will please him.'

'Thank you,' both Cindy and Micky said at the same time. They stepped outside and said goodbye. They crossed the road and climbed back into the truck. For a few seconds neither of them spoke. Then Cindy said, 'It's Frank.'

'What?' Micky looked at her with confusion on his face.

'It's Frank.'

'What's Frank?'

'He did it. He ran Dougie over. It's revenge.'

Micky looked at her completely shocked. 'How do you know?'

'I know Frank, that's how I know. He's been biding his time. He never gives up.'

'But you can't be sure, Cindy. It sounds a bit farfetched.'

'No. Not where Frank is concerned. I know how he thinks. He would have had Dougie's placed watched. A quiet road like this: you'd hardly expect anyone to get run over here. And the neighbour said the car came from nowhere and had no lights. He was parked and waiting. I know that's what happened. I know, Micky. Trust me.'

'We must inform the police.'

'That's no good. They'd laugh at us. We can't prove anything.'

'Okay, if what you say is true, the police will find the vehicle and get DNA from inside, and it's probably damaged outside.'

'He's so cunning, Micky. He'll have taken the car somewhere and set fire to it. There'll be absolutely no trace. He'd never forgive Dougie for what he did to him. He's capable of murder.'

Micky blew out a long and noisy breath. 'There's nothing we can do then.'

'Let's hope that Dougie makes a full recovery. But I don't think we should tell him what I've just said. It'll only lead to more trouble.'

'I think you're right. He's unlikely to try and get him again anyway.'

'Not Dougie, no. We'll be the next targets.'

'Us?'

'You and me, Micky. He'll definitely want revenge on me and you because you've taken me in. We'll have to be on our guard.'

'Christ, do you think he will?'

'It's all my fault. I've brought this on you and Dougie.'

'No! You mustn't think that Cindy.'

'It's true though.'

'Dougie did what he wanted to do when he hit him. And that bastard Frank deserved it. You're with me because I want you to be. I'm not going to be intimidated by that bully. Let him try his dirty tricks if he wants to. He'll get more than he bargained for.'

'Oh, Micky. I love you, but we've got to be careful.'

'Don't worry. We're going to be all right. Come on, let's go home.' He leant across to her and kissed her. Then he switched on the ignition and pulled away. He was smiling, but inside, a germ of concern began to gnaw away.

***

Frank got out of his car and looked up and down the street. It was empty. Carrying his canvas bag he walked up the garden path, put the key in his front door and went in. He had a quick look in the living room, the dining room, the kitchen and finally the small box room. Everything was in order. Although he had not expected anything otherwise, there was always a little voice at the back of his mind reminding him that that little bitch Cindy might try and break in again even though there was nothing in the house of any use to her. At least nothing that she knew about because he'd made sure that she never knew about where he kept the drugs and money. Big mistake. She knew exactly where he kept his swag. He rolled back the carpet and lifted the two loose floorboards. Underneath there was half a box of E tablets which amounted to several hundred, about a quarter kilo of cocaine, a small bag of heroin, a bag of flour and a wad of notes also wrapped in a plastic bag, to the tune of over £50,000. There was also a little note pad containing several pages of names and addresses of customers showing what they normally had, how much they paid and in some cases whether they owed him any money. Against one or two names there was a cross indicating there was a problem with getting payment. They would have to be visited and shown that sort of thing mustn't happen. Lenny would arrange those visits, though sometimes he went himself – just for the fun of it. He opened his canvas bag and took out a well-wrapped parcel containing a kilo of cocaine and a smaller parcel with cannabis. He placed the parcels next to the other cocaine and put back the floorboards. When he'd finished disposing of that little lot, his wad of notes would increase, which would provide him with more opportunities to expand in the future. And that of course would bring him greater power, greater prestige and greater happiness. Life was good. He came out of the box room and made his way to the kitchen. His mobile phone rang. He took it from his pocket and looked at it.

'Hi, Lenny.'

'Did you pick it up okay?' said Lenny's voice from the other end.

'Sorted. No problem.'

'I'll be over later.'

'Okay. Heard anything?'

'No. We're cool. Nothing left of the Rover. They've got nothing.'

'What about the big guy?'

'Hospital. Pretty bad I should think unless he's a goner. D'you want Gus to get in there and poke around?'

'No. Too risky. Doesn't matter anyway.'

'What about the other two?'

'There's no rush. We'll talk about it later. We'll deal with Cloth Ears first. Once he's out the way, we can pick that little bitch up any time.'

'See yer then.' The phone went dead.

Frank put his phone back in his pocket and opened the fridge. He took out a bottle of beer and moved into the living room. He picked up the remote and threw himself into the sofa, sprawling his legs out wide in front of him. The television came on and he took a swig of his beer.

'Nice one,' he said with a grin and enjoyed watching the screen.

Chapter 12

Linda pulled off Bush Lane and drove to the end of the cul-de-sac at the foot of Costers Hill. She felt sure the tiny house on her left was Micky's, which he had described to her, and which she had noticed many times in the past. His truck was parked outside so she hoped that he and Cindy would be at home. She walked up the little front path and jangled the bell that hung from the wall. A few moments later the door opened and Micky stood there. From the surprised look on his face, she could tell that he didn't immediately recognise her.

'Hallo, Micky.'

The penny dropped. 'Of course. Sorry. I knew you but seeing you here, I couldn't...'

'I know what you mean.' said Linda, 'We last talked at the hospital.'

'Stupid of me. Come in,' he said and stood back for her to enter.

'I'm not barging in on anything, am I?' she said as Cindy came in from the kitchen, but Cindy recognized her immediately.

'Hallo, Linda,' she said smiling, but trying to pat her shirt smooth as if she needed to look respectable for this visitor. Murphy wandered over to her, wagging his tail. Linda bent down and stroked him.

'Hallo, Murphy. You're a lovely dog. I hope you don't mind me calling in just like this.'

'Of course not. Sit down. Would you like a cup of coffee? Come away, Murphy,' offered Micky.

'That's kind of you, but I can't stay. I'm on my way to the Centre.'

'I could do it quickly. It's no trouble,' said Cindy nervously or desperately wanting to please.

'Truly. I'd love to stop, but I'm running late. You've got a wonderful, cosy little place here.'

'We're going to make it bigger one day.'

'That'll be even better.'

'Got to make the money first,' said Micky.

'Well, you're young. I'm sure you'll do it.'

'Have you some news on Tom?' asked Cindy.

'I haven't brought you very happy news. I'm afraid he died earlier today.'

Cindy immediately reached out for Micky's hand. She couldn't speak.

'In the end it was a peaceful death. I was lucky to be at his bedside. He was in no pain.'

Micky put his arm round Cindy. 'I think we both knew it was inevitable, that it would be soon. We wanted to hope otherwise, but really we knew.'

'He was much too young to die, and he was such a lovely man. He was the greatest friend I ever had, and he gave such a lot of kindness to so many people.'

'Thank you for coming to tell us.' again it was Micky who spoke.

'You did say you would like to go to his funeral. I can tell you already it will be next Friday at 2.O.clock in the afternoon. He was a humanist and will be buried in Ladybrook Woods. You'll be very welcome.'

'You go, Cindy. It can only be one of us. I'll look after the bar.'

Cindy nodded and squeezed his hand. 'Thank you,' she whispered.

'Well, I'll get off. I'm so sorry my visit to you didn't bring better news,' said Linda.

'It's kind of you to come. It can't be easy for you either,' said Micky.

Linda just nodded and turned for the door. Micky moved ahead and opened it.

'Thanks again,' he said as she stepped outside. 'Come again any time.'

'I'd love to.' Linda turned away and walked to her car. Micky and Cindy watched her drive away.

**

A gust of wind blowing a burst of rain on to the window woke Cindy. She lay with her eyes awake, staring into the darkness. Micky's breathing was soft and even. He seemed to be able to sleep soundly through anything. Thoughts began drifting into her mind. At first they dwelt on Tom's death. Even though she knew that it hadn't been long since she saw him, it had still been a shock. She'd never cared about anybody dying before. If it had been her mother or father, she would have acknowledged it and then not given it a second thought. She had hardly known Tom, and yet she felt a deep heartache. There had to be all sorts of reasons for that, and maybe many of them were complicated, but she wasn't going to try and delve into those. She simply knew that she felt a deep sadness. He was a man who had been kind to her. She had been drawn to him and felt a real fondness for him, and now he was dead. Beginning and end of story.

She turned on her side and decided to try and drop off. It was useless. But it wasn't because of thoughts about Tom. The thoughts that were really grinding away at the back of her mind, and it was the same during her daytime hours, were trying to figure out Frank's next move. Of one thing she was certain, and that was he would definitely set out to get her and Micky, but how would he do it and when would he do it? And what form would it take? He'd dream up something painful. Violent. And he'd do it in such a way that the finger of guilt couldn't be pointed at him. And how soon would he make his play? He was a very patient man, so it may not happen soon. But it could. It could happen tomorrow. There was absolutely no way of knowing. He'd probably try and take them separately. It would be easier. And it would also have the effect of sending a message to the last one that they were going to be punished too. They'd have that fear constantly hanging over them. They couldn't turn to anybody for help. The police wouldn't be bothered. They'd have nothing to go on anyway. No, they'd have to look out for themselves. And Cindy knew there was only one way they could do that. More accurately there was only one way she could do that. Micky was big and strong, but being involved with scum like Frank was totally unfamiliar to him. If he got hurt it would be because of her. It was going to be her responsibility to deal with Frank and there was only one way she would be able to do it. She'd have to be smarter than him, and she'd have to do whatever she planned before he made his move. It was going to be no good being defensive, just waiting for him to carry out his plan. She would have to go on the attack. He simply wouldn't expect that. He'd be sitting back with his cronies, thinking he'd got all the aces in his pack and that he could act whenever he felt like it. A big mistake. A whopping mistake. He may think of her as no more than a squirt with small tits (which he had always tried to bate her about), but she was going to outsmart him and make him pay for the misery he had caused her, Murphy and Dougie. She could do it. All she needed was a plan and the courage to carry it out.

She lay awake for another hour with a hundred thoughts tumbling about her mind before she had got the rough shape of the plan together. It was clever. Ingenious. But it would have to be carried out in stages. The downside was that it could be very dangerous. Any one of the stages could go wrong. If that happened and she got caught, she'd pay a terrible price. She would need to think about each stage, one at a time. Make sure she carried out each one successfully. She would need to act quickly, but the trouble was the whole plan would take a little time. It was no good her becoming impatient. She would simply make a mess of it. Above all she would need luck. Lots of luck. And she knew there were specific places where she would need it. But she could do it. She had to do it. And the only way would be to keep her mind completely focused. She must never doubt her ability or lose her nerve. She would need to have total faith in herself. If she could do that, she could pull it off, and she could deal with Frank once and for all.

She turned on her other side, and this time she fell asleep.

***

Micky pulled into the car park of the Royal Hospital and found a parking slot. He turned off the engine and reached his hand across to Cindy. They both felt nervous. When Andy had turned up at the bar with his mates earlier in the day, he had been able to tell them that Douglas had regained consciousness the day before and that it would be possible for them to visit him. Julie hadn't been able to give him any details about his injuries, but he was in fairly high spirits. Of course Micky and Cindy wanted to know as much as they could, but now that they were at the hospital and about to go in, they were feeling anxious about what they might be confronted with.

'If he's in high spirits, that's a good sign,' said Micky.

'That's typical Dougie. He'd always try and make light of anything bad happening to him.'

'At least he must be on the mend so that sounds good.'

'Don't say anything about Frank being responsible, Micky. Is that okay with you?'

'That's fine, if you feel sure it was him. We can't really say for certain.'

'Yes we can. I promise you I'm not wrong.'

'If you say it was him, then I accept that. I won't say anything. It'll be interesting to hear what Doug thinks of what happened.'

'Come on then. I hate going into hospitals. They give me the willies,' said Cindy as she got out of the truck. He followed her over to the main reception and they went in. The foyer was large with several people, some visitors, others medical staff, who moved about as if they all knew exactly where they were going.

'Andy said the name of the ward was Lavender,' said Micky and looked around at the large number of notice boards giving directions to the wards and different specialist areas.

'There it is,' said Cindy. 'Upstairs.' They followed the sign until they got to the first floor where they saw another sign pointing the direction to Lavender ward. They moved along the corridor and saw a sign above swing doors indicating the ward they wanted. They pushed them open into a ward that had about ten beds. On their left there was a counter with a couple of nurses behind it. Micky led Cindy over to it.

'Excuse me. We're looking for Douglas. Big chap. Was knocked over by a car.'

'Ah, yes. End bed on the right,' said the nurse pleasantly but then turned back to the heap of papers in front of her.

Micky and Cindy made their way up the ward until they got to Douglas's bed. They were relieved to see he had no other visitors. He was on his back and his head was resting on two or three pillows. His arms were heavily bandaged and spread out on top of the covers. There was a hoop lifting the weight of the blankets off the lower part of his body. His face was severely bruised with some lacerations reaching up into his hair on the left side of his head. He looked as if he'd been hit by a steamroller, but as soon as he saw them he smiled.

'Hallo, Dougie,' said Micky

'Hi, Dougie,' said Cindy.

'You haven't brought a burger, I s'pose,' said Douglas through half open and swollen lips.

'Sorry, mate. No such luck.'

'Thanks for coming.'

'How are you doing?'

'I've had better days.'

'You going to be in here long?

'Dunno. I've got to have a couple of ops. Fix my leg and one of my arms. Elbow I think. At least my brain box is okay.'

'Probably had a job to find it,' said Micky, attempting to make a joke which he immediately knew must have been made a hundred times before.

Cindy turned and looked around the ward at the other patients.

'What's it like in here?'

They're looking after me. Can't complain.'

'Dead rough luck, Dougie. What happened?' asked Micky.

'Don't ask me. Bloody thing came from nowhere. Bastard never stopped.'

'They could have killed you.'

'Damn near did. Not so easy.'

'Be some time before you get back to work, I s'pose.'

'I won't be going back to work. Not that job anyway.'

'Course you will. Why not?'

Douglas didn't answer for a little while. He stared back at them with a smile. 'They can only do so much with this leg,' he gently patted his right leg. 'And my left arm is never going to be what it was before. I couldn't handle that kind of work again.'

'Bloody 'ell, Dougie, I'm sorry,' said Micky and laid his hand down on Douglas's bandaged arm in a gesture of compassion.

'Not to worry. I'll get by. Julie's pretty broken up though. And the kids. They don't want to see their father like this.'

'You'll get back on top, Dougie. You're tough as old boots, mate.'

'I s'pose there's nothing we can do to help.'

'Having you visit is plenty.'

For a little while there was silence. It was fine. There was no need to speak. He lying there, they standing by the bed. It was enough. They trying to inject strength through their sense of caring and bond of friendship, he drawing strength from them.

Micky broke the silence. 'Are the police still looking for them?'

'They've talked to me, but I couldn't tell 'em anything. Bloody mystery. Came from nowhere. Pretty fast. Probably stolen. Kids most likely having a joy ride.'

Cindy said nothing.

'Won't change anything anyway,' said Douglas.

'You'll be fine,' said Micky, wanting to believe in what he was saying but thinking that his words sounded hollow.

'I miss the lads. Andy's been. I hope they're not making too many cock ups in my absence.'

'We all miss you,' said Cindy. 'It's not the same not having you turning up at the bar.'

'Don't worry about me. You two look after yourselves.' At that moment Julie entered the ward with her two children and came over to Douglas's bed.

'Hallo, you two. Have you been cheering him up?' said Julie and bent over Douglas and kissed him. 'How are you, luv?'

'Fine.'

'Hi, dad,' said his daughter who also bent over and kissed him.

His son stood at the bottom of the bed, obviously trying to hide the pain he felt at seeing his father in such a state. 'Hi, dad,' he said.

Douglas winked back at him with an encouraging smile. 'I'm fine, lad. Not to worry.'

'You've not met our children, have you,' said Julie, looking at both Micky and Cindy. 'I shouldn't say children any more. This is Lizzie and Jimmy. Lizzie's sixteen, Jimmy fourteen.'

'Hi, guys,' said Micky. 'You've got a great dad. He's going to be fine.'

'They run the burger bar I've told you about,' said Dougie. 'Now I'm not eating what they cook, I'll probably live a lot longer.'

Everyone laughed.

'We'll get off and leave you to your family, Dougie,' said Micky. 'We'll come and see you again.'

'Thanks for coming.'

Cindy suddenly felt an overwhelming sense of awe at the scene before her. It was the view of something she had only ever dreamed about. A complete family. Something that had always been a fantasy for her and didn't, or rather couldn't, exist. Douglas was a lovely man with his own quirks and warts of personality and nature. He was simple and honest and uncomplicated, and he was surrounded by a loving wife and two children who cared so much for their father. The thought that Frank could have inflicted such misery on them filled her with a terrible rage and thirst to make him pay. She hesitated a moment and then leant forward and kissed Douglas. The others could see that she was forcing back tears.

'Steady on, Cindy. The wife's watching,' said Douglas in an attempt to lighten the momentary emotional mood.

'Thank you for coming,' said Julie quietly and with a nod. Micky nodded back in a way that had a wealth of meaning and then took Cindy's hand and walked away.

***

The three of them were sat round a table in a corner in the Queen Vic. They were huddled together as they leaned on the table, speaking in hushed voices. They were known by Tony, the publican of the pub. They regarded him as a team member. A big chap, eighteen stone of blubber. Probably drop dead over his counter one day. He acted as a conduit to pass on messages to Carl, who in turn represented the Big Man who always remained in the shadows. Tony acted not out of evil intent, but because he was a man who was intimidated by Frank and wanted to curry favour with him so that in return he would have protection. There were other customers in the pub who also knew, or knew of, Frank and his other two friends. The customers knew of them from hearsay or myth or related stories of how aggressive or vicious they could be. They were shunned by some and smiled at by others. Their presence was always felt, and their absence always a cause for relief.

'What's the word on the big guy?' said Frank.

'You didn't kill him anyway,' replied Gus.

'Too bad.'

'Broke him up though. He'll never be the same again.'

'Oh well, that'll do.'

'He had it coming, Frank. Brought it on himself,' said Lenny who took a long swig of his beer and then wiped his mouth with the back of his hand.

'Don't they all,' grinned Frank.

'The old bill's got nothing.'

'Not worried about them. Couldn't find their way out of a paper bag.'

'What about Big Ears?' asked Lenny.

'What you got, Gus?'

'Nothing's changed. He and the bitch get to the bar early. He goes off sometimes. Takes the truck and does jobbing work in private houses. He comes back and picks her up about half past four, five. Most days they're both at the bar though.'

'You sure they haven't seen you?'

'No way.'

'Many people about when they pack up?'

'Not a lot. The merchants close at five, and most of the staff piss off quick.'

'What about the car park? Many cars left?'

'A few. One or two employees leave late and the odd customer takes their time.'

'They shouldn't be a problem, Frank,' said Lenny.

'I'd prefer to get him on his own; when she's not around. I want no witnesses. We can pick her up any time once he's out the way,' said Frank thoughtfully.

'May be some time before we get him on his own. She sticks to him like flies stick to shit. And she's a slippery little bitch,' said Gus.

'Don't worry about her, Gus. She's a female. They've got no brains. She'll slip away some time. We've just got to watch.'

'Could be a long wait though.'

'That's no problem, Gus. We've got plenty of time. Patience. That's the secret. Patience.' For a little while none of them spoke. Lenny and Gus watched Frank. They could see he was thinking and didn't want to interrupt his thoughts. He had the brains. He knew what he was doing. He was clever and wouldn't take shit from anyone. He was their leader. He was the man.

'Enough about Big Ears. I need you to make a couple of other calls.'

'Just say the name, Frank.'

'That toerag in Ermin Street. He's beginning to annoy me.'

'Foster. It'll be a pleasure,' said Lenny.

'Nothing heavy. Pay by tomorrow or there's nothing more for him. That'll have more effect than a whacking, and it's not in my nature to be a man of violence.'

195

'I swear to God he's got the money anyway. He's just a slime ball that doesn't like paying.'

'Who else, Frank?' asked Gus.

'Down The Grove. Jacobs. You can knock him about if you like. But not too much. Just enough to let him know I like being paid on time. He'll probably snivel. No need to break any bones. He'll get the money all right.'

'When shall we do it?'

'You can get off now. I've got things to do.' Frank stood up. 'I'll see you guys later.'

They all sank the last of their beers and went out.

Chapter 13

Micky flashed his indicator and pulled the truck into the kerb. The traffic behind him swung out and drove on past him. He'd come through town, but the last shop was behind him. It was 5:15 and beginning to get dark. The clouds were low, threatening rain, and a moderate north wind was getting up.

'Why don't I come with you?' said Micky to Cindy sitting next to him.

'Better if you don't, Micky.'

'It's risky. I shall worry.'

'The bike's on the back. I'll take that and be home within the hour. You can get me a lovely dinner.'

'They may not welcome you.'

'Look. When I was on the street, they were good to me sometimes. I just want to say hallo and see how they are getting on. I'll only stop a few minutes, and then I'll be home.'

Micky began to breathe heavily as he struggled to come up with a good argument for him to go with her. 'I could easily park down the road. Wait for you. I needn't come in if you think that'll make them uncomfortable.'

'You mustn't worry. Trust me.'

'If anything happened to you, Cindy, I'd never...' She leant across and stopped him with a kiss on the mouth.

'Nothing's going to happen to me. Go home and start cooking,' she grinned at him impishly.

'Oh Christ, what chance have I got. You and your magic charms.'

'I only use them on you.'

'One hour. A minute longer and I shall come looking for you.'

'I promise,' she said and climbed out of the truck. He got out his side and lifted the bicycle off the back of the truck.

'The lights are okay, but be careful. There's bloody mad drivers about.'

'I'll get going 'cos it looks like rain.'

He leant forward and gave her a kiss on the cheek. 'Be careful, babe,' he said and climbed back into the truck. He flashed his indicator and drove off. She watched him disappear into the stream of traffic.

She let out a long sigh. She hated lying to him – it cut her to the quick – but she had no choice. If she had told him the truth of what she was up to, he would never have let her go. He would have said she was crazy, and that it was far too dangerous. Well it was dangerous; she knew that. Hellishly dangerous. And she probably was crazy, but she had to go. She had to go because it was the first part of her plan. She couldn't have told him about that. It wouldn't be right. She didn't want to involve him. She had to do it herself. If Frank was going to be stopped, then this was the only way, and it was all down to her. She didn't kid herself that it wasn't hair-brained and full of risks, but she could pull it off. She needed to keep a cool head and not take unnecessary risks. Some risks, yes, but not stupid, unnecessary ones. But the whole thing depended on her getting the money. Without that the whole thing fell to bits. And it was big money which she didn't have. And Frank had money. Plenty of money. And she knew where he kept it. Of course, he didn't know that. He thought he was so bloody smart, he didn't know that she had often seen him stash it away under the floorboards in the box room. Well, that's where it was, and that's where she would get it. It was going to be a brilliant stroke of irony that she was going to use his own money to get her revenge on him.

She mounted the bike and went back through the town until she picked up the road that lead to the Cherry Tree Estate. Fifteen minutes later she stopped at the beginning of Cherry Tree Road. The corner house was empty. She dismounted the bicycle and pushed it into the front garden, laying it down behind a conifer tree. Hardly anyone was about, and they wouldn't see it there anyway. She rested down on her haunches while she got herself together. This was the part where she would be entering the danger zone. There was time to pull out and forget the whole thing. To acknowledge that when she had first thought up the plan it seemed simple, but that now she was actually embarking on it for real, it seemed crazy. Crazy because there were too many ifs and buts, but also because she could get herself beaten up or killed. Poor Douglas had suffered terrible injuries. He hadn't deserved that. He'd suffered them because he had protected her. She owed him. He wouldn't say that, wouldn't want that, but she owed him just the same. She'd made up her mind anyway, so nothing was going to stop her now.

She went over timing in her mind. It would probably take her ten, maybe fifteen minutes, to get in and out. The first problem would be getting in and out in a way that didn't leave signs of a break-in. That was crucial. She needed to get in and take what money she reckoned would be enough and get out so that he didn't know he'd been robbed. He rarely counted the money, so if she only took what she needed, he wouldn't suspect anything. Breaking a window to get in the house as she had done before was out of the question. There was just the chance, a small one, that there was another way. This was the first bit of luck she would need. There was a side window in the wall down the passageway at the side of the house. It gave some light in the hallway. It was never opened and never closed. It was a metal-framed window that had slightly rusted at the bottom, and she remembered it had never been closed tightly. There was a chance she could pull it open and close it again without Frank ever being the wiser.

She stood up and moved to the pavement. She could easily see as far as number 18 and was pleased that Frank's car was not parked outside. Nobody was about. She began to advance down the street, welcoming the fact that the one street light between her and number 18 was not working. As soon as she drew level with the passageway between Frank's and the next-door house, she quickly darted down and stood still, listening. Silence. No lighting on inside. It was now or never. If Frank came home while she was inside, she'd never get out before he caught her. She'd never get out the window quickly enough, and by the time she'd unlocked the back door and tried running down the garden to get out the garden gate, which would be bolted, he'd have her, and that would be the end of her. So be it. It was now or never.

She reached up and managed to get her fingers between the narrow gap of the window and the window frame. To her surprise it moved easily and began to open. But after a couple of inches, it stopped. Something was jamming it. She tugged again but to no avail. Then she realised that it must be the locking arm that had caught the locking pin in the first hole. Her hands were small, and she was able to reach in and lift it free. So far, so good. She stood still again and listened. Nothing. Suddenly the silence was shattered by her mobile ringing. She dived into her pocket and pulled it out. Obviously Micky checking that she was all right. She switched off and hoped he'd understand and not try again. If he kept on trying and got no reply, he'd begin to panic. The sooner she got back, the better. She put both hands on the sill and pulled herself up. No problem. She was lithe like a panther. She pulled herself through and landed on the other side. Moving the window had disturbed the rust and caused some crumbs to drop on the sill. She brushed them off with one hand into the palm of the other and threw them out the window. She was immediately conscious of the smell that she recognized was so peculiar to Frank's house. It suddenly sent memories rushing back of the months she had spent living there, after the first couple weeks when he had seemed a kind person who wanted to help her, to the instant change into the vicious thug that he really was who forced her to have sex any time of the day whenever the mood took him. He'd even forced himself on her in front of his cronies. Sometimes he'd turned on the charm, even the suggestion of camaraderie with her, as if they were colleagues in his drug dealing business. She'd never stepped out of line. She'd never nicked his money, never failed to pick up the packages, always been reliable and prompt, and above all kept her mouth shut. And in return he'd hit her, raped her, screamed at her and forced her into a life of constant fear. Fear of not knowing what was coming at her from one moment to the next. As the memories somersaulted round her brain, they hardened her resolve to see he paid.

She quickly made her way to the box room and turned the door handle. The second bit of luck. The door opened, and she went in. He probably never bothered to lock it now she wasn't living there. She pulled the chair back and lifted the rug. She held her breath and lifted the floorboards. Easy. There were the drugs. There was the polythene bag containing the wad of money. She lifted it. 'Bloody 'ell,' she whispered to herself, 'there's got to be fifty grand in here.' She unfolded the bag and slipped out two bundles of £20 notes. She was certain that each bundle contained £1000. How much should she take? How much was she

201

going to need? She had no idea what the cost would be for what she wanted. Five hundred? A thousand? Surely not that much. What the hell, she'd take two. It was his money, and she felt certain it would be enough. No, she wouldn't take more than what she thought she needed. Not for herself. Not this trip. Next time maybe. She rolled up the bag again and put it back in exactly the same place from where she'd picked it up. If he happened to look in there tomorrow or the next day, he wouldn't notice anything amiss, and he'd have no reason to suspect anyway. She put the floorboards back, folded over the carpet and pushed the chair into the position she had found it. Christ, she thought, it had been as easy as taking sweets off a kid. Then she heard the car door slam, and she froze. It came from immediately outside the house. It had to be Frank. Then she heard his voice. Heat instantly rushed to her face. Move! Fucking move! She skipped from the room, remembering to close the door behind her. She was in the hallway and saw the window still open. Beyond it was the front door. Frank would come in that way. Could she get up and through the window before he opened the door, or would he step inside and see her rear end staring him in the face as she tried to slither through? As her hands grabbed the sill, she heard feet walking up the path. The key went into the door, and she dropped to the ground on the outside. Now she could hear more clearly Frank speaking round the front of the house. She reached up and pushed the window shut. She stood rigid against the wall of the house. She'd either hear him shouting or there would be nothing. Her heart pounded, and her breathing was as if she'd just run flat out for a mile. And then she heard the sounds of quiet voices speaking and knew that Frank had not detected anything wrong. She moved out of the passageway and ran down the street back to her bicycle. A moment later she was pedalling out of Cherry Tree Road, gleefully looking forward to Micky's promised dinner.

***

It was the last Friday in February, and it was the day of Tom's funeral. It was a cold day. There was a heavy frost that glistened in the sunshine which shone from a clear blue sky. The weather forecast had suggested that later in the day there would be rain, and Cindy was hoping that it wouldn't come before Tom's funeral had ended. She had never been to a funeral, but the thought of standing next to Tom's grave in pouring rain as he was lowered into the ground filled her with sadness. She knew it would make no difference to him, but she desperately hoped that the sun would shine long enough until the ceremony was completed. She wasn't worried about having to stand about in the cold, even the wet, if it did begin to rain, because she had experienced far worse through freezing nights when she'd slept rough.

Her mood was mixed. She was still buoyed up from the success of her break-in at Frank's. Micky hadn't a clue what she was up to, and she'd managed to hide the £2000 pounds in an old tin at the back of the outhouse. It meant that she could now attempt the second part of her plan. There were risks, but they were of a different sort to those of being caught at Frank's. She had a rough idea of how she should handle it but had to admit that she was pretty much out of her depth in trying to get what she was after. She might be questioned in detail if she ever got to Carl and would have to be evasive with her replies. He wouldn't be able to resist the money – that would be her ace card as far as he was concerned – but she'd have to be sure that Frank didn't get the slightest whiff of what she was up to. If any of it got back to him before she was ready, she would be a goner. There were a lot of ifs and maybes before she could execute her plan, and she'd have to keep faith in herself and hold her nerve. She didn't think that Tony, the publican of the Queen Vic, would betray her. He may raise his eyebrows when she asked him to contact Carl, but she felt certain he wouldn't ask questions or say anything. He liked her and thought she shouldn't be involved with the likes of people like Frank. And anyway, she'd often gone through him to contact Carl when she was representing Frank in the past. It had to be well known that she was no longer with him, but it was the norm for people not to ask questions. In any case, she had no choice. She would just have to play it by ear when the time came.

The other part of her mood was overshadowed by thoughts of the funeral itself. She wouldn't know anybody there except Linda. People would probably stare at her and wonder who she was or what she was doing there. At the best of times she wasn't comfortable in the company of lots of people. She had no confidence, what the psychologists called a lack of self-esteem: a sense of little worth. She couldn't help it. It was because of her background, her upbringing, what there was of it. She'd always been at the bottom of the heap and had believed that was the rightful place for her. She'd only begun to realise that was wrong, that it was crap, a load of bollocks, and that was since she met Micky and Dougie and his friends. They had begun to make her feel better about herself and that it was people like Frank who were the real trash. She was better than them and could hold her head up high. But she wasn't there yet. The funeral would be an ordeal anyway because she knew that, underneath her sometimes hard exterior, she was a softie. She'd probably cry. She wouldn't want to, but she wouldn't be able to help it. It was no good worrying about it. She was a big girl now and would have to deal with things as best she could.

She was grateful that Linda had dropped a note in the house saying that, if she could be at the Samaritan Centre by 2:15, she would give her a lift to the Ladywood Chapel where a short service would take place before they walked the short distance through the woods to the spot where Tom was to be buried. Linda was kind and understanding and would stand with her throughout the whole proceedings.

In spite of the many thoughts crowding her mind, she worked with Micky all morning, chatting with customers and trying to make the occasional joke. Micky was aware that she was tense underneath because of the funeral and constantly whispered words of encouragement into her ear. Andy gave them an update on Douglas's progress and learned that he he'd had an operation on his leg, which was successful, and that he was slowly on the mend.

At 2 o'clock she combed her hair, put on a pair of below-the-knee boots and a half-length, thickly-lined puffer jacket which Micky had bought for her as a present. It was the warmest piece of clothing she had ever had. She was ready to go. She'd insisted on cycling to the Centre so that Micky wouldn't have to leave the bar. She'd call him later on her mobile and let him know what time she should be back. Probably before he finished clearing up for the day. He kissed her and smiled as she stuck up her arm to wave without turning round as she cycled away.

***

On the other side of the car park, just inside the entrance to Clarkes, Gus also watched her leave. He took out his mobile and punched Frank's number.

Frank answered. 'Yeah?'

'She's just cycled off. Got a new coat on. Unusual for her to go. Could be she's not coming back.'

'Well done, Gus. Hang on there. Let me know if she comes back. This may be our chance.'

'I'm on it.' Gus snapped his phone shut.

***

It took Linda twenty-five minutes to drive the eight miles from the Centre to the Ladywood Woodland Chapel on the edge of the memorial woodlands. Cindy had arrived at the Centre by 2:15, but they hadn't got off until twenty-five past. For most of the journey they had made little conversation. Cindy was still feeling nervous and a little shy, and Linda had not wanted to ask questions about Cindy for fear that she would appear to be prying. As was the practice of Samaritans, it was always better to listen when a companion wanted to speak rather than force the conversation. In spite of her shyness, Cindy felt at ease with Linda and was thankful that Linda had offered to take her to the funeral with her.

As they pulled into the car park at the side of the chapel, Cindy was surprised to see such a large gathering of people walking towards it. She immediately noticed that none were wearing black, and they were all chatting away with each other.

'They're nearly all volunteers from the Centre. They all loved him, and we're a close lot,' said Linda as she got out of the car. Then she added quickly, 'Don't worry. You won't be made to feel an outsider.'

The two of them wandered over to join the others as many of them called out her name in welcome, some of them waving and all with big smiles. Cindy felt the mood was relaxed – subdued but happy. There was no tight-lipped and unnatural conversation with people not knowing where to put their hands or whether they were speaking too loudly. In some ways it made her think she had joined guests for a wedding. The chapel was a plain stone building with a high-pitched roof. Inside, it was bright with wide, high windows and white walls. The roof exposed huge supporting timbers. The floor was flagged with random paving stones on which were placed rows of chairs. There was a plain altar at the far end which could be converted to suit any particular religious faith or none. The whole surface was decorated with flowers. On every chair there was placed a card showing the order of the ceremony that the guests would follow (Linda had told Cindy that Tom had wanted those who attended to think of themselves as guests rather than mourners). When everybody was seated, a woman moved to the pulpit. She was about forty-five with long dark hair. She was attractive and wore make-up, but it was tasteful and simply enhanced her good looks. She had a lovely smile and a soft friendly voice. She introduced herself as the Funeral Celebrant for this, Tom's funeral. She welcomed everyone and explained that the service would be carried out exactly as Tom had requested. It would be a short celebration of his life.

The service began with the recording of John Lennon's 'Imagine'. When it came to an end, Cindy was surprised that Linda stood up and took her place in the pulpit. She told everyone that he had asked her if she would say a few words about him but made her promise she would keep it short, and he insisted 'short', and not make him sound as if he had been virtuous as he suspected she might do.

'It would be very difficult for me to talk about Tom without reminding everyone what a lovely man he was. But I know that none of us need reminding of that,' she said and everyone smiled with nods.

'I'm going to comply with his wishes and simply remind us of the many hundreds of acts of kindness that we will have witnessed from Tom but not talk about them individually. I know that many of you will want to come up here and do that for yourselves. He was a simple man who genuinely believed that if one treated others as you would want to be treated yourself, there would be less strife between individuals and also between nations. He would want me to say how grateful he had been to have experienced this life, with both ups and downs. He had been blessed with his dear wife Janice and lovely baby daughter Jessica, both of whom he will lie next to in the woods.'

Cindy hung on to every word that Linda spoke. She was brief but managed to convey the image of a man whose plea was for more compassion in the world. He believed that compassion was greater than love because, whereas love could make huge demands of selflessness, sacrifice, and courage, it could also be clinical and considered. His passion was for compassion and she said that Tom had written a poem about it which she said she would like to read. She unfolded a sheet of paper and spoke in a quiet but firm voice.

Compassion is the purest of love.

It springs to life from the heart,

It does not shy from the sharing of tears

Sometimes seen, sometimes hidden.

It is soft and kind and full of tenderness.

It is spontaneous and given with feeling.

It is given without judgement of another,

It is gentle and selfless and over flowing with warmth

It is not done for preservation of conscience

Nor in fear of being watched by an omnipotent being.

It is not done in judgement of merit.

It is not calculated or planned or measured.

It is not done for self-gratification

Or to seek honour.

It is not given in response to a set of rules

Or pledge to any hierarchical law.

It is not done for reward

Or as an antidote for punishment.

It is not done in response to another's example

Nor to set one.

It is not done for morality, ethics or duty.

It is simply the response of the heart

From one human being to another

Whether stranger, friend or foe.

It is the ultimate purity of love.

As soon as she had finished she said that over the many years that Tom had been a Samaritan volunteer, he had learned that the one thing that all their callers wanted to feel was the warmth from another human being. Cindy knew that she had experienced that warmth from him, herself.

When Linda came back to her seat, those who wanted to were invited to come up and speak about their own experiences with Tom. Cindy felt overwhelmed that so many came forward and related their own stories of kindness that they had witnessed with Tom. Some brought tears. Others laughter.

Throughout the service there were no pleas for mercy from a deity, nor reference to sin, leaving time only for expressions of love and thanksgiving for his life.

When the service was completed, the guests followed a cardboard coffin resting on a cart drawn by a horse to the open grave about a hundred yards further into the woods. As soon as everyone had assembled at the graveside, which was alongside Janice's and Jessica's, both marked with small headstones not much higher than nine inches tall, the coffin was lifted off the cart and lowered into the grave. For a little while people stood by, and for the first time there was a dignified silence. There were some tears, and although Cindy felt a deep sadness that Tom had died, she also felt uplifted by having been privileged to have known him. After a little while the empty cart was drawn away and people began to move off back to their cars.

'There is a wake, Cindy. It could have been here. They have facilities, but Tom had asked if it could be held at the Centre. We have a very large room there which is used for training and various meetings. Volunteers have provided a huge array of cakes and goodies. Do come back with us,' said Linda as they walked over to her car.

'I'm no good in crowds,' said Cindy.

'You'll be fine. Tom would have wanted you to come. He liked you. You're a friend.'

Hearing that Linda called her a friend of such august company gave Cindy a feeling of pride. Did Linda really mean that any or all of those people would come over and chat to her, just like they would to each other or anybody else? She said, 'Thank you, but I won't stop long. Micky will be worried about me.'

'You stay as long as you like.' Linda smiled and they both got into the car. On the journey back they chatted more easily, sometimes referring to the funeral but mostly about things relating to their daily lives. Linda was keen to know all about Micky's snack bar and how it all worked. It wasn't long before Cindy got carried away with enthusiasm in relating how it was run and with comical stories about some of the customers. The journey passed quickly, and by the time they reached the Centre, Cindy felt really relaxed, losing many of her misgivings about going in and mingling with the others. She told herself she could do it, even enjoy it.

'You go in, Linda. I'm just going to ring Micky and tell him what I'm doing. I'll follow you.'

'Okay. See you in a bit,' said Linda and disappeared into the building.

Cindy took out her phone and punched the code for Micky. She heard it ring twice and then he answered.

'Hi, Cindy. You all right?'

'Fine. I'll tell you all about it when I see you.'

'I'm just clearing up. Do you want me to wait for you?'

'No, Micky. I'm just going in to have some food. If it's okay I'll go straight home from here.'

'That's good. I'll see you at home then. Take care. Bye.'

'Love you. Bye.' Cindy closed her phone and went into the Centre.

***

Gus took out his phone and punched a number. Frank's voice came on the line.

'What you got?'

'She's not back. He's just had a phone call. I'm guessing it's from her. I don't think she's coming back?'

'What's going on there?'

'Not a lot. Clarkes have just closed. Staff are going home. Big Ears is clearing up. He normally takes about fifteen, twenty minutes.'

'We'll do it. See you in five.' Gus snapped his phone shut.

***

Micky gave a final wipe round the surfaces. He collected up cloths to take home for washing and made sure everything was neat and tidy in readiness for tomorrow.

'Think that's okay, Murphy?' he said looking down at the dog. Murphy looked up at him and wagged his tail.

'I'll give a quick sweep up outside and then we'll be off.' He collected a broom and moved outside. He took a look around the car park. Across the way he could see that most of the lights had been turned out in Clarkes. Either cleaners or management staff would still be in there, but being Friday, even the management wouldn't want to pack up late. About half a dozen cars were dotted around the car park. He noticed a kid close to the entrance of the car park playing with his skateboard. It was beginning to get dark and spit with rain. Micky picked up the odd dog-ends and a couple of disposable cups and threw them in a litter bin. Murphy suddenly gave a quiet soft growl. 'What's the matter with you, grumpy?' Micky looked down at the dog and saw him staring across the car park.

He didn't notice the three men who watched from the car at the entrance of the car park. There was no conversation. Frank half turned to Gus in the rear seat and nodded. Gus got out of the car and quietly called to the boy on the skateboard. The boy glided over to him.

'Do me a favour, kid. Here's five quid. I'm a bit worried. I've just seen what looked like an injured cat go round the back of that snack bar. Tell that guy over there to check it out, would you, and then piss off,' said Gus. The boy barely looked at Gus. He took the money and rolled over to Micky who was just locking up.

'Hey mister, I just seen an injured cat go round the back of your van.'

'Really? Thanks, I'll have a look.' Micky put the key in his pocket and made his way round the back of the bar. He looked from left to right but couldn't see the cat. 'Can you see it, Murphy?' Micky asked distractedly and bent down to peer under the bar. 'Come on, cat. Where are you? Let's have a look at you. Not going to hurt you.' Murphy growled. 'Quiet Murphy. You'll frighten it away.'

Micky bent low and moved backwards along the bar trying to see the whole of the area underneath. Murphy gave another snarl and then an unusually vicious bark.

Micky began to straighten up and turn when he felt a massive crash and splintering pain explode in the valley caused by the base of his neck and shoulder. He vaguely heard Murphy make a terrible snarling noise followed by a man's voice cry out in pain and then swearing. As he felt himself sinking to the ground, he half swung round and saw a glimpse of three men in balaclavas. As he hit the ground, he saw from the corner of his eye Murphy spring at one of the men and sink his jaws into his thigh. The man screamed. A moment later the dog gave a terrible howl as a baseball bat swung from nowhere into his side and sent him hurtling across the ground. The dog whimpered and lay still. Micky instinctively rolled to one side but was met with a crashing boot into his chest, followed by one to his head, then one into his kidneys, then another one to his head, then two more into his arms as he held them up to protect his head, then more kicks to his legs and back and chest, and then another blow from the baseball bat to the side of his head. Then it suddenly stopped. Micky lay still, his face scuffed into the tarmac, blood and spit seeping from his mouth; his eyes, already beginning to swell, hardly open. There was silence. He heard no voices. Then everything went black and he became unconscious.

The three men pulled off their balaclavas and calmly walked in silence back to their car. Hardly anybody was about, and those that were scarcely noticed them. The men got into their car and pulled out of the car park.

Gus suddenly began to moan and look down between his legs where he saw blood seeping through his trousers. 'Jesus, that fucking dog took a chunk out of me.' He wriggled his trousers down to his knees and looked at the gaping wound. 'Christ, I need a doctor on this.'

'Bollocks,' said Frank without turning to look. 'You'll live. Can't risk it. We'll patch you up when we get back.'

'Another good job done,' said Lenny.

'One more to go. I'm starving. Let's go and get something to eat.' He put his foot down and accelerated. He and Lenny looked happy. Gus whined in pain.

***

The three men had driven away twenty minutes ago, but Micky still remained unconscious. A few feet from him, Murphy was also stretched out. He whimpered quietly and tried to stand up but found he couldn't because the side of his body was on fire. He lifted his head and saw Micky lying still. Very slowly and painfully, he began to drag himself over the tarmac towards him. Occasionally his whimpers became louder as pain surged through him. Eventually he reached him and lay alongside him. He whimpered again and began to lick Micky's face. His eyelids suddenly fluttered, and one of his eyes partially opened. He made a sound, but it wasn't a word because he couldn't form words. Then he made a grunting sound and tried to move his lips to say 'Murphy'. Murphy whimpered again. It began to rain, and a wind started to sweep across the car park. Micky began to hear a strange noise. It was a quiet noise, almost like a rumble but softer than that. It suddenly seemed close, but then it stopped. He was able to turn his eye in the direction where he had heard it.

'Bloody 'ell', said a boy's voice. 'You okay, mister?'

Micky heard the quiet rumble again, moving away this time, and a boy's voice calling out for help. Then everything went black again.

***

Cindy had enjoyed herself, but it was a kind of enjoyment she hadn't experienced in her past life. She had never mixed with a lot of people before and had never wanted to. The most she had ever been with was no more than four or five at any one time, and that was too many. Too many because she had always been used or abused by one or all of them at some time. Conversations were hard and coarse with everyone trying to stake their own importance. If she was ever spoken to, it was usually because she was the butt of ridicule. But this was different. People had chatted with her and smiled at her and said how pleased they were that she had come to the funeral. She hadn't actually minded telling them that she had called at the Centre and that Tom had been kind to her. They were so pleased that things were better for her now and wished her well for the future. They didn't look upon her as some nonentity.

She was offered sandwiches and cake and coffee or wine and didn't have to ask for any of it. Linda frequently came to her and asked her if she felt comfortable, and then she would introduce her to other people there. She had found herself laughing and joining in conversations, and those who she was talking to listened to what she was saying in exactly the same way as they listened to each other. Time slipped by, and she realised she must be on her way. She took Linda to one side and thanked her.

'I was glad you came with me,' said Linda, 'and it was kind of you to come.'

'I suppose one shouldn't enjoy a funeral, but I did enjoy it.'

'That would please Tom. Take care.' Linda kissed Cindy on the cheek and showed her out. She collected her bicycle and set off into what was now heavy rain. Her new coat gave her a lot of protection, but twenty minutes later, as she made her way up Bush Lane and reached Micky's house, she was wet but warm. She pushed her bike round the side of the house and put it in the shed, but the first thing she noticed was that Micky's truck wasn't parked outside, and there were no lights on in the house. She had assumed he would have been home ages ago. She went into the house and took off her wet coat. She suddenly felt cold. That was odd. A moment ago she was warm. But this was an odd coldness. It was a coldness she had experienced before but couldn't remember why. Then it suddenly came to her: she felt like this when she was frightened. Why should she feel that now? She began to panic. Something was wrong. Something terrible had happened. Micky was coming straight home over an hour ago, but he wasn't there. Why? Why wasn't he there? She took out her mobile and punched the number. She heard the connecting buzz and then got the recorded message to call again later. She began to pace up and down, struggling to think of a reasonable explanation and also trying to calm herself. Where could he be? Where? There had to be something wrong, otherwise he would have rung her and let her know what was happening – why he might be delayed – but there was nothing. What could she do? She had to do something. To sit around on her own just waiting would drive her crazy. She'd go back to the bar. He couldn't possibly be there, but she'd go there anyway. She grabbed her coat and went out again. She got her bicycle out of the shed and set off. A strong wind had got up, and the rain was unrelenting, but twenty minutes later she pulled into the car park at Clarkes. There were only three cars there and Micky's truck. She felt a dreadful sinking feeling in her stomach. None of it was making sense. She pushed her bicycle over to the bar and climbed the step to the door. She didn't have a key. She called, 'Micky! Micky, are you there? Murph? Where are you?' She listened but all she could hear was the rain pounding on the bar roof. She moved down the steps and looked around her. There was nobody. The area was stark and forbidding. Micky wasn't there. He wasn't by her side. She began to feel really scared. Alone. Vulnerable and exposed to danger. What should she do? Go back to the house? Go to the police? What could she say? My

216

boyfriend has been missing for an hour? They'd laugh at her. She wouldn't want to go there anyway. She'd always had an antipathy towards the police. It wasn't her fault; it was because of her childhood, the way she'd been nurtured. Nurtured? That was a laugh. She started mumbling Micky's name, and then a thought came into her mind. Frank.

That bastard Frank. It had to be him. There was no other explanation. He'd moved quickly, made his second strike. He'd beaten her to it and come for Micky. Poor Micky. Where are you? What have they done to you? Kidnap? No, they wouldn't try that. Too complicated. Messy. They must have got Murphy as well. They will have killed him. For sure they will have killed him. And Micky. Would they have gone the whole hog and killed him? They'd tried to kill Dougie. They were capable of it. They'd enjoy it, and they could get away with it.

Her heart was pounding like a piston out of control now. She needed to calm down. Calm down and think. Right. It was obvious. If they'd beaten him and left him, someone would have discovered him and called an ambulance. Or maybe they were scared off. Either way an ambulance would have been called. That means the only place he could be was in hospital. That settled it. At least if she didn't find him there, she could guess he might not have been injured, that he was okay and that there was some other reasonable explanation. She jumped on her bicycle and set off for The Royal. She cycled like a maniac, twice nearly having a collision with a car. Horns blared at her and drivers swore, but she raced on uncaring about them. The Royal was only a few minutes away, and she was quickly in the car park and approaching the A&E department. She rested her bicycle against the wall and, without bothering to lock it, went in. A few people were sitting around in a waiting foyer, but immediately on her right was an enquiry window. She walked over to it and the nurse on the other side spoke.

217

'Can I help you?'

'My boyfriend. I think he may have been beaten up. Can you tell me if he's been brought in?'

'Can you tell me your relationship?' The nurse was pleasant but firm.

'I've told you. He's my boyfriend. His name is Micky. We're partners. We live together. For Christ's sake, is he here?'

'A young man was brought in who had suffered a beating. I haven't yet been passed any details about his identity. He had a dog with him.'

'That's him. Murphy. That's our dog. He was with him. Please. Tell me what's happened.'

'If you take a seat, I'll get someone to come and see you.'

'Just tell me where he is!'

'Please, go and sit down, and I'll get someone to come and see you as soon as possible.'

Cindy wanted to scream. She wanted to smash the glass separating her from the nurse the other side.

'Please. I'll do my best.' The nurse spoke in a kindly way, and Cindy wilted in a kind of submission. She simply nodded and went and sat down. She would have to wait.

***

Gus eased himself high up on to the pillows, leaving his upper body uncovered by the sheet and blankets. The electric clock indicated the time as 13:10. He felt cold and shivery, yet he also felt hot. The pain in his leg was becoming unbearable. He switched on the bedside lamp and threw back the blanket covering his legs. The leg with the dog bite was wrapped round with a towel. He folded it back and inspected the wound. It was oozing blood and puffed up. The whole of his thigh had doubled in size, and his lower leg was swelling up.

Ellie stirred next to him and turned over towards him.

'Are you all right?' She was still half asleep.

'My leg. It's killing me.'

'You're a bloody nuisance.' She sat up and leaned across him to inspect his leg.

'Jesus. That looks bad. You need the hospital.'

'It'll be fine. I'm not going there. Frank says to keep away.'

'Frank says.' She spat out the words with contempt. 'And he's a fucking doctor and knows about these things, does he?'

The very mention of Frank's name always got Ellie riled up. She knew him for what he was – a scumbag. Mean and vicious and a blight on decent society. She'd never claimed to be an angel, but she was honest and would rather be poor than resort to thieving and being part of a life that was connected to Frank. Gus was naïve, easily led and hadn't got the brains to see that Frank just used him for his own ends. She had never minded that Gus was just a simple guy. When she first met him, she had never seen in him an aggressive streak, and he had never hit her. With her money that she had earned from the hotel together with his from driving for a local builder, they had rubbed along together just fine. They were satisfied with going out once a week and having a load of laughs with some good friends. But then Frank had come on the scene, and the rot had set in.

'We've got to be careful.' Gus winced as he hissed out the words.

'Careful. So what's he dragged you into this time?'

'It's business.'

'Business?! You make me sick. You run around that scumbag like a little puppy. You could be dying and he wouldn't care. Get away from him, Gus, or he'll drag you down with him.'

'He's a good mate. We had to deal with something.'

'Yeah, I bet you did. I'm going, Gus. My sister's got a small boarding house in Devon. I told you. She and Robby are making a go of it and want me to join them.'

'You won't go, will you? Devon? What kind of a dump is that?'

'Of course I'm going, and you should come with me. Get away from that toerag.'

'I can't. He relies on me.'

'I bet he does. To do his dirty work. And what do you get for it? Handouts when he's in the mood. Dirty money he makes from drugs. I'm going, Gus. I'm slaving my arse off at the hotel day after day for a pittance. I've had enough, and I've got the chance.'

'You fucking stay here with me.'

'Not any more, Gus. You've got to make your mind up: stay here and work in the sewer, or come with me and start a new life. But I'm definitely going.'

'And what am I supposed to do?'

'You start acting like a decent grown up. A fucking man. If you hang on to Frank's apron strings, you'll end up in prison. And it'll serve you right.'

Gus flopped back on the pillows. His world was falling to pieces. Why the hell couldn't she understand his position? If he left, he'd be letting Frank down. He couldn't do that. Frank was the man. He was going places, and Gus was going to go with him. That's how it worked. Devon. That was a place in the back of beyond. And anyway, if he went to Devon, Frank wouldn't be very pleased. Ellie should understand that. Okay, yeah, she was a good woman, he'd grant her that. But she was so stubborn and had no ambition. The trouble was she hated Frank and thought he was just a vicious tosser. What the hell did she know? One had to fight to survive in this world. She'd already admitted she had to work like stink at the hotel. So what kind of a life was that? It was stupid. Frank understood the world. He knew what made things tick. He'd always proved that women didn't have a clue about these things. They were always getting above themselves and causing trouble.

He let out a long sigh again and looked down at Ellie who had turned away and was dropping off to sleep. What the hell was he going to do? He needed her. She'd stuck with him for eight years now, and the thought of not having her around had to be a no-no. Christ, he'd never manage without her. She was always there. She was a good screw and was always up for it. She was a bloody good cook too. That was good. He liked his food. She'd always given him a bit of cash too if Frank had been short and couldn't pay him. Shit! What the hell was he going to do?

He wrapped the towel round his leg again, slid back down into the bed and tried to turn on his side which would not squash his injury. He'd never known such pain. All because of the bloody dog. They shouldn't have bothered with Big Ears. What was the point? They'd got the big guy and should have left it at that. Now he wants to go after that little bitch. What was that going to achieve? Sod all. It was such a waste of time and energy. Ellie wasn't completely wrong. Frank could be a right wanker sometimes, though it was more than his life was worth to tell him. Trouble with Frank was he had no sense of humour and a short fuse. If you didn't agree with him, then watch out. Oh well, if he did go after the girl, he'd have to bail out. He could barely walk, let alone stand on his leg. He'd just have to manage with Lenny. So what was the problem? Two blokes against a skinny little bitch like that. A right laugh that was. Sod it.

He needed to forget all about that shit and try and get some sleep. Yeah, hell might freeze.

***

Cindy opened her eyes and frowned. It took her a few moments to remember where she was, but then she saw Micky lying in bed, and it came back to her all too quickly. The nurse at reception had been as good as her word and got someone to come and see her within ten minutes which was a lot less than she had expected. She didn't know anything about the ranking of nurses but guessed that this one was probably a top dog, most likely a Sister. She was pleasant but business-like, the sort that wasn't going to take shit from anybody.

She didn't know anything about how it had happened or who had done it. She'd understood that Micky had been found in a car park. He was unconscious and had suffered a severe beating. An ambulance had been called, and he was brought in. He'd suffered massive bruising and lacerations to his head and body. They didn't think there was internal bleeding, but there was considerable bruising round his kidneys. He was concussed. The police had been, but questioning him would not be possible until tomorrow.

As soon as Cindy heard that he'd been beaten up, she knew beyond any doubt that Frank had been responsible, that he'd come for Micky much sooner than she'd imagined.

'Is he going to be okay though?' asked Cindy, fearing the worst.

'Well, it'll take a few days, but he's a big strong lad. He should make a full recovery. We had to stitch up some of his face which doesn't look very pretty at the moment. Try not to be too shocked when you see him. It will heal up in time.'

Cindy sighed with relief and then had an afterthought. 'There was a dog with him. He's our dog. Do you know what happened to him?

'I did hear there was a dog with him when they found him, but I can't tell you anything more. I'm sorry.'

Cindy had felt a sudden sensation of dread that Murphy had been caught again or even killed. Better perhaps to be killed rather than taken back with Frank. She couldn't bear to think what might happen to him if that were the case.

The nurse had kindly brought her to this private room where they had put Micky for the night and told her she could stay if she wanted to. When she had come in, she had had to stifle a gasp at the sight of Micky's face even though the nurse had warned her. She couldn't see his body below the bedclothes, but his face was raw. His lips and eyes were swollen and the rest of his face covered in cuts and grazes. He had been asleep and had remained so until she herself had dropped off after a couple of hours and had now woken up herself. She wondered what time it was. Everywhere was very quiet, and the main lighting in the big ward was turned down. She tried to get her thoughts together. That scumbag Frank was obviously still hell bent on revenge, and so far he'd done it without any problems. He would have been laughing at how easy it had been. There was no way he could be blamed. The police would have nothing, assuming they bothered to investigate, which she believed would amount to no more than asking a few useless questions. They'd be back in the morning to talk to Micky, as long as he was able to by then, but he wouldn't be able to tell them anything. She could just hear the copper asking Micky if he could think of anybody who might have given him the beating. Of course he could: a man named Frank, who was very well known to them, but no, he couldn't actually say why. And he couldn't identify him or the others with him because they would have had masks on and they'd crept up on him from behind. They didn't open their

223

mouths so he couldn't identify their voices. So yes, he knew exactly who was responsible but the police would never be able to prove it. How could he be so sure then? Because, well, Frank was pissed off because he, Micky, had shacked up with his girlfriend. And of course one didn't upset Frank like that. The police interrogation would be useless, even though they'd do their best. Of course they'd have to go through the procedure to show that they wanted to do something, and they'd be more than happy to stick something on Frank because, yes, he was very well known to them, but so far he'd managed to slip through their fingers.

One thing was certain: Frank was now on a mission to get them all and wouldn't stop until he'd got her. He'd kept her until last. He'd be puffed up with confidence. He could pick his time and moment. Every moment of every day she'd have to look over her shoulder. Even when she felt safe, she would probably still be in danger. He was as slippery as an eel. She could be walking along the street, and he could jump out of the pavement beneath her feet. If he did get her, she was certain he'd damn near slaughter her, judging by what he had done to Dougie and Micky. She knew now, even if she hadn't really known before, that without any shadow of doubt, it was going to be useless for her to try and escape, to spend the rest of her life trying to avoid him. He'd get her in the end unless she got him first. The plan she'd already started to put into operation couldn't be delayed any longer. Could she pull it off? She had to. She had to make herself strong. Mean. Vicious. She had to be like some boxer who could be gentle and friendly out of the ring but inside become a killer who wouldn't be stopped by anything. That was the only way she was going to find enough self-belief and courage to see it through. It was going to be all down to mental strength.

Micky gave a weak cough, and she sprang out of her chair and went over to him. His eyes opened to slits, but it was enough to see her. He formed the suggestion of a smile.

'Micky. Oh Micky – those bastards,' she whispered and laid her face very close to his.

'Some water please.' His voice was an even quieter whisper.

She picked up the half glass of water from his bedside table and lifted it to his lips. He took a sip, spilling only a little down his chin. She gently wiped it and smiled down at him.

'You must be careful now,' his lips barely moving.

'You mustn't worry. I shall be fine.'

'The bar. Leave the bar.'

'I can manage it, Micky. The men rely on us. You mustn't worry.'

'He'll come for you. Tell the police.'

'Shshshshsh, I'll be fine. You must rest and not worry.'

'Murphy. Is Murphy all right? He did his best.'

'He's fine. Don't worry.' The words came out without thought. Automatically. She didn't know if he was all right or not, and it was another worry for her.

'You must get away or he'll get you.' He tried to lift his head, indicating his strength of feeling.

'Shshshshsh, you must rest. All you must think about is getting better.'

He relaxed his head back on the pillow and closed his eyes. She stared down at him for a few minutes and then realised he had gone back to sleep. She pondered for a few moments and then decided she would leave. He was in safe hands where he would be looked after. She had work to do. She needed to find out about Murphy, and she needed to try and get some rest before snack bar first thing in the morning. Also, she couldn't put off another day before executing the second part of her plan. She would have to see Tony at the Queen Vic and get him to contact Carl. God, that was another bit of the plan she dreaded. Still, stay mean. Tight-lipped. Hard. She could do it.

She made her way out of the ward and back to the reception waiting room where she had come in. The nurse behind the glass at the reception counter beckoned her over.

'I managed to make a couple of enquiries about your dog. I've been told that he was injured but taken to the animal shelter.'

Cindy heaved a huge sigh of relief. He'd survived Frank and was alive.

'I knew it. Thank you. Do you know how badly he was hurt?'

'That's all I know. '

'Okay. Thank you,' said Cindy and went out relieved that he'd been taken to the animal shelter but desperate to know how badly he was hurt. It would have to wait until tomorrow. The clock in the reception room had said 2 o'clock. She felt exhausted. She collected her bicycle and set off for home. She had to get some rest.

Chapter 14

The two police detectives stood next to Micky's bed. One was a woman, the other a man. Micky was slightly propped up on his pillows and was awake. He'd eaten some breakfast and indicated that he was prepared to talk to the police.

'I'm DC Collins, and my colleague is DC Foster,' said DC Collins and indicated the woman DC. 'Do you feel all right to answer a few question?'

'I'll do my best,' said Micky with slightly slurred speech because he had difficulty in opening his mouth very wide.

'We'll try and keep this short.'

'It's okay. Call me Micky.' His mouth was working marginally better than the night before.

'Any idea who could have done this to you?'

'Dead right I have, but you'll never prove it.'

'Let us judge that Micky.'

'Frank. I don't know his other name. I think it's Lewis.'

The two detectives looked at each other with knowing nods.

'What makes you think that, Micky?'

'It's complicated. Cindy, she used to be his girlfriend – slave more likely – she left him. Got away. She's with me now. He's pretty pissed off.'

'We know him,' said DC Foster. 'When you were attacked, could you see them? Could you identify them?'

'They wore masks. They crept up on me from behind. I've no proof it was them. I'm more worried about Cindy. They'll go after her.'

'You own and work at the snack bar in Clarke's car park, is that right?' asked DC Collins.

'Yeah. She'll be there today. We run it together now. He knows where to find us.'

'He's a slippery lot, Micky. We'd never make it stick in court unless you've anything else.'

Micky remained silent.

'There were three of them, is that right?'

'Yeah. They came up from behind, but I'm sure there were three.'

'And you've no idea who they were?'

'I haven't a clue. His cronies, I s'pose.'

'Did no one say anything, speak, in a way you could recognize a voice?'

'No. One of them cried out when my dog bit him, but that was all. I'm worried about Murphy. He was injured. Do you know what happened to him?'

'We've got your dog, Micky,' said DC Foster. 'He was injured, but he's been taken to the animal shelter. They'll have known what to do with him.'

'Christ, they won't put him down, will they? He's Cindy's dog really. That would break her heart.'

'I don't think they're going to do that.'

The two DCs were silent for a little while. They felt sorry for Micky. They wished they had more evidence on

Frank. They knew all about him, all right. They'd love to get him off the street. They knew he was into all sorts of crime and that he was a vicious thug, but knowing that and proving it was another matter. They'd get him in time, but they wished that time was now.

'We'll leave you to rest now, Micky. May want to talk to you again when you're a bit better. Get you to make a statement,' said DC Collins.

'What about Cindy? You've got to look after her.'

'We can't watch out for her all day. We'll do our best. We'll pay Frank a visit.'

'He'll laugh in your face.'

'You get some rest.' The two DCs turned and walked out.

Micky sank back into the pillows. They'd never stop Frank. It wasn't their fault. What the hell could they do? He couldn't expect them to provide round the clock security for Cindy. If they saw Frank, he'd only deny everything and dream up some alibi. If he got Cindy and hurt her, he didn't know what he'd do. Yes he did. He'd kill the bastard and take the consequences.

***

Frank stared in the bathroom mirror and examined his face. He swore under his breath. His nose was never going to be any different now. Revenge on the big guy wasn't ever going to change that. He wished he had killed him. That would have been the end of him. Maybe he'd go for him a second time, later on – there was no rush – and he'd finish him off for good. There was a bang on the front door, and he heard Lenny call out. He went downstairs and opened the door.

'Come in, Lenny.'

'Hi, Frank.'

Frank turned away, and Lenny followed him into the living room.

'Slept like a log,' said Frank with a grin.

'Me too,' replied Lenny with an equally broad grin. 'Where's Gus?'

Frank scoffed. 'You tell me. He hasn't showed.'

'Shit. I'm late myself.'

'I tried ringing him, but it was dead. I'll try once more.' He flipped his phone and punched the number.

A voice answered. 'Hallo.'

'Gus?'

'No it's Ellie.'

'I want to speak to Gus. It's Frank.'

'I know who it is. You can't.'

'Why not?'

'He's sick.'

'What's the matter with him?'

'He's got a bad leg.'

'He speaks with his mouth, doesn't he? Not his leg.'

There was a pause at the other end of the line, and Frank knew that Gus's pain-in-the-arse partner was scowling.

'He was bitten by a dog. But I suppose you know all about that.'

'I want to speak to him.'

'You can't.'

'Why not?

'Because I say so.'

'You give him his fucking phone. I want to speak to him.'

'Piss off, Frank.' The phone went dead.

'The bitch. She cut me off,' said Frank.

'I know that one. I've met her. Bloody 'ell. Gus ought to get rid of her,' said Lenny and then saw the rage on Frank's face.

'If I get hold of her, she'll know all about pissing off.'

'That's Gus for you, Frank. Ruled by a woman.'

'I want him here. Never mind about his poxy leg.'

'He won't be any good if it's bad.'

'The guy's a wimp. He's part of the plan to get the girl.'

'Already?'

'No point in hanging about.' He suddenly heard a noise and moved to the front room to look out of the window. 'It's the filth, Lenny,' said Frank as he came back into the living room.

'Shit. What do we do?'

'Nothing. They've got nothing on us. Keep calm and leave it to me.' He suddenly noticed the bloody baseball bat on the floor. There was a knock on the door.

'Here, give me that,' said Frank indicating the baseball bat. Lenny handed it to him. 'Wait here, Lenny.' He walked out of the room and into the box room. He placed the bat behind a bookcase and then came out into the hallway to open the front door. The two DCs who had interviewed Micky were on the doorstep.

'Well, if it isn't the Old Bill,' said Frank.

'Mind if we come in, Frank?' said DC Collins, pushing by before getting an answer.

'Come in. Make yourself at home.' He didn't hide the sarcasm in his voice.

'Ah, one of the others here too. Hallo, Lenny. Still haven't changed your friends then,' said DC Collins.

231

'What do you want?' asked Frank in a much harder voice.

'Where were you last night between five and six?'

'Me? Let me see now. Oh yes, I remember. I was just getting myself a nice supper here in the kitchen.'

'Any witnesses?'

'Well, Lenny was with me. I'd invited him round for the evening. We were going to have cocktails and a pleasant evening watching the television together.'

'Yeah, that's right. We were here together,' said Lenny.

'Yeah? What about the other one?'

'Other one? What other one?'

'The third one. Your other lackey?' said DC Foster.

'I don't know who you mean. Just the two of us together here all evening.'

'So you don't know anything about beating up a guy in the Clarkes car park?'

'Did you hear that Lenny? Us? Would we do a thing like that?'

'Definitely not. Where's Clarkes car park anyway?'

'Can't say that I really know,' said Frank, theatrically stroking his chin.

'Okay. Have your laugh. But let me tell you this, Frank. If anything nasty should happen to your ex-girlfriend, we'll come looking for you.' DC Collins stared hard at Frank, who didn't bat an eyelid, but he noticed Lenny partially look away.

'We'll see ourselves out,' he said, and the two of them walked through the house and out through the front door.

'Shit! Are they on to us, Frank?'

'Of course not. Fishing, that's all.'

'But the girl. What are we going to do?'

'Changes nothing.'

'But if anything happens to her, they'll come for us.'

'Let 'em come. We'll cover our tracks as usual. They won't be able to prove anything. I keep telling you, Lenny, they can't do a bloody thing without proof. All it needs is careful planning. We'll leave things for a couple of days and then we'll get Gus. Just leave it to me, Lenny.'

'If you're sure.'

'Have I ever failed?'

'No.'

'Right then. Come on. Let's go out. I want to make a few calls,' said Frank and made his way to the front door, picking up his coat on the way.

***

Although she had only managed to get three hours of sleep, Cindy was up by 6:00 AM on the Saturday morning. After she had showered, she grabbed an apple, drank a cup of tea and was able to open up the bar by 6:45. She quickly had everything on the move and was frying up and ready for the first customers by 7:30. As it was Saturday, the flow of business was small. Bob was the only one of Dougie's crew who came in. Dougie was still in hospital. Andy had gone down with flu, and Joe had to sort out problems about getting his elderly mother into a care home. She was able to briefly tell Bob about Micky's mugging. The shock on his face illustrated just how much he and his other mates liked Micky. He could only respond by spitting words of venom for those who were responsible, mixed with others of frustration and concern both for Micky and Cindy.

'I'll go and see him over the weekend, Cindy. And I know you haven't got your licence yet, so if you want me to drive you anywhere, especially first thing in the morning to pick up stock for the bar, I'm your man. I mean it. Just say the word.'

His offer of genuine help brought a lump to her throat as well as a sense of relief, because getting fresh food to the bar might become a problem she hadn't worked out how to solve. There was a delivery twice a week to the bar, which provided ninety percent of what they needed, but sometimes she or Micky picked up odd items from one of the supermarkets. She had more or less made up her mind to drive the truck if it had been necessary which she knew was a bad idea. She was capable of driving by now but still hadn't taken her test and got her license. If she had got picked up by the police with no license and no insurance, it would not only be bad for her but also for Micky who would either have to say she drove the truck with his permission or that she had stolen it. Bob's offer could be a godsend and provided a bright spark amongst the many other issues that were cramming her mind. She was desperate to go and see Micky, and while she was at the hospital, she could take time to see Dougie who was still there. She also needed to find out more about Murphy's injuries. Last of all, and most urgent, was her need to see Tony at the Queen Vic. She dare not delay seeing him another day. She was convinced Frank would be coming for her soon, probably within the next two or three days, so she had to beat him to it by outsmarting him.

By 1 o'clock she had closed the bar for the day. All morning she had constantly scanned the car park, watching to see if there was any unusual movement. She couldn't imagine what that might be and realised she was becoming paranoid, but she knew she couldn't take any risks.

She collected her bicycle and gave a final look round before setting off to the hospital. Every time a vehicle drew alongside or passed her, she glanced out of the corner of her eye, half expecting one of them to be Frank trying to run her down. With a sense of relief, she reached the hospital and went inside. To her surprise she found that Micky had been moved from the private room into the main communal ward and, to even more surprise, placed in a bed next to Dougie.

'Well, well, you two know how to pull strings,' she said and immediately bent over Micky and kissed him.

'Ouch!' he exclaimed, pointing to a tender spot under the bedclothes.

'Sorry. I'm only a featherweight. Does it hurt that much?'

'Bloody right.' They were both joking with each other but she knew that he was trying to be bright for her benefit whilst she, on the other hand, guessed from the sight of his face, let alone the injuries she couldn't see to his body, that he must be in pain.

'How are you feeling?' she asked and reached for his hand.

'I'll be all right. What about you? Did you manage this morning?'

'Everything is fine. Bob has offered to drive his car for me at any time I need. I hope it won't be necessary, but you never know.'

'Bloody hell. That's good of him.' His words were slurred because of his still swollen lips, but she was thankful that he was mentally in better shape than she had expected.

'He's a good lad. I'm pleased he's helping.'

'How are you getting on, Dougie?'

'Just a question of time now. Everything is healing up, and I should be allowed home in two or three days. My kidneys are pretty bruised, and I'm passing a little bit of blood, but I'll be fine.' He smiled at her.

'Oh dear. Are you sure?'

'Of course. Sounds worse than it really is.'

'The police came by and asked me questions,' said Micky.

'What did you tell them?' asked Cindy.

'Nothing. What could I? I didn't see 'em. They jumped me from behind.' He gave her a sideways glance and slight shake of the head to let her know that he had not mentioned Frank. They were adamant that it was best not to let Dougie think that what had happened had anything to do with Frank because it simply wouldn't be of benefit. They knew there was no way the police could prove anything, and it was possible that Dougie's family might begin to worry that they could be future targets. Knowing Douglas as they did, he might decide to take matters into his own hands, and that would almost certainly lead to a bad ending for him and his family.

'Fancy the two of us getting injured at the same time and ending up in hospital side-by-side. Who said coincidences never happened?' said Dougie.

'That's life, mate. You never can tell,' said Micky.

'What did the police say, Micky?' asked Cindy

'They couldn't say much. They said they'd ask around, but they had virtually nothing to go on.' He didn't tell her that he'd told them he suspected Frank as being responsible. 'They said they may come back and ask more questions, but I don't think they will.'

'They've taken Murphy to the animal shelter. I'm going down there after leaving here.'

'Ahhh, he's a lovely boy. I know he got one of them before they clobbered him. Do you know how bad he's hurt?'

'No, Micky, but I'm worried. Those bastards were vicious.'

'He's a survivor, Cindy.' He could see she was worried and trying to cover up her distress at what had been done to him. He reached out for her hand. 'Hey. Everything is going to be fine.' He smiled at her and she smiled back. 'How did the funeral go?'

'Considering it was a funeral, it was wonderful, and I met so many people. If I hadn't stayed on and gone to the wake afterwards but come back to the bar, this probably wouldn't have happened to you.'

'You can't say that, Cindy. I'm glad you didn't come back, otherwise you might have got the same treatment.'

'He's right, Cindy,' Douglas called across from his bed. 'You'd have been another casualty.' She almost blurted out that it was because of her that both of them had suffered anyway but held back knowing it would sound futile.

She lingered for two hours at the hospital, torn between the wish to stay on and the desperate need to get off and find Murphy before carrying out her visit to Tony at the Queen Vic. Micky understood that she had plenty of things to attend to without knowing of her visit to Tony, who she had never told him about anyway, and insisted that she didn't return later that evening but come again tomorrow after she'd had a good night's sleep.

As she bent down to kiss him goodbye, he whispered, 'Keep your eyes in the back of your head. When you get home make sure everything's locked up. You'll find an old baseball bat in the shed. Take it up with you to bed. I don't believe he'd try and break in, but use it if you have to.'

'I shall be fine. Don't worry about me. You get well quickly. I'll see you tomorrow.' She kissed him as gently as she could on his swollen lips. She said goodbye to Douglas and left the two of them to talk.

Outside she climbed on her bicycle and set off for the animal shelter which she knew was on the outskirts of the town off Compton Road, which she was pleased to remember was not far from the Queen Vic. It would make the travelling to visit Tony much easier. As she cycled along she still kept casting her eyes in all directions thinking that Frank might have known she had just come from the hospital and was following her, biding his time, ready to strike. She knew her nerves were getting the better of her but couldn't help herself and reckoned it was better to be paranoid than too laid back. The sight of what they had done to Micky made her feel sick but also a manic determination that she would take Frank down, even if she herself took a beating or even lost her own life in the process.

As she rode up the track off Compton Road, which led to the animal shelter, she could hear dogs housed in the kennels. She reached the building, leant her bike against the wall and went into the reception office. A young woman in a dark blue uniform was sitting behind a counter. She had a friendly smile. 'Can I help you?'

'I'm looking for Murphy. He's a bit scruffy. Quite big. Thick, brown-grey coat. I was told he was brought here last evening.'

'I know who you mean. Poor thing had a couple of cracked ribs.'

'Oh Christ. He's already recovering from cracked ribs. Are these different ones, do you know?'

'As far as I know, he only has two that are cracked, so they must be the same ones. I believe the injury was fairly acute so that would explain.'

'I think somebody hit him with a baseball bat. My boyfriend was mugged and Murphy tried to help.'

'Oh dear. I'm sorry. He was x-rayed and seen by the vet. He's very sore, and it's painful for him to stand or walk, but he's on pain killers and he'll need lots of rest.'

'I was frightened he might be worse or you'd put him down,' said Cindy.

'I'm afraid we do have to put many dogs down. Mostly strays that are unclaimed. That might have happened eventually if nobody came to claim him.'

'Do you charge for – well for what you do?'

'We are charity, and there are standard charges for most things, but usually people pay what they can afford.'

'I want to pay but may not be able to pay at the moment.'

'I'm sure we can make an arrangement. Do you want to come through and see him?'

'Thank you,' said Cindy, feeling relieved that at least Murphy was going to be fine. 'I can't take him with me today. I've come on my bike.'

The assistant talked as she led the way through the maze of kennels. 'He'll be fine here for a couple of days if that will help.' She eventually stopped at a kennel.

'Here he is.'

Cindy looked through the wire grill and had to force back tears as Murphy looked up at her and struggled unsteadily to stand and give his tail a wag. The assistant opened the door, and Cindy went down on her knees to gently hold Murphy to her. 'You lovely brave boy, Murphy.' Then a couple of tears did flow.

'He's obviously yours,' said the assistant, smiling. 'We get a lot of sad endings. It's lovely to see a happy one.'

Cindy remained for a few minutes, holding and petting the dog, and then had to leave. 'I'm coming back for you, Murph. It won't be long. You'll be safe here.' She stood up and hurried back to the reception. She thanked the assistant, and after giving details about her address and other red tape details, she left the building. She was beginning to feel better. Murphy was going to be okay, and although it had been an awful shock to see the terrible beating that Micky had suffered, he would recover. Her number one priority now was to avoid Frank before she could make her own strike. As she cycled the short distance to the Queen Vic, she tried to prepare herself mentally for the first stage of the most difficult part of her plan so far. A lot depended on it going smoothly. She'd broken in to Frank's and got the money, and she'd managed it without a hitch. The next bit wouldn't put her in danger, at least not immediately. She simply needed to keep calm and be absolutely determined.

As soon as she reached the Queen Vic, she stopped on the edge of the car park and scanned the area. It was still only early evening and unlikely that Frank would be there, but she wasn't about to take any chances of bumping into him in the bar. There were very few cars but no sign of Frank's. She pushed her bicycle across the car park, leant it against the wall and, without bothering to lock it, went inside. Being so early in the evening, there were hardly any customers. There was a barmaid behind the bar chatting to a customer, and at the far end she saw Tony standing alone. She casually walked across to him, trying not to draw attention to herself from the other customers.

'Christ! Cindy! What are you doing here?' His expression was more of alarm than surprise.

'Thanks for the welcome, Tony,' said Cindy, quietly.

'I thought you and Frank were…'

'I'm not here for Frank. He knows nothing about it.'

Tony quickly scanned the bar as if he was being watched for doing something wrong. 'What are you up to?' he asked in a hushed voice.

'I want your help, Tony.'

'What do you mean? What kind of help?'

'Get hold of Carl for me. Arrange a meeting.'

'What's this all about?'

'There's nothing for you to worry about.'

'What about Frank?'

'Don't worry about him. He doesn't have to know anything about it.'

Tony started moving his head from side to side, and she realised how nervous he was. 'I dunno, Cindy. I like you, you know that, but I don't want any trouble.'

'You're not doing anything wrong. This is simply a meeting between me and Carl.'

'He won't agree. He must know all about you and Frank.'

'Just tell him there's nothing to worry about. Tell him he'll benefit from it.'

'How do you mean, benefit?'

'Don't ask questions, Tony. Just tell him what I've said.' She could see his mind beginning to race and realised the terrifying hold Frank had got over him. Even speaking to her without telling him would probably invite a punishment. She felt sorry for him but had to get him to play ball with her.

'When do you want to meet him?'

'Tomorrow.'

'Tomorrow. Christ, it's Sunday.'

'I'm sure he won't be going to church. Get hold of him tonight.'

'That's such short notice, Cindy. I may not be able to.'

'If you try hard, you will. If Frank asked you, I'm sure you'd manage it.'

'Okay, okay. I promise to get hold of him. But I can't promise he'll agree to come, and he may not want to make it tomorrow.'

'No, it has to be tomorrow, Monday Try and sound firm, Tony. Tell him I said the deal's off if he doesn't make

241

it tomorrow, and he'd be the loser.' She was determined to make the meeting tomorrow. Every day delayed gave Frank more opportunity to get her. But more important was that she wanted to execute the whole of her plan before Micky came back from hospital. She didn't know when that would be, but she didn't think they would want to keep him there for long. If he was in no danger, he would simply be able to recover at home. As long as he was in hospital, she had freedom of movement to do what she wanted without him asking questions, which she would find difficult to answer without lying and she didn't want to do that.

'What are you up to, Cindy?'

'Don't ask me any questions, Tony. You should know that. Just do as I ask. Please.'

He sighed, blowing out his cheeks. 'I hope you know what you're doing. How have you been?' His voice sounded softer, more caring.

'Things are good, Tony. I'm gonner be all right. You take care of yourself. Don't let Frank bully you so much.'

He pushed aside the air with his hand as much as to say, 'D'you think I don't know that.'

She put a small piece of paper on to the counter. 'This is my telephone number. Call me tonight. Just give me the time and place. Text might be better.' He took the piece of paper and nodded.

'Thanks, Tony. I owe you.' She smiled and then walked out of the bar. She picked up her bicycle but pondered for a few moments. There was always the chance that Tony might betray her. That his fear of Frank would get the better of him and he'd tell him that she'd been in and wanted to see Carl. Frank could easily let the meeting take place, in collusion with Carl, and grab her when she turned up. Was that a real possibility? Would Tony really do that to her, or was her paranoia driving her over the edge? Well she wouldn't know the answer to that until her meeting with Carl – assuming he agreed to meet her.

She suddenly felt drained. She'd had little sleep the previous night, and it had been a tiring day. She needed food and rest.

She climbed on her bicycle and set off for home. When she reached the house it was in darkness, which was no surprise, but it suddenly gave her a feeling of isolation. She quickly put the bicycle away in the shed and went into the house. Again more darkness, and very quiet. If she had been with Micky she would have hardly noticed, but he wasn't there and neither was Murphy. As soon as she'd turned on the lights, she made sure all the doors were locked. The fire was already laid so she put a match to it, and the dead wood quickly began to spring to life with yellow flames. Inside the fridge there was a chunk of quiche that Micky had made and was left over from the night before. She took it out and put it in the oven to warm up. She unhooked a frying pan hanging from a rail against the wall and put it on the cooker. She washed her hands at the sink and cut a slice of bread. It was a makeshift meal but luxury compared to much of what she'd had to eat in the past. She cut up half a courgette, which Micky had introduced her to, and put the rounds in the pan. It didn't take them long to cook and for the quiche to warm up. She was soon sitting at the table eating. It all tasted good. When she'd finished she made a cup of coffee and then sat down in front of the fire. She turned on the TV, but her mind was too full of what she'd done during the day, and what she had to carry out in the next two or three days, to pay much attention to what was on the screen. She turned and stared at the fire, watching the flames dance and listening to the wood occasionally crackle. In a very short time, her lids became heavy and she dozed off. It wasn't until two hours later that she was woken by her mobile alerting her to a text message. She opened it and read: 'Tomorrow. 7pm. Usual place.' Her whole body instinctively relaxed, and she smiled. Good. Carl had agreed to meet her. She was in business.

The fire had gone out. She went to bed.

Chapter 15

Gus sat down at the table with a glum expression on his face. His leg was killing him with pain, he felt sick, and he'd been rowing all night with Ellie. At one stage she was screaming at him, and he only just managed to control himself from hitting her. He'd never done that before, but he'd come damn near close to it this time. She'd gone on and on about Frank and what a scumbag he was; that he was a menace to society; that people like him should be thrown in jail and left to rot. It cut her to the pit of her stomach to see how Gus, the man who she had lived with for over eight years, the man who she had been loyal to, had supported him through bad times and had loved so much when they first met, could have now sunk so low and become no more than one of Frank's lackeys. He'd become weak and pathetic in his hero-worship of a vicious thug. And what had he got out of it? Nothing. Had he got rich? That was a laugh. Had he made any money? If he had, she hadn't seen any of it. Had he got stability? Security? If that's what he had wanted, he might just as well have spat in the wind. The one thing he had acquired was the hatred of other people with whom he had any connection. Because of his association with Frank, they had no friends. The ones that they'd previously had had drifted away. One or two had tried to be loyal to her because they felt sorry for her. They pitied her. What kind of a friendship was that? She was humiliated and miserable. He'd almost brought her life to ruins. She was going to get out as she had promised. She was definitely going down to Devon and joining up with her sister. She was going to start a new life and forget all about Gus. He could come with her and they could both make a fresh start if he wanted to, or he could stay and hang on to Frank and go down the sewer with him. But he should be in no doubt she meant what she was saying. She was definitely going.

He was definitely feeling ill. He'd never felt more ill. Ellie didn't seem to understand that Frank was doing his best. He only turned on people who tried to do him down. He stood up for himself and should be admired for that. The police were always badgering him and giving him a bad name. It was only fair that he should try and protect himself. Stories of him making thousands of pounds by dealing in drugs and causing misery to so many others were exaggerated. Also exaggerated were the suggestions that he beat up people who crossed him. It was true he had had to defend himself against people who had attacked him, but what else was he supposed to do? She had absolutely no understanding.

She put a plate of steaming hotpot, complete with dumplings, on the table in front of him. He loved hotpot, especially with Ellie's dumplings, but he didn't want it tonight, not now, because he felt so ill, and the rowing had exhausted him, and he was almost falling asleep. Another surge of agonizing pain clawed at his leg. Suddenly the kitchen door burst open and Frank was standing there, and he could see the rage on his face. Christ, he was in trouble. He should have gone to Frank when he called. Frank had needed him, and he had let him down. He tried to stand, but his bad leg wouldn't let him. Sorry, Frank, I'll make it up to you mate. Just give me a chance and I'll do what you want. The thoughts stampeded through his brain. He heard Ellie screaming and swearing at Frank to get out of her house, but he took no notice and swung his fist at Ellie, knocking her to the ground. As she tried to get up, Frank kicked her in the face, and she fell back with blood pouring from her mouth. Gus pushed back his chair to try once more and get up but felt a thundering blow to the side of his head, sending him hurtling to the floor. This was followed by a vicious kick to his head, which sent flashing lights across his vision as he tried to roll over and protect himself. He heard Frank call out some kind of command, and he instantly saw a massive brown bear come through the kitchen door and stand with snarling bared teeth. Frank barked out an order, and the bear leapt at him, clawing his face and digging massive teeth into his bad leg so that he screamed out in agony. Then he woke up. His body was on fire, and he was soaked in sweat. His heart was pounding, and he couldn't stop shaking. Ellie stirred next to him and sleepily asked, 'Are you okay, Gus?'

Gus groaned. 'I'm sick, Ellie. And I've had a terrible dream. A nightmare.'

'Must be nearly eleven. I can hear the church bells.' She threw back the bedclothes and stood up from the bed. 'I'm going to the bathroom.' She padded across the room and went out.

Gus lay back, trying to stop shaking. A moment ago he was on fire, he still was, but he was trembling with cold too. What the hell was the matter with him? He thought he was going to cry. He felt frightened. He couldn't exactly say why, but he was definitely frightened. He felt so ill. Was he going to die? He didn't want to die. That wasn't right. Why should he die? He wanted to live.

Ellie came back into the room, naked except for a towel wrapped round her waist. 'Are you going to get up, Gus?'

'I can't, Ellie. I feel too ill.'

'How's your leg? Let me have a look. She pulled back the bedclothes and saw a dark stain on the surface of the towel that was wrapped round Gus's leg. She gently unfolded it, leaving it spread under his leg to protect the sheets.

'My God, your leg is the size of a house. Turn on your side so I can see the wound properly.'

Gus rolled on to his side so that the side of his thigh was uppermost.

'Jesus Christ, Gus. That's bad. You could lose your leg!'

***

'They've said they'll keep Murphy until you get back home,' said Cindy, sitting next to Micky's bed.

'That's great. They've said I can go home tomorrow.'

'So soon. Will you be all right?'

'Of course.'

'Bob's agreed to take me in his car to collect Murphy. He'll be company for you at home until you're better.'

'Oh I shall be fine in a couple days, Cindy.'

'Not unless you do as you're told and rest. Don't get any ideas about coming back to work yet.'

'I can't lie about all day. I'll go nuts.'

'You talk to him, Dougie. I've got no control,' said Cindy, turning to Douglas in the next bed.

'I've got enough trouble with my own wife. Don't drag me in,' said Douglas as he sneaked a sideways glance at Micky.

'All you guys stick together.'

A nurse suddenly appeared and began to pull the screens round Douglas's bed. 'Time to inspect your injuries, Douglas,' she said with a smile. A moment later he was lost from view.

Cindy leant across to Micky and put her face close to his cheek. 'How are you?' She kissed him gently.

'I'm doing great. I just need to get out of here.'

'Tomorrow will soon be here.'

He pulled her in closer and secretively. 'I've got something to tell you,' he whispered.

She frowned. 'What's happened?'

'It's not me. It's about Dougie. He told me in confidence. He doesn't want Julie to know. Not yet anyway?'

'What is it?'

'It's his left leg. He's got to have another operation. Maybe two. But they can only do so much. It means he's going to be a bit of a cripple.'

'Oh no.'

'He's worried about the future. He'll never get his old job back. There'll be no insurance claim because the driver's unknown. And he doesn't have a private policy.'

'That bastard Frank.'

'We've no proof. Wouldn't help anyway. He'd be an uninsured driver if it was a stolen car.'

For a little while neither of them spoke. They just let the enormity of Douglas's situation sink in.

'What's he going to do?'

'He'll get a job all right, but it won't be what he wants, and he probably won't earn as much. Julie has a part time job, but it'll be hard for them.'

'Frank's caused so much misery.'

'Are you going to be all right? I'm worried about you.'

'I'll be fine.'

'Don't come back tonight. I don't want you out in the dark. It'll be too dangerous.'

'I should come and sit with you.'

'No. Dougie and I keep each other company. Julie will be in too.'

'All right. I'll stay in and put my feet up.'

For two hours the conversation continued light-heartedly, each concealing their own worries. He had told her that he was worried about her and that she should be careful, but he had not revealed the degree of his anxiety for her safety. If Frank was responsible for what had happened to Dougie and his own beating up, then it was certain he would be out to get Cindy. She'd be so vulnerable. Frank could even kill her. Whilst he hid his true fears for her safety, she couldn't shake off her own fears for her meeting with Carl later that evening. Her mind kept wandering and imagining all sorts of horrific scenarios. The worst would be if Tony had betrayed her and Frank was there, waiting to grab her. But there were other more likely dangers. That world of drugs and shady deals was always suspicious and protective of itself. Although Carl knew her, she had had always represented Frank, simply handing over money and picking up packages. They would meet, exchange a few words and then depart. This time she would be going for herself, and her request might put the frighteners on him. She'd no idea how he would react. She had to rely on the money she'd nicked from Frank. That was her only weapon to pull it off. Money always talked and made deals genuine. And he'd be greedy like the rest of them and wouldn't be able to resist it.

'Are you okay?' said Micky.

'Sorry, I was miles away.'

'You're tired. You get off home now. You've had to deal with a lot.'

'I'm dismissed,' she called across to Douglas who had had his screens pulled back.

'Quite right. You don't want to spend all day in a place like this. Not unless you have to.'

Cindy smiled and bent down to kiss Micky. 'Okay. I'll see you tomorrow.'

'Be careful now,' he said and shooed her away. When she got to the far end of the ward, she turned and waved. Then she was gone.

Chapter 16

Ellie pushed the key into her front door and went inside. Ellie was a good-looking woman. Her dark brown hair was naturally wavy and thick, and the bone structure of her face was the kind that many a model would die for. Her teeth were good and even, and she had an infectious, flashing smile. She was only thirty-seven but as she entered the house, at that moment, she felt and looked twice that age. She felt both physically and emotionally exhausted. She flopped back on to the sofa and closed her eyes. She'd given her all to Gus over the last eight years, but now it was going to come to nothing. She'd watched him change (she really wanted to use the word 'disintegrate'), from a cheerful, happy-go-lucky man with a generous nature, into a selfish, weak-kneed, heartless thug because of a sickening worship of a monster named Frank. Over the years she had begged and cajoled him to get away from him before it had all ended in disaster. Her efforts had achieved nothing. So be it. She had to think of herself as well. She'd told him she was going to her sister's in Devon, and that is exactly what she was going to do. She'd given in her notice at the hotel and had brought any outstanding bills up to date. Once she'd gone, Gus would have to handle everything himself. God knows how he would manage because he'd always left the running of their home affairs to her. He hadn't a clue. He'd very quickly have to find out what needed to be done.

They were tedious and boring, but everybody had to do them. Maybe his dear friend Frank would help him out.

She pushed herself off the sofa and went into the kitchen. A mobile phone rang. It was Gus's. She picked it up and looked at who was calling. Her jaw tightened with anger but decided to answer.

'What do you want?' she said in a cold, flat voice.

Frank's voice replied. 'Do you have to answer Gus's phone?'

Again, 'What do you want?'

'I want to speak to Gus.'

'You can't.'

'Why not?'

'Because he's not here.'

'Where is he?'

'He's in hospital.'

There was a long silence. Eventually: 'What's he doing there?'

'He's sick.'

'What d'you mean, sick?'

'His system's full of poison because of a dog bite.'

There was another long silence. Then: 'A dog bite?'

'That's right. But I'm sure you know all about that.'

'Why would I know? I'm not a dog and I didn't bite him.'

'No. If you bit him he'd probably be dead.'

'You want to watch your mouth.'

'And you want to clean yours out. Now piss off.' She snapped off the phone.

***

Cindy decided it was time to go. It would only take her about ten minutes to get to the gardens. She knew them well. Unless she'd been told otherwise, it had always been the place she had met Carl in the past. They were small gardens well-maintained by the council. The flower beds were kept immaculate and the lawn regularly mown. There was a small pond and fountain in the middle. Around the edges of the garden, there were seats and wooden benches. This time of year they were rarely busy. Occasionally people would walk through them, going from one place to another. When it was dark, as it was now, hardly anybody would be in there though they were open twenty-four hours a day.

She put on her thick warm coat that Micky had bought her and stuffed the £2000, which she'd wrapped in a polythene freezer bag, into one of the pockets. She had deliberately wrapped the money in a freezer bag so that Carl would be able to see the money without her taking it out to prove she'd really got it. She left a couple of lights on and went out.

The gardens were actually close to the shops, and there were still a number of people about even though it was Sunday. Later in the evening the town would become much more crowded with people going to the pubs and clubs. As soon as she reached the entrance to the gardens, she dismounted and pushed her bike along one of the paths that circumscribed the whole area. It was not so dark that she couldn't see around her. The fountain was turned off, and everywhere was quiet. She saw Carl sitting on a seat about twenty yards ahead. She couldn't see anybody else around. She took a deep breath to calm herself and then walked over to him. She rested her bicycle against the back of the seat and sat down next to him. For a long while there was silence.

Then he spoke. 'This had better be good.'

'Thanks for coming.'

'What do you want?'

'I want you to get me something.'

'You're not here for Frank. Can't be done.'

'Never mind about Frank. I want you to do business with me.'

He gave a snigger. 'And what makes you think I'd want to do that?'

'Money.'

There was a silence and then he turned his head slightly towards her with a disdainful smile.

'And you reckon you've got enough money?'

'That's right.'

He sighed as much as to say he was wasting his time.

'What is it you want for your money?'

'Firstly I want a gun.' Her voice remained flat and calm, and she noticed a sudden shift in his body. He hadn't expected this.

'You want a gun?'

'That's what I said.'

'What kind of a gun?' His tone was patronising.

'One that fires bullets.'

'Don't be smart-mouthed with me.'

'One that fires lots of bullets. Heavy maybe. A big gun.'

He sighed. He'd had enough of this rubbish. 'Go home, you stupid girl.'

She stood up. 'Fine. If you can't handle it, I'll go somewhere else.'

'Hang on.'

She hesitated for a few moments and then sat down again. 'And I shall want plenty of ammo to go with the gun. And don't try and tell me that's an extra.'

'Jesus, have you any idea how to load a gun, let alone shoot one?'

'Let me worry about that.' She sat down again.

'How much have you got?'

'That's not all I want.'

'You want more than a gun.'

'I want two hand grenades as well.'

'Jesus Christ! You starting a war?'

'Can you get them?' She still kept her voice cold and calm.

'You're crazy.'

She took the money out of her pocket and marginally held it out to him so that he could see it. 'There's £2000 if you get what I ask.'

He paused before speaking. 'Coming up in the world, aren't we.'

'I don't know what these things cost. Five hundred for all I know. I don't care what you do with it. Pay what you have to and keep the rest for yourself. This is between you and me.'

'I don't know that I can trust you.'

'No, you don't. And I don't know if I can trust you either.'

'There can be no comebacks. No tracing.'

'Of course. And when I say it's just between you and me, I mean that includes Frank.'

'These things are not that easy to get.'

'I want them tomorrow.'

'Impossible.'

She began to stand up again.

'Wait. Day after tomorrow. That's the best I can do.'

She didn't reply. She wanted them tomorrow before Micky got back. It made things harder once he was home. She'd have to make excuses for going out which sounded plausible, and that would be difficult. Still, she had to be realistic. It was probably asking a lot to expect him to get the weapons by tomorrow.

'Very well. The day after tomorrow. Tuesday.'

'Not here. There's a lay-by a couple of miles out of town on the A41 to Tewkesbury. Seven o'clock. The day after tomorrow.' He reached out for the money.

'You have this when I get what I want. Don't worry. You'll have it. There's one other thing. I've fixed an insurance. If I don't return after the deal's completed, then things will happen.'

'You said no one else knew about this.'

'They don't. I've left a sealed envelope that can be found. As soon as I get back, I'll destroy it. Nobody else will be the wiser.' It wasn't true of course, but he didn't know that.

He stared at her without speaking. Then he turned and walked away. As she watched him disappear, she could feel her heart pounding in her chest. Christ, had she actually pulled it off? Did she know what she had pulled off? Had she any idea what the hell she was getting into? Buying guns. Hand grenades. This was serious crime. She was getting into something way over her head. If anything went wrong, if she got caught, she would face a long prison sentence. Maybe she should pull out now before it was too late. Walk away. Call the whole thing off. She'd been lucky so far with the early stages of her hair-brained plan, but the worst part was yet to come. If she thought about that too much, it simply terrified her. And so it should because if it all went wrong then that would be the end of her. She wished she could share her worries with Micky. Tell him all about what she was doing. It was impossible of course. She could never do that. He'd a have a fit. And he'd never allow her to attempt it. No, she'd have to stick to her resolve and do what she had set out to do, in secret. She had to keep telling herself she could do it. That it only needed self-belief and nerve.

She put the money back in her pocket and set off for home. She needed a good night's rest.

Chapter 17

Micky laid back and stared at the ceiling. The lights had been turned down, and the ward was quiet. The day had dragged and been disappointing. Douglas had had an operation on his leg and was asleep. He was worried about Douglas. Life was going to be a bit different for him when he got out of hospital. He'd be okay, Micky knew that, because Dougie was that kind of guy. Any kind of difficulty that came along, he'd overcome and not make a fuss. He'd got a good wife too so they would support each other, but it wasn't going to be easy for them.

Micky had expected to have been going home today, but they'd discovered he'd a slight temperature and were concerned that he might have some bleeding from a badly bruised kidney. There was no cause for alarm, but it meant he would have to remain there for another two or three days. He'd had to tell Cindy who had visited earlier, but he didn't let her stay more than an hour because she needed to get back and rest after a busy day running the bar. At least she was fine and had seen no sign of Frank. But every day he remained in hospital meant that she was on her own, and the thought of something terrible happening to her constantly ground away at the back of his mind.

As it had not been possible to talk with Douglas very much because he was either in the theatre or sleeping, he had tried to distract himself by walking up the ward a couple of times to chat with some of the other patients. Two patients had gone home, but there was a new guy who had come in late yesterday afternoon. He didn't know what was wrong with him because, as often as not, many patients wanted to keep their conditions to themselves. One of the patients who had gone home earlier had said that he'd heard a nurse say something about the guy having a wound on his leg which had gone badly septic, causing what he assumed was blood poisoning. Whatever it was he was pretty sick, and when he had seen Micky, he had reacted as if was looking at a ghost.

'Do I look that strange?' Micky had joked.

'No, mate,' the guy had stuttered. 'No, no, of course not. Sorry. No offence.'

'None taken. Are you okay?'

'Yeah, yeah, I'm fine.'

He had thought the guy was terrified and wanted to give him some encouragement. 'You'll be out of here in no time. They look after you really well.'

'Yeah, I s'pose.'

'D'you live local?'

'Um... Um... well, yes and no. I mean I'm moving. Should have been on my way.'

'That's bad luck. Anywhere good?'

'Devon. Probably crazy, but my girlfriend is dragging me down there.'

'It's a nice county. Trust your girlfriend. They always know best. Anyway, good luck.'

Micky had walked away and chatted to other patients. He was grateful that, compared to most of them, his problem was small. But he felt frustrated at not being able to go home, especially as he felt so well. Cindy was having to run the bar on her own, and she was in constant danger.

He had to get out, and get out quick. In spite of his mind running wild with thoughts, he dropped off to sleep.

Next morning he woke very early. The lights were still down, and there was little activity. The night staff hadn't yet changed. He immediately began to wonder about whether he would be allowed home today. He'd had enough lying about.

He suddenly heard Douglas's voice. 'Hey, Micky, you awake?'

'Yeah. I thought you were still asleep.'

'Woke up ages ago.'

'How you feeling?'

'I've been better.'

'You in pain?'

'No. But I'm worried.'

'You'll be fine.'

'I shall get through this, yeah, but what the hell am I going to do when I get out of here?'

'You're strong, Dougie. You'll soon get fit and back to work.'

'Don't kid me, Micky. I can never go back to construction work. I'll be stuck with a desk job if I'm lucky. I'm no good at that. Haven't got the brains.'

'That's bollocks. You may not be as good as you were, but you'll still be good. You've got a lot of experience.'

'Won't be enough. I'll find work, but it won't pay the same. I want the kids to go to uni. That costs a fortune today. I don't want them taking out bloody great loans.'

'Wait and see. It's early days. You could recover nearly hundred percent,' Micky tried to encourage.

'If I'd been injured at work, things would be different. I'll get nothing out of this.'

Micky didn't reply. What could he say? He wasn't going to insult him by saying he had nothing to worry about. He knew as well as Dougie that things were going to be tough for him. The really galling thing for Dougie was that there would be no compensation. Where would it come from? Nowhere. The villains had done a runner, and there would have been no insurance anyway. Maybe he was being too pessimistic. Maybe Dougie wouldn't be too much of a cripple. If he ended up with no more than a slight limp, then maybe he could go back to his old job. He could still be very active, and he was very strong. Dougie was a fighter all right and wouldn't throw in the towel unless he had absolutely no choice. He began to feel angry. Those bastards had done a terrible thing and had got away with it. If only there was some way of proving they were responsible, some way of making them pay. If only there was some piece of evidence that they had overlooked which now came to light so that they could stick the guilt on them. He sighed. Thinking like this was just going round in circles. He threw back the bedclothes.

'I'm going for a pee,' he said and eased his feet on the ground. He slowly made his way up the ward and stopped when he reached the last bed. The screens were pulled round it, but the porters were wheeling out a stretcher. On it was a body covered by a sheet from head to toe. He watched them as they pushed it out into the corridor. A nurse began stripping the bed.

He caught her attention. 'Did he…?' he whispered.

She nodded. 'It was not expected, but these things happen. Sepsis. He was too far gone when he came in.'

'Poor chap. He was hoping to start a new life in Devon with his girlfriend.'

He stood for a moment then carried on walking to the toilet.

***

During her short life, Cindy had experienced many days of tension and fear, but she'd never experienced anything like she had experienced today. Even the customers at the bar had noticed she was jittery and making mistakes with their orders. She'd been friendly but seemed on another planet. They had all thought it was due to her being worried about Micky, which was understandable, and had brushed it aside without making comment. But her concerns hadn't been about Micky. They had been because of her worries about closing the deal with Carl that night, and then she was going to carry out the final stage of her plan. As the day had worn on, thoughts of disaster had thrashed around in her mind. Her mood constantly changed. One minute it was buoyant with confidence, the next full of failure and terror. She kept telling herself she had to get a grip. If she was going to be in is such a state of panic before she even set off, she'd forget something or become sloppy and make some dreadful mistake which would turn the whole thing into disaster. She'd gone over what she had to do a thousand times, but she still worried that she could have easily overlooked something. It might be something small and totally unexpected, but it might make all the difference to success or failure. And she would need lots of luck. So far she'd had it, but it couldn't last forever. She knew it was bad policy to rely so heavily on luck, but what option did she have? It was either that or give up the whole idea. But if she did that, it would mean she'd have to sit around day after day, looking over her shoulder, waiting for Frank to come and get her. And he would get her, she had no doubt about that. Micky would try to protect her, but it wouldn't be enough. Frank could take his time and pick his moment. It would be so simple for him. Well, she wasn't going to let that happen. He'd be totally unprepared for her to try anything. He would think she was some stupid female who was incapable of trying an attack on him, let alone dreaming up how to do it. Big mistake. She was going to show him just how wrong he was.

As soon as she'd got back from visiting Micky on her way home after closing the bar, she'd got herself a quick snack and hot drink. She had really needed a proper meal, but she felt too sick with nerves to attempt that. It had been a struggle to even eat a sandwich with a hot drink of coffee.

She collected her canvas knapsack, which the woman from the garage had given her. During the day, she had managed to find a quiet moment and slip across to Clarkes. She bought a reel of 50mm wide duct tape and a 12m length of 6mm nylon rope. On her way home, she had called in to a chemist shop and bought some surgical rubber gloves and then gone on to Tesco and bought a couple of basic mobile phones that were on offer. She'd purchased a SIM card and paid out £10 to provide pay-as-you-go. She put all the items in the bag with Micky's baseball bat. She pulled on her warm coat and put the bundle of money in her pocket. It was twenty-five minutes to seven. The lay-by where she was going to meet Carl was two miles out of town, but by the time she had crossed town, the overall distance would be nearer three. If she took it steady she'd be there by 7 o'clock. She turned off the lights and stood for a few moments in the dark. Amazingly she began to feel calmer than she had experienced all day. Right. This was it.

She stepped outside, shutting the door behind her. It had been pouring with rain all day, but for the moment it had reduced to a murky drizzle. She particularly noticed that the thermometer hanging on the outside wall of the bar had not dropped below 10°C, which was not cold for February, and the weather forecast had suggested it would remain much the same all night. She smiled to herself. It was only fair that Frank should have a little bit of luck. She couldn't expect to have everything her own way. She slung the knapsack across her back and set off.

As she had anticipated, it took her just under twenty-five minutes to reach the lay-by where she'd agreed to meet Carl. In spite of keeping her mind focused on what she was doing, she still kept a wary eye open for anything suspicious that might warn her Frank was close by or ready to jump her. The lay-by was on a stretch of dual carriageway alongside farmland. There was only moderate traffic on the road at the best of times and even less in the evening or at night.

As she drew near she saw a car parked without any lights on it. She glided up slowly behind it and dismounted. She could see the shape of a man in the driver's seat. He wasn't moving or turning to beckon her. She laid her bicycle on the ground and slipped her knapsack off. She moved round to the passenger side of the car, tapped on the window and then opened the door. She was relieved to see it was Carl sitting there. She slipped into the passenger seat, holding her knapsack on her lap, and shut the door.

'Have you got the money?'

'Have you got the weapons?'

He half turned and reached for a holdall on the back seat. He lifted it over and rested it on his lap.

'Where's the money?'

'Let me see what I'm buying.'

He unzipped the bag and lifted out a handgun which he rested on his knee. Then he took out the two hand grenades. 'I don't like handling this stuff. I don't trust it,' He put the grenades and gun back into the bag and zipped it up.

'What kind of gun is it? Is it good?'

'It's a Ruger SR40 pistol. There are four magazines in the bag. It's good.'

'Magazines?'

He frowned and raised his eyebrows in disdain. 'The ammo. They each hold fifteen rounds.'

265

It sounded good to her, but what the hell did she know? It was a gun, and that's all the mattered. She took the bundle of notes in the plastic bag out of her pocket and handed it to him. He opened the bag and took the money out which was made up of £20 notes.

He flicked through the bundles to check there was no fiction amongst it, followed by a cursory count. He nodded satisfaction. He dumped the holdall with the weapons in it on her lap. 'You can have the bag, no extra charge.'

'You won't see me again,' said Cindy and put her hand on the door catch.

'I hope I don't,' he replied.

She pushed open the door and stepped outside carrying her knapsack and the holdall. She shut the door and banged on the roof. A moment later he turned on the engine and pulled out on to the road. No other cars came by. She watched him disappear in the distance. She took her surgical gloves out of her pocket and put them on. She took the automatic weapon, hand grenades and ammunition out of the hold all and transferred them to her knapsack. She flung the holdall over the side of bushes in the adjoining field. She took the gloves off and put them back in her pocket. She paused for a moment as she contemplated what was now in her possession. If she got stopped by the police, the crime of carrying a knife would sound laughable compared to what she had. She had to get off the lay-by. She was too conspicuous. Just cycling along the road wouldn't draw any attention. She slung the knapsack on her back and set off. She had originally planned to go home first and then go to Frank's later but now decided there wasn't any point in that. Her blood was pumping. The adrenaline was up. She would go straight to Frank's and get the thing done. She knew that Tuesday was a night he usually stayed home on his own. Even Lenny stayed away. His usual practice was to get a DVD and drink a lot of beer, even falling asleep on the sofa until 2 or 3 o'clock in the morning. It had always been a time when she herself had kept out of his way, and he had never bothered to check up what she might be up to. Usually she had stayed in her room and gone to bed.

It was a dark night and this part of the road had no street lighting. Visibility was worse because of the murky fine drizzle which hung over the area like a cloak. The lamp on the front of her bicycle made a narrow shaft of light as it pierced the gloom. The occasional car swooped past making her keep tight into the kerb. The last thing she wanted was to have an accident at this stage of the game. Her thoughts were in turmoil as she realised how far she had got with her plan. She was committed now and she couldn't pull out even if she wanted to.

She hadn't gone very far before she suddenly became aware that the headlights of a car behind her hadn't moved on and passed her. There wasn't a vehicle coming towards them so there was no reason for it not to pull out and overtake her. Irrationally she pushed hard on the pedals and half looked back but she couldn't see anything except that the glare of the headlights shone on her faced. In a sudden surge of panic she realised that the vehicle behind her was deliberately following her. Why? Christ, was it Frank? No, it couldn't be. Or could it? Had Carl ratted on her after all and told him what was going on? Why would he do that? He'd nothing to gain. He'd got two thousand quid in his pocket. He wouldn't want to jeopardise that. There was a sudden single blast from a police siren indicating that she had to stop. The police?! Jesus, why were they following her? She'd had it. The game was up. They were on to her. Carl had done the dirty. He'd made an anonymous call and they were definitely on to her. He was in the clear with two thousand quid and she was going to end up in prison with a minimum stretch of twenty five. For a few moments she kept peddling as if pretending she hadn't heard or didn't know what she was supposed to do. Oh Micky, what the hell had she got herself into? He'd be devastated. There was nothing for it. She'd have to face the consequences and it served her right. She squeezed the brakes and pulled into the kerb. The police car stopped behind her, still with its headlights on and the blue light flashing on the roof. There were fields on her left. Maybe she could make a run for it. She was fast. They'd never catch her. They didn't know who she was. They hadn't seen her face. They wouldn't have a clue. She'd be far away and there'd be no comebacks. Stupid girl. Making a run for it was the worst thing she could do. The headlights were suddenly doused. The side lights remained on and the blue light continued flashing. There was no pavement so she held her bike and stood back on to a narrow verge. She slipped off the knapsack and put it on the ground by her feet. Maybe they wouldn't notice it. Again, stupid girl. They'd want to know what was in it all right. A moment passed and then the passenger door opened and a policeman stepped into the road. Her heart crashed around in her chest as she watched him put on his hat and walk towards her.

'Do you want to get yourself killed miss?' There was no smile on his face but his voice was not unpleasant.

'Sorry?'

'You've no rear light on your bicycle. This is a fast road. Dark. Weather like this you could easily get run down.'

'No light? But I have…?' suddenly confused she looked down at the light unit on the rear of her bike but nothing shone from it. 'Well, it was working when I set off.' She bent down and banged it with her fist. Immediately a red glow sprang to life. 'Sorry, I didn't know it had gone out.'

'It'll be the connection. You'd better get it fixed when you get home. Have you got far to go?'

'No. Just a few minutes from here. I'm really sorry.'

'Okay. Just be sure you get it fixed.'

'I will, yes. Thank you.'

He bent down and lifted up her knapsack,

'Heavy.'

'I can manage.'

'Here.' He lifted the knapsack up to her and helped her sling it on her back.

'Books'

'Hmmmm,' he nodded. 'Student?'

'Er...yes.'

'You take care.'

'Yes, I will. Thanks.'

He nodded again and turned back to his car. She waited a few moments and gave a brief wave as the car moved off. She realised her hands were shaking and grasped the handlebars tightly to try and get them under control. Jesus Christ, this was becoming a nightmare. She'd got the wrong temperament for this kind of thing. Still, it was no good whining now. She'd have to pull herself together. If she didn't see it through and get Frank she was a gonner. Well that settled it. She clamped her jaw tight and pushed off.

It took her just over twenty-five minutes to reach the entrance to Cherry Tree Road. The murky drizzle had persisted and begun to descend like a cloak and made it look forbidding and eerie in the poor street lighting. She dismounted and pushed her cycle to the first house, which was still deserted. She moved round the back of the fir tree in the front garden and laid it down. There was no point in delaying and begin doubting her plan. She'd gone over it in her mind hundreds of times and knew exactly what she had to do. She moved to the pavement and checked that the road was empty. It was clear. Keeping close to the boundary fences – those that hadn't been broken down – she made her way to Frank's house. She noted with satisfaction that lights were on and his car was parked outside. She turned into the passageway that divided it from the neighbouring empty house. She paused to calm herself. She smiled at the rusty window through which she had climbed when she last broke in. Her plan was different tonight. She moved down to the 6ft high wooden gate and put her knapsack on the ground. She caught hold of the top of the fence and pulled herself up and dropped down the other side. She could see that the kitchen light was on, but the room was empty. She slipped the bolt on the gate, opened it and collected her knapsack. She stood back in the garden and shut the gate again. She undid the knapsack and placed it on the ground against the bottom of the boundary fence. Everything inside it was ready. For a few moments she stood quietly, taking in deep breaths and exhaling slowly. At last she was ready. She picked up a small stone and threw it at the window. It seemed to make a deafening clatter in the stillness, but it caused no movement in the house. She picked up another stone and threw it. This time she could see Frank coming into the kitchen and look around. Because the light was on, he could only look into blackness outside. She picked up another stone and threw it at the window. She could see then that he realised something was being thrown at the window. She watched him move forward to the back door and open it. Immediately a shaft of light reflected on the fine drizzle and spread down the garden, and although it wasn't bright, it managed to pick out, what appeared to Frank, a dark form that he couldn't immediately identify. He squinted in confusion at the ghostlike shape, which he instinctively knew must be a person standing at the bottom, facing the house. Frank stepped outside and stared down the shaft of light. Cindy could tell that, at first, he couldn't quite comprehend what he was seeing. She appeared as a lone figure standing in the darkness and murky drizzle. Who was this figure, what was it doing there and how the hell did it get there? But then he took a step forward and he could immediately see who it was.

'You!' It was a roar of anger but came out as a hiss.

'Yes, Frank. It's me, Cindy.' She saw him hesitate and try to look into the darkness left and right of the shaft of light to see if she was alone. 'It's all right, Frank. It's only me.'

He gave a quiet chuckle. 'Got you this time.'

She didn't move but stood quite still, her hands gently clasped behind her back.

'No, Frank. You haven't got me.'

'How the fuck did you get in?'

'I climbed the fence, of course.'

'You won't escape. You're dead.'

'Don't you want to know why I've come?'

'I don't really care.'

'But you should do. It'll be of big interest to you.'

His prime instinct was to charge forward and beat her to the ground with a single blow and then drag her into the house where he could take his time on deciding what particular punishment he would inflict on her. But there was something about her stance, her calmness and the total unexpectedness of seeing her there that caused him to hesitate. She couldn't get away, so he could afford to take his time.

'I don't think anything you say will be of interest to me.'

'I've brought you two messages.'

'Messages?' Although he replied with a sneer and his usual smug bravado, he couldn't conceal the hesitancy in his voice.

'Yes.'

'I'm not interested in your messages.' He took a menacing step forward.

'Hold it!' She was surprised at the bark in her own voice.

Frank stood still, surprised and taken aback.

'You must hear the messages first.'

'What are these fucking messages? What are you on about? Who are they from?'

'The first one is from Murphy.'

'Murphy?! He's a fucking dog.'

'Yes. He wants you to know that he was very upset by the way you treated him. Making him stay out here in the garden in freezing rain with a kennel that had holes in the roof and no bedding. He had to stand or lie in squelching mud and his own shit. He wants you to know that it was terrible for him, and he's very annoyed.'

'You're crazy.'

'And so he's asked me to come to you and give you the same treatment so that you know what he had to suffer.'

Frank took two more menacing steps closer. 'You skinny piece of shit, don't try and take the piss with me.'

'Wait! You haven't heard the second message. It's from the big man who you tried to kill by running him down because you were too cowardly to face him man-to-man, and also it's from my boyfriend because you and your pieces of shit beat him up. They want you to know that they are going to be all right but that you are now going to have to pay.'

Frank made no reply other than to give a roar and leap forward to grab her. In a flash her arm came round from her back and shot forward like a piston. In her hand was the pepper spray. She immediately released a blast of it into his face from only 12 inches away. He let out a terrifying scream and threw up his hands to his face. He doubled over, holding his head in his hands and gasping for breath as he struggled with his breathing.

'I can't see! I can't see! You've blinded me you bitch!' His words came out in choking gasps as he fought for breath and he rolled around, not knowing which way to turn. Cindy calmly reached down into her knapsack and lifted out Micky's baseball bat. She moved up behind Frank and gave an almighty swipe across the back of his legs, catching him just above the back of his knees. He let out another scream amid his choking and coughing and fell down onto his knees in the mud, all the while holding his hands up to his face. His wailing and coughing continued remorselessly. He was completely defenceless. Cindy reached down into the knapsack and took out the reel of duct tape and moved round to behind him. Quickly grabbing his trousers, she forced his legs together and deftly wound the tape round his ankles several times. She knew that now he was down and secured at the ankles, he would not be able to get up. It was an extra precaution because she knew he wouldn't have been able to catch her anyway because the spray had temporarily almost blinded him. There was no longer need for panic or rush. She had him at her mercy. Once again she reached into the knapsack and took out the 12-metre length of rope. Taking one end she made a slipknot and created a large loop similar to a hangman's noose. She picked up the baseball bat again and whacked it across the back of his hands that still covered his face. For a second he dropped them with a scream of pain, and as he did so she slipped the noose over his head and pulled. His head jerked backward. She wound the loose end of the rope between his ankles and wrapped it round them two or three times to make it secure. He could almost straighten his body from the knees but he couldn't lean forward very far without tightening the rope round his neck.

'I don't think you are going to kill me now, Frank, do you?' She pushed him with her foot, and he rolled on to his side in the mud. 'I know how you must be feeling, and that's just how poor Murphy felt.' He continued to choke and gasp for breath. 'You mustn't worry about your eyes, Frank. The effects will wear off in about forty-five minutes, maybe an hour. Doing that to you was a necessary part of my plan. But you understand that sometimes these things are necessary.'

Again she took the roll of duct tape and, knocking his hands away from his face, quickly slapped it across his mouth and jerked it round the whole circumference of his head. 'Don't want you screaming out too loudly. Might disturb the neighbours, and that wouldn't be very considerate.' She cut the tape, and as he put his hands up to his face again, she slipped it round his wrists. Once she'd got it round once, she had better control and wound it round another three or four times. 'Nearly done, Frank. Just one more thing. How do you think I'm doing? I'm doing well, aren't I? Not bad for a skinny little bitch.'

She took the length of excess rope, trailing from his ankles, and slipped it under the bottom of the 6ft gate. She stepped outside, threw the end over the top and then came back in and pulled the latch down to shut the gate securely. There was no way he'd be able to lift it. Then she pulled the loose end of the rope down and tied it to the rope where it ran under the gate. 'I've left you a bit of movement, Frank, but I don't want you wandering around the garden. I'm probably being over-cautious but better to be really careful, don't you think?'

Frank could only respond by making pathetic sounds.

'All I need now, Frank, is your mobile phone.' She felt around in his pockets until she found it. 'I'm not going to steal it, Frank. I wouldn't do anything like that. I'm just going to turn it off in case some of your buddies ring you. Not that you could do much. Silly me. I'm being over-cautious again. Still, what can you expect? I'm only a pathetic female. Right, I'm going home now Frank. Much warmer indoors. Still, you'll manage out here just as Murphy had to. You're lucky though, Frank, because the weather's not freezing tonight. Still, it won't be very pleasant, and I don't want to kill you anyway. I've got other plans for you. This'll just give you enough discomfort for you to crave the arrival of morning when you might hope for rescue. Of course that may not come, and you'd be stuck here for days. Bye, Frank. I'll see myself out.'

She put the baseball bat and remains of the duct tape back in her knapsack and moved over to the back door. Before going in she slipped off her shoes and put them in a plastic bag which she took out of her knapsack. Once inside she closed the door. So far, so good. She put her hand in her pocket, took out the rubber surgical gloves and put them on. She looked down at her hands and wondered if she was being dramatic. Did she need them? Probably not. She'd seen them do it too many times in thrillers on TV. Still, it was fun. Added to the excitement. She turned off the kitchen light and then made her way to the box room. The door was closed but not locked. Why would it be? No one else lived in the house. She turned on the light. She put her knapsack down and looked around. She knew what she was looking for and was pretty certain where to look. She took a couple of paces to the bookcase and reached behind. She immediately felt Frank's baseball bat and pulled it out. She inspected the end. Just as she had expected – blood stains. And she knew whose blood that would be. Stupid, arrogant Frank. He should have wiped it clean. Plenty of DNA there. She put the bat down and rolled back the carpet to expose the loose floorboards. She lifted them up and put them on one side. Firstly, she took out the large bundle of money wrapped in the plastic bag. She undid it and lifted out the money. It was made up in bundles, which she could tell were each £1000. There were fifty-four bundles. Even more than she had realised. She pondered for a little while, wondering how much to take. She needed to leave some to make the evidence she was leaving as bad as she could. She put forty-two bundles in the knapsack, two in her pocket, and the remaining ten back under the floor boards. She didn't touch the drugs but was glad to see that he must have recently stocked up. She picked up the baseball bat and laid it alongside the drugs. She took out the little notepad and flipped through the pages. She glanced through the lists of names. Some were crossed out and others had ticks against them. She flipped through until the last page, which was blank. She took a biro off his desk, printed '68 Vernon Street' and put a tick against it and a jagged line through it. Underneath she printed Micky's Burger Bar and put a tick against it and a similar jagged line. She smiled. Unless the police were completely dumb, they'd work it out. She put the notebook back. Finally she took the automatic gun and magazines and the two grenades and baseball bat and placed them under the floorboards. She replaced the boards and rolled back the carpet. Right. She'd done everything, and it had only taken her a couple of minutes. She looked about her to check that nothing had been disturbed and that there was no mud on the carpet or any sign that would suggest the room had been entered or tampered with. She didn't want Frank going in there and finding out about his presents before she was ready. She turned off the light and closed the door behind her. She went into the living room and turned the volume of the television down but didn't turn it off. There was a small table light on, but she left it. She came out of the room and moved down to the front door. She opened it and stepped outside. It was still drizzling. That was okay. Frank wouldn't freeze to death, but it would be cold enough for him to think about poor Murphy. Perhaps he'd roll in the mud to keep warm like lots of animals did. She put her outdoor shoes on again and closed the door. She slung her knapsack over her back and walked off back down the road. She saw no one. She collected her bicycle and set off home. She didn't bother to keep a wary eye open for Frank. Even he didn't have enough tricks in his bag to allow him to jump out of the road in front of her. All the way home she kept her head down and her eyes on the road in front of her, keeping her mind blank. There would be time enough to go over everything later. As soon as she reached home, she pushed her bicycle into the shed and then went into the house. She took off her coat and quickly put a match to the fire. The dry kindling wood quickly sparked and crackled, giving the room a welcoming glow. She boiled the kettle and made herself a coffee, then sat down with it in front of the fire. She flopped back and closed her eyes. Her heart was beating quietly, but she felt ill. Not ill exactly. More like a strange feeling that she had never experienced before. She instinctively knew there wasn't anything physically wrong with her, so it had to be in her mind. She was in shock. That was it. It had to be. A reaction to suddenly realising the enormity of what she had just carried out. She felt an overwhelming compulsion to pull herself away from her emotional motivation and look at it dispassionately as one would from outside. In spite of her desperate efforts to resist this, she found an irresistible force dragging her back to confront the truth of what she had done and been capable of. Not only had she involved herself with villains of serious crime, acquiring weapons that were manufactured for the purpose of maiming or killing others, but she had engineered the infliction of pain and suffering on a fellow human being. She had carried it out with cold and calculating efficiency. True, she regarded Frank as a monster, but that made no difference. What kind of person could do that? Surely only a cruel and sadistic specimen of humanity. Was that her? Was that what she had allowed herself to become? Had she become so consumed with hatred for Frank that she could now behave in exactly the same way as he did? She screwed up her eyes and squeezed the fingers of one hand into the other, in torment at the

277

sudden spectre of what she might be. Were such feelings of self-hatred enough in mitigation to exonerate her actions? Were her feelings of regret sufficient? Yet in her heart of hearts, she had no regrets. She had found courage and belief in her cause. She was a tiny warrior of justice who had administered revenge for those she loved and put in place the trap that would, in the end, remove some vermin from society. It had demanded of her a strength that she had not known she possessed. The deed was almost done. Let it proceed to its final end so she could hear trumpets in her ears. She leaned forward and threw a log on the fire. Sparks exploded and she smiled.

***

Cindy woke early. She got up straight away and showered. She'd slept soundly, although she had not expected to, thinking that the events of the night before would keep going round and round in her head. As she got herself some breakfast, she felt calm, relaxed. She'd almost completed her plan, and it had gone without a hitch. The knowledge that Frank wouldn't be able to get her was a big relief. She would give Lenny a quick call later, and he could go and rescue his leader. What a shock he was going to get.

As soon as she'd finished her breakfast, she collected the bundle of money she'd taken from Frank and put it on the kitchen table. She pondered. Forty-four grand. Well, she would need two thousand for herself. That should cover everything. She had to buy two more items on the way home later, but they wouldn't cost much. By the time she'd finished, she'd probably have a few pounds over. She gathered the other forty-two bundles together and wrapped them up neatly in brown paper, sealing the package with Sellotape. She put the package in her knapsack and saw the surgical gloves in there with Micky's baseball bat. She'd forgotten about those items. That was sloppy. Still, it wasn't a big mistake, and it was excusable considering the stress she'd put herself through last night. She would easily dispose of the gloves in a litter bin on the way to the bar that morning, and she'd throw the baseball bat back in the shed when she collected her bicycle. Right. That was everything. It was time to go.

Chapter 18

It was just after ten past nine when Lenny woke to hear his mobile phone bleeping. He slowly threw back the blanket and reached for the phone. He opened the text messages to see who was calling, but there was no name. He opened it up and read: 'Get to Frank. He's in big trouble. Enter by side gate.' The caller left no name. Lenny swung his legs off the bed and scratched his head. What the hell was that kind of message? Some stupid wind up? He tried to get his thoughts together. He wasn't thinking properly. It was too early in the morning. He threw his phone on the bed and went into the shower. Ten minutes later he was out, dried and properly awake. He picked up his mobile and decided to check it out. He flipped Frank's number and waited. Nothing. The damn fool. He'd turned it off. He went back to the message and read it again. There was nothing for it. He would have to get round there and see if some idiot was playing silly buggers. He made a quick cup of tea, scoffed a piece of toast and then went out to his motorbike. It had drizzled most of the night, but now it had stopped and only dark clouds drifted across the sky.

It took him only five minutes to get to Frank's. He parked his bike in the front garden and looked up at the house. It looked quiet enough. He noted that Frank's car was parked outside, so he should be at home. He rattled the front door knocker and called Frank's name through the letterbox. He heard nothing. The message had said enter by the side gate. He'd never done that before, and it was always locked anyway. He shrugged and walked down the passageway between the two houses until he reached the gate. Immediately he spotted the piece of rope coming from underneath and carrying on up over the top. He tried the latch and felt the gate shift, telling him it wasn't bolted. He suddenly became wary and eased it inwards slowly. He only had to open it a foot wide before he saw the trussed up body of Frank lying hunched in the mud. He instantly stopped dead in shock and tried to register some glimmer of comprehension of what he was looking at. Then he leapt into action, jumping to Frank's side.

'Frank! Jesus Christ!' He ran round to face him and unwound the tape going round his head and covering his mouth. 'Who did this?!'

Frank moved his lips but made no sound. He half opened his eyes with heavy lids, and he leaned heavily into Lenny's side. 'You must be frozen. Got to get you inside and warmed up. You're plastered in muck. They're bastards who did this.'

He took a penknife from his pocket and cut the tape round Frank's ankles and hands and then slipped the rope that was round his neck back over his head. 'I'm going to get you inside, Frank. How long have you been here?' Lenny slipped his arm round Frank's back and dragged him to his feet. Frank managed to find enough strength in his legs to hold himself up, but his joints had almost seized because of the almost fixed position he had remained in during the night. By hanging on to Lenny, he got through the kitchen door and along to the living room where he eased himself down on to the sofa. 'Let's get these shoes and clothes off. You're plastered in mud and shit. Christ, you stink.' This stuff will have to be burnt.' Frank made no resistance as Lenny took off his shoes and clothes. 'Back in a sec.' He ran upstairs where he rummaged through drawers in Frank's bedroom until he found clean trousers and heavy sweaters and then, with the blankets which he pulled off Frank's bed, ran back down stairs. He pulled Frank's filthy clothes off and threw them on the floor. He piled the blankets over him and got him to lie back on the sofa. 'You're not too bad, mate. You'll soon warm up,' said Lenny, hiding his concern. Frank made a weak attempt at being dismissive at Lenny's fussing by holding up his hand and grunting, but he was savvy enough to know that he would be in deep shit without Lenny's help.

'Drinks, that's it, I'll get hot drinks going.' He moved into the kitchen and filled the kettle to make tea. While it was heating up, he found an electric fire that Frank kept under the stairs and put that on close to Frank's trembling body. As soon as the kettle had boiled, he made tea and poured two mugs, with lots of sugar in Frank's. He handed him a mug, and he managed to reach for it with trembling hands and hold it unsteadily to his mouth. He gave a mild cough as the liquid caught in his throat, but Lenny took it as a sign that he was fighting back. He pulled up a chair close to the sofa where he could watch Frank for signs of improvement and also try to give him encouragement by saying he was going to be okay, whilst at the same time swearing and cursing those who had carried out this heinous crime, and what would be done to them to make them pay.

***

Cindy was grateful that she had been busy all day. It had helped her to keep her mind off what she had done the previous night. Everyone enquired as to Micky's progress and asked for their good wishes to be passed on. Occasionally, when there was a lull in customers, her mind wandered back to everything that had happened the night before. She knew that Lenny would have rushed round to

Frank's after she had sent him the text and discovered him trussed up like a chicken. Once he'd got him into the house, Frank would gradually thaw out as the day went on. His sight would be back to normal, and tomorrow he'd be fit enough to come after her. That was all right with her. She'd already laid the trap to beat him to it. There was a possibility that he would go into his box room and lift the floorboards to see if everything was there, but it was unlikely. He'd have no reason to suspect anything. He was still under the impression that she knew nothing about his hiding place, and he'd be far too preoccupied with getting over the previous night's ordeal to think about anything else. By evening he would be raging with anger and planning what he was going to do to her. After tomorrow it would be too late.

At 3 o'clock Micky came through on her mobile. 'How are you, Micky?'

Micky's voice replied, 'I'm coming home.'

'That's wonderful.' Her face lit up with excitement.

'I'm in the clear. Julie's going to give me a lift.'

'Good on her. I can't wait. What time are you coming?'

'I'll be home by five. Will you be back?'

'Soon after. I've just got to get some bits.'

'Don't be long. See you later.'

'Can't wait. Bye.'

She pondered for a few moments. With Micky coming home that afternoon, she'd have to get everything finished off quickly, which meant she needed to finish early so that she would have time to make her calls.

Almost as if a guardian angel knew what she needed and was looking after her, the customers fell away earlier than usual, and although she expected there would be the odd one or two that would drift in until late, she decided to close up shop and they'd just have to be disappointed. She cleared the deck, put everything away so that it would be shipshape for the next day and then locked up. She collected her knapsack and checked that the £42,000, which she had wrapped up in brown paper before setting off first thing, was still there. Of course it would be, but she still felt the need to check. As soon as she got outside, she pulled out a plastic crate from under the bar. She moved over to her bicycle and managed to secure it to the handlebars with some thick string. She placed an old blanket in the bottom and had decided to use it to carry Murphy home when she collected him from the animal shelter rather than worry Bob for the use of his car. Satisfied that it was secure enough, she set off. Firstly she headed for the town centre and then directly to a hair salon, the kind of which she had never entered in her life. In fact, she'd never been in any salon but assumed that what she needed she would find in the one she had selected. There was the odd smell of shampoos and hair conditioners filling the air and the tinkling sound of chatter and laughter from women sitting in chairs having their hair put through torture. At least that's how Cindy viewed it, except that she knew there was no feeling in hair. There was a heavily made up woman behind a counter at the far end of the salon, and Cindy went up to her. She noticed that the woman didn't make a very good job of concealing the way she looked Cindy up and down.

'I'm afraid we can't take any more customers today,' said the woman with a poker face.

'I don't want my hair done, thank you. I want a wig.'

'A wig?' The woman's eyes opened in surprise. 'What kind of wig?'

'One that goes on my head.'

The woman glowered in response but did not comment. 'Of course. I understand. But do you want it long or short, blond or dark?'

'I don't mind what colour. I want it to make me look completely different. With a fringe might be a good idea.'

'We have several to choose from. If you'd like to go into the booth, I'll bring some in.'

She indicated a booth at the opposite side of the salon to where the women were having their hair done. Cindy pushed back the curtain and went in to be confronted by a massive mirror on the wall in front of her. A moment later the assistant came in with an armful of wigs. She handed her one that was long and black with lots of waves. Cindy pushed her hair up and pulled it on. She moved her head from side to side to try and get an all-round view from the mirror but quickly made up her mind she didn't like it and took it off. On the fourth try she found one, mid-brown in colour. It had a fringe which reached down below her eyebrows, but just above her eyes, and the back of it to just above her collar. It was thick and wavy and made her look very different. The transformation surprised her.

'What do you think?' she asked the assistant.

'Very fetching, but not cheap.'

'I'll have it.'

'That'll be a hundred and twenty five pounds,' said the assistant smugly, expecting Cindy to look at her in shock and change her mind.

'Fine. Can you see that I've got it on properly please? I want to wear it out now.'

The assistant suddenly gave a warm smile and started pushing her fingers round Cindy's head to make sure her own hair was concealed.

Cindy concealed her contempt for the woman's supercilious attitude but retaliated by taking out a wad of notes from her pocket with exaggerated show and peeling off seven £20 notes which she handed to the assistant. The parcel containing £42,000 was still in her knapsack. The assistant went out and came back with £15 change.

'Thanks,' said Cindy and walked out.

Once outside she paused and smiled to herself. Hmm, she thought she looked rather nice. Maybe there was something in this beauty game after all. She collected her bicycle and pushed it along the pavement past half a dozen shops until she reached the opticians. She rested her bicycle and went in. There was a huge array of spectacle frames fixed to the walls. The shop was empty, and an assistant immediately approached her.

'Can I help you?'

'I want a pair of thick rimmed glasses with plain glass. It's for a disguise.'

The assistant was surprised at the blunt request but did her best to conceal it. 'I'm sure we can find something for you.' She moved back to behind her counter, opened a small cabinet and took out a dark spectacle frame with large lenses. Cindy took them and tried them on. Tiny bit big, but good enough.

'They'll do. How much?'

'Forty two pounds."

'Okay.' She pulled out her wad of notes and gave the assistant two £20 notes and a £5 note. She gave the money to the assistant who put it in the till and then gave her back change.

'Thank you.' She walked out of the shop.

Right. She was ready to make her first call. She put the spectacles in her pocket, worried that they might drop off, and then set off through town. Fifteen minutes later she pulled into Vernon Street. She cycled someway down it and stopped at number 40. She dismounted and leant her bike against a front garden wall. She took the brown paper parcel out of her knapsack, smoothed her coat, put on the spectacles and walked down to number 68. She was pretty sure Julie would be out at the hospital visiting Douglas and waiting to take Micky home. She hoped that the two children would be at home.

She walked up the front garden path and rang the front door bell. Julie's daughter, Lizzie, opened the door.

Cindy said, 'Hallo. I've got a parcel here for your mum and dad.'

'Oh, thank you,' said Lizzie reaching for it. 'My mum's visiting dad at the hospital at the moment. Who shall I say it's from?'

'Well, they don't know me. Just tell them that I'm someone who recently won the lottery. I'm just helping out one or two people who I've heard about who have fallen on bad times.' She could see that Lizzie was momentarily knocked off balance and stuck for words.

'Oh gosh. Well he was run over you see and…'

'Yes, I know.'

'Will you come in? Mum will be home soon.'

'No, thank you. I have to be on my way.' Cindy began to turn away.

'Can you give me your name?'

'No need,' said Cindy with a wave of her hand as she hurriedly walked away down the front path and back up the street to her bicycle. She removed her wig and spectacles before mounting it and sped off back towards town. She couldn't stop smiling. That went well. Thank you, Frank. That was kind of you. She would love to see the look on Julie's and Dougie's faces when they opened the parcel, but she'd just have to imagine it. It would remain a mystery to them where the money came from, but of course they must never know the truth. After the initial surprise they would gradually accept that it had simply come from a generous lottery winner. She was certain that Julie's daughter didn't recognise her.

She was soon back in town and quickly headed for St Catherine Walk. As soon as she got there, she made her way into the vet office where she had taken Murphy when he was injured. There were a number of pet owners with their animals sitting in the waiting room. She went up to the reception desk and spoke to the receptionist. 'I'd like to speak to Richard.'

'What's your pet's name?'

'Murphy. Never mind about that. I need to see Richard, and it's quite urgent.'

'Can I have your name?'

'Cindy, but I don't think he'll remember my name.'

'He's very busy with a patient at the moment.'

Cindy knew she was being unreasonable but she was in no mood to wait. 'I need to see him now.'

The receptionist stood up. 'I'll see what I can do.' She walked out to a back room. Cindy felt the eyes of those in the waiting room boring into her. She turned round and glared, and they all looked away. A moment later Richard came in. As soon as he saw her, his face dropped.

'I can't do anything more for you,' he said with a touch of finality in his voice.

'I don't want you to do anything.' She slapped one of the bundle of notes, still with a rubber band round them to hold them together, on the counter. 'There's a thousand quid. I promised I'd pay you. You said it would cost hundreds, what with the operation and x-rays and drugs and everything. If this is too much, then keep what's over for any poor bugger who comes in and hasn't got enough to pay.'

Richard stared at her in disbelief and couldn't open his mouth to speak.

Cindy held up her hand. 'It's okay. Thanks for what you did. He's fine now.' She turned and walked out. Good, that's the second one dealt with. Good old Frank. Her sense of euphoria was growing by the minute. She mounted her bicycle and was just about to move off when the door opened and Richard stepped outside. 'Wait!' he called.

Cindy stopped and turned. Neither of them spoke. They both stared at each other for several moments. Then he gave a nod. 'Good luck,' he said. She nodded back then turned away and moved off.

One more to go.

She headed for the other end of town. As soon as she'd left the shops behind, it only took her three or four minutes to reach Compton Road. She cycled half way up it and turned down the track that led to the animal shelter. She could hear the dogs making a terrible racket. She pushed the door open and went up to the reception. The same assistant that she had seen before was behind the counter.

'Hi. I've come for Murphy.'

'That's good. He's doing fine, but I'm sure he'll be glad to see you.'

'I can't wait.'

'If you hang on a minute, I'll go and get him.' The girl departed through a rear door and Cindy took out the loose notes left in her pocket. She counted out twenty-five £20 notes and put them on the counter. She'd paid £1000 to the vet, £125 for the wig and £42 for the spectacles and now £500 for the animal shelter. That still left her £333. While she waited she decided she'd call in at the garage which offered showers and free meals for the homeless and give them £300 and stick the odd £33 in their tin at home. She'd think of it as expenses and gave a quiet chuckle at the irony of it. A moment later the assistant returned with Murphy who, in spite of still being in some pain, trotted up to her with his tail wagging excitedly.

'Hello, my beautiful boy. We're going home, and nothing bad is ever going to happen to you again.'

'We get far too many strays and dogs that we have to put down. It's great to see a story with a happy ending.'

'Thanks for everything you've done. There's five hundred quid to cover the costs of his keep and any medical care that he needed. What's over, put in the kitty. I expect you can use it.'

'We certainly can. That's very generous of you.'

'It's okay. The money comes from a friend of mine who can afford it,' said Cindy with a wide grin.

'Well, do thank them. That's really kind.'

'It's no problem to him. He'll be thrilled to have helped.'

'Well, thank you anyway.'

'We'll be off then. Good bye and thanks.' She turned and went out with Murphy at her heels.

'I've got to put you in this crate, Murph. There's a blanket in the bottom so don't complain.' She picked him up but had forgotten how heavy he was. It was only after her third attempt that she managed to tip him into the crate she had secured to the handlebars. She mounted the bicycle and set off down the track. She had to take it slowly because the weight of Murphy in the crate made steering very precarious. At the end of the track, there was a large skip full of rubbish. She pulled up alongside it and unhitched her knapsack. She took out the spectacles, wig and surgical gloves and threw them in with the rubbish.

'Okay, Murphy, we're done. Let's go home.' She set off down the road.

***

At number 18 Cherry Tree Road, time dragged on, but very slowly life began to grow stronger in Frank. His sight was back to normal, though his eyes were still slightly bloodshot. His shivering had stopped, and his muscles loosened. He began to move his fingers, then his arms and legs, around with ease although most of his joints still ached. His hatred of Cindy and rage at what she had managed to do to him had helped to give him the will to pull through the night. The fact that the temperature was well above freezing gave him no comfort. As far as he was concerned, it had been the most dreadful ordeal he could ever have imagined going through. And his physical suffering was matched only by the humiliation she had inflicted on him. By lunchtime, and after three hot drinks, he was sitting down to scrambled eggs and making conversation which consisted, for the most part, of short sentences of venom towards Cindy. As he related the details of how she had managed to overcome him by firstly blinding him so that he couldn't defend himself and then bringing him down with a blow from a baseball bat, Lenny's own sense of outrage began to rise.

'She meant to kill you, Frank. She wanted you to die a horrible death.'

'When I find her she will pray for death.'

'I can't believe she had the nerve.'

'It's only because she had that spray. Without that she had nothing.'

'That was a filthy trick.'

All day long they fed off each other's anger and outrage, knowing that their response for what she'd done must be total. The bitch had to be annihilated. Wiped off the face of the earth. She must be removed and never found. And it must never be known what she had inflicted on him. It had to be known that he must be avoided by the weak and approached with fear. And those that dared to cross him must know that they would have to pay a terrible price.

Chapter 19

The customers at the bar were really pleased to see Micky back, and he took it in good heart when they made remarks about the improvement to his face. Cindy had been worried about him coming back too soon, and earlier on she had tried to persuade him to stay at home a bit longer.

'Don't try and stop me. I'm definitely coming with you today,' Micky had said as he leant his backside into the sink and put the remains of a slice of toast in his mouth.

'I don't think it's a good idea,' replied Cindy, who was sitting at the table finishing her puffed wheat. 'You need to rest. You only came home yesterday.'

'I'm fine. Nothing's busted. And it's not heavy work.'

'It's tiring though. And I can easily manage. And you've still got stitches in your face.'

'That doesn't matter. And the bruising is going. The customers look at you, not me.'

Cindy knew she wasn't going to win the argument and that he was mostly concerned for her safety. He was certain that Frank would try and grab her, and if that happened the consequences would be terrible. The thought constantly gnawed away in his mind.

'Okay, but you come home if you start to feel funny.'

He moved over to the table and kissed her. 'You know you want me there really,' he said with a smile. 'And you too, Murphy. You're coming.'

Now that he was there with her, she was happy and secretly admitted that she had probably been too protective. Of course, he wasn't to know that Frank wasn't going to be a threat any longer. At least he wouldn't be once she'd executed the final part of her plan. It was great to be working in the bar together, with the friendly chatter to the customers and having Murphy lying at their feet.

She wanted to tell Micky that Frank wasn't going to be a threat to her any longer. In fact he wasn't going to be a threat to anyone once she'd delivered the final blow in her plan. She couldn't have told him about what she was planning before she'd carried it out because he'd never have allowed her to put herself at such a risk. He'd have thought the whole thing crazy anyway and that she'd never be able to pull it off. That would have been fair because she herself had thought the whole thing crazy a lot of the time and believed deep down that she had been very lucky to have carried it out without something going wrong and ended up being beaten up or dead. She thought she would tell him, maybe in a few days, once the dust had settled. She wouldn't go into too much detail, just the bare facts. He'd probably be cross with her for taking such huge risks, but she'd understand that. What worried her mostly was the chance that he might not love her any more once he knew of her dealings with Carl and the harsh treatment she had meted out on Frank. Would he then think of her as a cold and calculating, hard-faced bitch? She decided she'd take the risk of that rather than go through the rest of her life having not been honest with him.

But the plan had not yet been completed, and when it was 9:30 she decided it was time to act. Micky had been serving and chatting away with no sign of strain, so she knew she could excuse herself for a few minutes.

'I've got to go to the loo, Micky. Will you be okay for a few minutes?' she said quietly into his ear.

'Sure. Go ahead. I'm doing good.' He smiled and winked at her.

She climbed down from the bar and made her way over to Clarkes. The manager had become friends with Micky and allowed him and Cindy to use the company's WC whenever they wanted. Just before going in she quickly doubled back and moved over to two giant skips that were half filled with rubbish and waste and stood between them where she couldn't be seen. She took out the mobile phone she had bought from Tesco and dialled 999. As soon as she got through she dived straight in, 'Don't ask me my name. There are two men brandishing weapons at number 18 Cherry Tree Road. I heard gunshots. Two men came running out and then went back in. I'm terrified. Please come quickly. And come armed.' She hung up before the voice at the other end could respond. She watched her phone and waited five minutes. Then she dialled Frank.

***

Frank sunk the last of his coffee and put the mug down on the kitchen table. It was 9.30. He'd spent all yesterday huddled up followed by a good night's sleep and although there was still some stiffness in his joints from the previous night's ordeal he was ready to wage war.

'I think it's time for us to make a little visit, Lenny.'

'I can't think of anything better. I've called in Ted and his brother Hal. I've said we'll pick 'em up on the way. We can deal with any trouble. It'll be a piece of cake.'

'Good,' said Frank and stood up. He rolled his shoulders and stared into the mirror on the wall. He nodded at his reflection with a smile 'Let's go and get her.' .His

295

mobile phone bleeped. He flipped it open to read the message: 'Lift your floorboards, stupid. C.' The blood suddenly drained from his face. 'The bitch! The bitch!' he screamed and ran out of the kitchen to the box room.

'What's happened, Frank?' whined Lenny with alarm and following close behind.

Frank threw back the carpet and lifted the loose floorboards. He peered in, his jaw dropping in disbelief.

'What the…?' He reached down and picked up the gun and stared at it in his hands. He handed it to Lenny and reached for the two hand grenades. 'Christ! Look at these, Lenny.' Lenny stared back with as much bewilderment.

There was a sudden crash on the front door and it burst open, allowing a group of policemen holding guns to spill into the hallway.

'Police! Put down your weapons and lay on the floor,' screamed one of the squad.

Frank looked up with terrified shock on his face.

'Put your weapons down and lay on the floor!' The command was loud and clear.

Frank dropped the gun and put up his hands whilst Lenny nervously put the grenades on the ground and then lay down on his stomach.

'Lay down on the floor!' screamed the voice behind the leading gun.

Frank eased himself down and laid face down on the floor.

As one of the squad stood over them with his gun pointing down, Frank turned his head slightly and looked out of the corner of his eye into the box room where two of the squad were lifting out from the floorboards what was there.

He was calling out, 'About ten thousand quid. A baseball bat – looks like blood on it – three full magazines, a notebook with names, a few hundred Es, bag of flour, one and a bit kilos of coke and a bag which looks like heroin. These boys are going to go down for a long, long time.'

***

Cindy took out the SIM card and stood on it. She threw it into the skip followed by the mobile phone she had purchased from Tesco. She walked back to the bar, smiling.

Chapter 20

Micky stood up and turned off the TV. They had just watched the local news.

'Good grief. I can hardly believe it. Fancy him being arrested for guns and drugs and what have you.'

'The police have been after him for ages. Of course I knew about his drugs business. But guns! Wow!'

'And bloody hand grenades. He'll be put away for ages.'

'Let's face it. He's got what he deserved.'

'Well, it's a big relief to me. I don't have to worry about you now.'

'You needn't have worried. I could handle him,' said Cindy with a smile.

'Yeah, I'm sure you could. Like pigs might fly.'

'They said it was an anonymous tip-off. Probably grassed by one of his cronies.'

'Probably.'

Micky threw another log on the fire and then lay back on the sofa next to Cindy. Murphy was sprawled out on the ground in front of them. They stared at the dancing flames and felt their warmth laying over them.

'Do you want to watch more telly?' Micky asked.

'No,' said Cindy.

There was silence for a little while except for the crackling of the fire. He sensed she was lost in thought. He took a pound coin out of his pocket and held it up to her face.

'A penny for your thoughts.'

'That's not a penny, that's a pound.'

'Okay. Tell me what's wrong anyway.'

'Nothing,' said Cindy, but he recognized a false lightness in her voice.

'You've been fidgeting all evening. What is it?'

'Truly, nothing.' She turned and kissed him on the cheek. He knew then for certain that something was on her mind and she was trying to get him off the scent.

'You may as well tell me. I know you want to.'

'I promise everything is fine.' He looked at her with a mildly disapproving smile.

There was a knock at the front door.

'Bloody hell. Who can that be?' said Micky and stood up. As he walked to the door, she stood up too so that she could see who was calling. Micky opened the door. Linda was standing there.

'Hi,' said Micky.

'Linda!' Cindy called with a big smile on her face.

'Hallo. Is it a good time?'

'Of course it is. Come in,' said Micky and stood aside for her to come into the room. 'Come over by the fire.'

Linda moved over to the fire as Cindy stepped next to her and kissed her.

'It's lovely to see you.'

'I won't stay long.'

'Sit down.' said Micky indicating his vacant seat on the sofa. 'Can we make you a drink?'

'No, thank you. Isn't it cosy here,' replied Linda, accepting his offer to sit.

'We do our best.'

'Are you well?' asked Cindy.

'I'm fine. How about you two?'

'Everything's great. Had one or two hiccups, but everything's good now,' said Micky giving Cindy a sideways grin with raised eyebrows.

'I s'pose it's not the thing to say, but I really enjoyed Tom's funeral. He must have been loved by such a lot of people.'

'He was. I'm glad you came. He would have been very pleased to know it.'

'I shall never forget him anyway.'

'It's really why I've come to see you.'

'Oh, dear. Have I done something wrong?'

'Of course you haven't. No, it's good news. As well as his solicitors, he made me an executor of his will. You'll be getting a letter from them, but I'm here to tell you he's left you some money.'

'Really? Surely not.'

'I can only tell you that he was very concerned for you. He had a daughter who died as a baby. Had she lived she would have been about your age. He had this huge desire to try and do something for you that he would have done for her.'

'I don't know what to say. What do you reckon, Micky?'

'If it's what he wanted. We can do with a few quid.'

''It's rather a lot.'

'How d'you mean?'

'Well, £100,000.'

300

There was silence.

'This must be a mistake.'

'It's no mistake, I assure you. There will be money also for others from the sale of his house. He's giving to the Samaritans and the women's refuge and one or two other charities.'

'But we can't take the money can we, Micky?'

'Of course you can. It was his wish,' said Linda.

'One hundred thousand,' said Cindy and stared at Micky.

'If it's really what he wanted, Cindy – bloody 'ell – we'll feel like millionaires.'

'I'm really happy for you,' said Linda. 'I only wish that Tom was here to give it to you himself.'

'But I never did anything for him,' said Cindy still in bewilderment.

'If it helps you to live a happy and good life, then you will fulfil what he wished for.'

Cindy reached for Micky's hand and then stared back at Linda. 'Thank you.' She had an utterly dazed expression on her face.

'I'll leave you now. You'll have a lot to talk about,' said Linda and stood up.

'Are you sure you won't stay?'

'Not now. Thank you. But I'll see you again soon.' She turned to go to the front door. Mickey stepped ahead to open it. Cindy followed and Linda kissed her.

'Good bye,' said Linda. Micky opened the door.

'Good bye,' he said.

'Good bye, and thank you,' said Cindy.

Linda smiled and walked away to her car. She got in and drove off. They turned round and came back into the house.

'Micky, we're rich,' said Cindy as they walked back to the fire.

'What are you going to do with it?'

'Not me. What are we going to do with it?'

'Probably be best if we do nothing for a bit. Get used to it and take our time to think.'

'I'll never get used to it. It's something I could never have imagined.'

'Well, this is real, Cindy. We can move if you like.'

'I don't want to move. I love it here. You said we could extend it.'

'Yeah, we could do that if that's what you want.'

'I do. We shall have to anyway to accommodate the three of us.'

'How d'you mean, three? Oh, I see: you mean Murphy.'

She made no reply but stared at him. He gazed back at her with a confused expression. Then his eyes widened and his jaw dropped.

'No. Really?'

'It's all your fault,' said Cindy with happiness dazzling across her face.

'Oh my God,' said Micky and put his arms round her, pulling her into him. 'I love you, Cindy. I'll always love you.'

She looked up at him. 'I dreamt about you when I was a child. Now you've come for real, and I love you for real.' She pressed her lips against his and held him tight. He eased her away and mischievously looked into her eyes.

'What do you want? Boy or girl?'

'I don't mind – as long as it doesn't have your big ears.'

'I'll settle for that, as long as it doesn't have your brains,' he replied and pulled her down on to the sofa. Murphy grunted and moved away, knocking the pound coin that Micky had put on the arm of the sofa on to the floor. It fell with the head facing up. Cindy glimpsed it from the corner of her eye. She could almost swear she saw the head of the coin smiling.

End